About Author

James Palmer has previously written several published short stories but now he devotes his time to writing full-length novels. He grew up in a small Yorkshire mining town during WWII and although he never knew his parents, winning a scholarship to a Grammar School gave him a sense of purpose and encouraged him to write. After marrying a Northern country lass and having various different jobs including farming and quarrying, James felt inspired to create fictitious worlds, and write about the family life that as a boy he never had.

TEN DAYS IN JUNE

James Palmer

This edition published in 2016 by Palmer Publishing

Copyright © James Palmer

First published in 2007

The right of James Palmer to be identified as author of this work has been asserted by him in accordance with the Copyright, Designs and Patents act 1988.
All Rights Reserved.

No reproduction, copy or transmission of this publication May be made without written permission. No paragraph of this publication may be reproduced Copied or transmitted save with the written permission of the Publisher, or in accordance with the provisions of the Copyright Act 1958 (as amended).

Any person who commits any unauthorised act in relation to this publication may be liable to criminal prosecution and civil claims for damages.

This novel is entirely a work of fiction. The names, characters and incidents in it are the work of the author's imagination. Some place names are factual but any resemblance to actual persons living or dead or any incidents or events, is entirely coincidental.

A CIP catalogue for this title is available from the British Library.

Cover image: © Michael Milner (Glasshoughton Pit Buildings)

ISBN: 978-0-9935566-0-9

Publication managed by TJ INK
tjink.co.uk

Printed and bound in Great Britain by TJ International, Cornwall

Dedication

Grateful thanks to my wife who patiently tolerated the hours I spent writing and rewriting this novel. She promised to be the first one to read the published result but sadly was not able to keep her pledge.

CHAPTER ONE

Mrs Next-door-but-one

Late May and a warm shimmering haze was making long rows of red clay chimney pots dance as they ranked like sentinels over the homes below. The only intrusion on the afternoon's stillness was from a group of young children engrossed in their game of hopscotch. However, the relative peace came to an abrupt end when a voice, often referred to as 'the fog horn' by neighbours, bellowed out a boy's name: "Billy!!" It was delivered with a force and a clarity that any drill instructor would have been proud to emulate on a barrack square. Its sheer volume caused startled house sparrows to take to their wings and rise above the slate roofs of the four rows of terraced houses forming Jubilee Avenue and Collier Avenue. Hardly had the birds time to resettle when they were disturbed yet again, only this time the voice was even more strident and "Billy" was transformed into, "Billeee ... where are you?"

The sparrows, from their new vantage points, could now look down on the cause of their involuntary flights and it was not on to some strapping sergeant major, but a diminutive housewife. There she stood, just five feet four inches tall, her hands on hips that were still trim even after bearing three sons and a daughter. Today she was dressed in a blue wrap-over pinafore, and her hair the colour of cinnamon was held tightly in place by a hairnet of similar hue; this revealed a frank, open face that glowed as if freshly scrubbed, and although devoid of any make-up, was not unattractive. The year was 1940 and here among the Yorkshire miners in their rows of terraced houses, the words 'belt-tightening', 'rations' and 'queuing up' always had real meaning. Annie Foster had no illusions about life or what it meant for her and those like her, because each day she was engaged in a private perpetual war. Not against Germany, but against the ever invasive coal dust from the pit chimney, existing from payday to payday while trying to be all the things a wife and mother was expected to be. But as she stood there with her hands on her hips, one instinctively felt she would cope with whatever was doled out in life's lottery.

"There you are, where have you been? On that tip again by the looks of you, just look at your knees."

Annie jabbed an admonishing finger towards the source of her exasperation while uttering loud tut-tuts. She paused for a moment, then in a somewhat softer tone, "Be a love and slip to Mrs Next-door-but-one, see if she'll let me have a cup of sugar till Friday; there's a cup on't table."

A skinny twelve-year-old boy was now at the entrance of the yard and he looked down at his blackened knees. 'If I didn't have to wear these short trousers out, I could play in my long ones and then my knees wouldn't get dirty,' he mused, but with a sigh he answered his mother. "Alright Mam, but that Pole is there again, I've seen his bike." As he spoke, he pushed his cap back, allowing hair to fall over his forehead to partially obscure a pair of dark brown eyes. These were set amid a mass of freckles and with teeth that looked too big in a face so young, he gave the impression of being constantly on the verge of laughing, and this had earned him more than one clout around the ear, albeit undeserved.

"How do you know that Pole is there?" the boy's mother asked, "How do you know it's his bike?"

Billy raised his hand to nearly shoulder height and waggled his fingers. "Cos it's an army bike and the seat's right up here." 'That Pole' they were referring to was a private in the Polish armed forces, stationed at a camp near Worksop and a regular visitor to Mrs Next-door-but-one. Mrs Barlow was a huge lady, now living on her own since her husband was also serving in the army, so she was deeming it her duty to be patriotic and look after the welfare of the lonely soldiers stationed nearby. Especially the lanky Stefan who spoke little English, stood six feet four in his socks was as thin as a rake and had acquired the name 'Bean Pole'.

"That woman goes short of nothing," muttered Annie to herself, but in a louder voice she addressed Billy again. "Anyway, Pole or no Pole, see if she'll let me have a cup of sugar till Friday; your Dad will be home shortly."

Billy went indoors and collected a cup, minus its handle,

from off a bare wooden table set in the centre of a fairly large living room. The place was clean and tidy but certainly didn't boast any luxuries apart from a wireless set on the sideboard, and although the day was warm, a coal fire glowed in the range, which that morning had undergone one of its weekly black leadings. A large oven, its heavy door gleaming from constant polishing, was positioned on one side of the open grate, while the other side of the fire accommodated a boiler for heating washing-up water. On its lid rested a large kettle, its sides blackened from contact with the coal fire, and at a moment's notice it could be moved across, atop the glowing coals, to provide boiling water for a brew of tea. Above all this, a mantelshelf was home to a couple of small chrome vases, a tea caddy, a box of matches and in pride of place were two photographs. One was of a young man in army uniform, with the numbers 1914-1918 printed along the bottom, and alongside was another photo, also of a khaki-clad young man, but beneath this soldier was printed K.O.Y.L.I. 1939. When asked their identity, Annie would instinctively draw herself up to her full five feet four inches.

"That's my dad and that one is our Jack." She didn't need to add anything further, the pride in her voice said it all.

It was towards the fireplace that Billy now moved; it was Wednesday and it should be meat and potato pie for dinner. He had a peek in the oven. Yes, there on the top shelf a large pie was browning nicely and there would be freshly baked bread to soak up all that lovely, thick brown gravy. Billy licked his lips in anticipation then went outside to carry out his errand. His mother was still there, having a word with a neighbour who was on the other side of the concrete road that separated Jubilee Avenue from Collier Avenue. Her arms were folded, her speech animated and accompanied by vigorous nods of her head; she was in garrulous vein.

"I wish I could get my hands on that Adolf; three quarters of an hour I had to queue this morning," and without turning or pausing for breath. "Don't be long, our Billy, I need that sugar for when your dad gets home." Her tirade then resumed.

"Yes, three quarters of an hour for a bit of stewing meat; rotten Hitler, I bet he never has to queue."

Billy hurried to Mrs Barlow's house; perhaps Stefan would give him a bit of chocolate if he was still there. He could see the bike just inside the yard, so a few steps to reach the back door and he raised his hand to knock, but it was already slightly ajar and voices were coming from the living room. Billy was about to call out but something about the tone of the voices silenced him. Instinct told him he should retrace his steps, but instead he held his breath and slowly pushed the door open. The kitchen was empty so he strained his ears; it didn't sound like a normal conversation and they certainly weren't arguing so something was going on. A short passage led from the kitchen to the living room and Billy tiptoed along this until he could peer round its corner, but the living room too was empty, or nearly so. What did greet his eyes made them open wide and a whistle nearly escaped his pursed lips but he controlled himself just in time. This room was in contrast to his own only by virtue of its decor otherwise it was identical, so he knew that the door from which the voices were coming, led to stairs. It was wide open and a pair of thin white legs protruded through the opening and into the living room. Army boots adorned two large feet showing below khaki trousers concertinaed around khaki socks, allowing a display of knobbly knees pressed against red linoleum.

'Oh, Mrs next-door-but-one and Stefan!' reasoned Billy, 'they must be, wow!' He looked round for further corroborative details to lodge in his memory bank, and a set of pink stays thrown hastily into an armchair caught his eye and yes, on the floor, huge pink bloomers. Billy enthused excitedly on his observations. 'Jimmy Keats reckons he's seen his brother and girlfriend at it, but I bet he hasn't seen owt like this, better not make a sound or these two will kill me.' He tightened his grip on his mother's cup.

The heads of the couple on the stairs were out of view, but the open door allowed a glimpse of a pair of chubby hands grasping a screwed-up khaki shirt halfway up Stefan's back. Billy heard a voice.

"You sod, Stefan, you just couldn't wait till we got upstairs could you?" The white knees pressed into the linoleum, a deeper voice gasped in broken English. "I no wait ... Stefan no can no can ... oh!!"

The words ended in a moan as the white bottom disappeared for the last time and ended its frantic journeying. The chubby hands screwed the shirt tail even tighter, while pink legs, partially clad in rolled down lisle stockings, overlapped bare white ones as if to embrace and secure them for all time.

Billy bit his lip – he knew he had to escape at once if he were to remain undetected – the activity on the stairs had ceased although there was still some muffled discourse taking place and the thin white legs were still enfolded by the chubby pink ones. Carefully he retraced his steps backwards through the passage then a slow quiet turn in the kitchen and he was out the open door. 'What about the sugar?' He clutched the cup as he tiptoed across the concrete towards the yard's opening; his mother was no longer talking so she must be indoors but he couldn't go home without sugar. Billy's mind raced then he clicked a finger and thumb together. 'Mrs Carter, she sometimes comes across to borrow things from my mam, so yes that would solve it.' He stepped onto the road separating the two rows of houses and hurried across to number 27 Collier Avenue, through another yard entrance, past a coalhouse, an outside toilet and finally to an open back door.

"Mrs Carter?" Billy waited a second then continued, "Mam says can you lend her a cup of tea till Friday, er no, I mean sugar. Dad's on days and will be home soon."

Poor Billy was still trying to collect his thoughts after his exposure to the facts of life across the way. There was movement inside the house.

"That you, Billy? Come on in."

Billy stepped inside, made his way past coats hanging on pegs in the passage and into Mrs Carter's living room. A middle aged woman was resting her bottom on a fireguard while holding a young child in her arms.

"Just a minute, while I see to Tommy." She looked down at the child. "I don't like his colour; he's a bit flushed."

She gently placed the tot in an armchair before turning to her visitor to give him a quizzical look. "Now then, is it a cup of tea or a cup of sugar?"

"Sugar please, Mrs Carter." Billy looked down at his feet as the cup was taken from his hand.

"You been up to something? You look more flushed than our Tommy."

Billy shook his head. "No, I've been running, that's all."

The cup was filled from a sugar bowl on the table then handed back. "Till Friday mind, tell your mam not to forget but I know she won't, Annie's not like that."

Billy took the cup and turned to leave. "Thanks, Mrs Carter, I'll bring it back Friday." As he was leaving, he called over his shoulder. "Hope little Tommy will be alright."

When he emerged from number 27, he took a sideways glance towards the Barlow residence and wondered what was happening in the living room now.

'Big pink bloomers,' he said to himself, grinning, 'and old rabbit arse Stefan.' Billy couldn't wait to see Jimmy Keats and he threw back his head, laughing as he ran the few yards to his own back door. When he entered, he found his mother laying plates and cutlery on the table.

"Been to Sheffield for that sugar, our Billy?"

"No, Mam," Billy shook his head vigorously. "I've just been having a look at Stefan's bike." The lie was delivered with consummate ease as he continued. "Do you think I could have one soon? Jimmy Keats has, it's a fixed wheel and got racing handlebars."

Annie looked at her young son then glanced towards a clock on the sideboard before answering.

"Hey, bikes don't grow on trees you know; we'll have to see what your dad says. Now go and see if he and our Les are coming; they should be out of baths by now."

Billy ran out of the house to make his way towards a miniature mountain of coal waste that ended some two hundred yards from the top of the avenues. It was a huge waste tip that started near the mine some quarter of a mile away and ran parallel to a newer one that was now nearly as long. Here and there wisps of smoke rose from the surface of the old tip and at these points a constant jet of water was being played on any particularly active hot-spot in an attempt to prevent a further rise in temperature, for this could result in combustion of coal waste within the slag heap. Areas could smoulder away below the surface for months then suddenly cave in to reveal a glowing sulphurous chasm that one could envisage as being a gateway down to hell.

The tip was Billy's playground but he was ever wary of any areas that felt even the least bit warm and he tried to steer clear of danger. The land adjoining the tips was gorse covered and bordered on to Pit Lane which ran past Bennington Main Colliery; it was across this piece of land, known locally as 'The Grips', that the miners took a short cut to and from the pithead. They were able to leave the baths and locker rooms of the colliery, hop over a fence then have only a short walk to reach the four rows of uniform houses that provided accommodation for them and their families.

Billy had now reached a vantage point that allowed him to see small groups of men making their way from the pithead baths and head towards the fence. Some had a dudley (a metal water container) slung from their shoulder and nearly all had snap tins tucked under their arms. He could remember when all the miners walked home with blackened faces and hands prior to the baths being built. Then it had been his task to look out for his father so that he could run home to let his mother know it was time to prepare the tin bath. Sometimes, he would lend a hand to scrub his dad's back and he would wash blue scars that were mementos of wounds caused by lumps of rock falling from the roof of the coalface. Thankfully, the tin bath days were gone but when he was not in school, he continued his lookout duty in order to help his mother gauge how long it would take his father and now also his older brother Les, to reach home so that a mug of tea was ready for them when they walked into the house. Several groups of men were already making their way across The Grips and some were just exiting the baths, and it was one of these groups that caught Billy's eye. He knew at once it was his dad, his brother Les and another young man who he recognized as their next door neighbour. The two younger men were in conversation, but the older man strode purposefully forward. His shift for the day completed, he could now look forward to a good meal, a few hours with his pigeons, then maybe a pint in the Working Man's Club later. John Foster was a quiet man, tall and strong with close-cropped sandy hair, and as usual he was wearing a wide leather belt and braces to hold up thick cord trousers, while his size eleven boots shone from the application of plenty of spit and polish. Prior to the baths being built, he had made an awesome sight striding home in his clogs, cap and muffler, and with hands and face the colour of jet, apart from white rings around the eyes.

His son and their neighbour were having to walk briskly in order to keep pace with him, and Billy guessed that the young men would be talking about the war, beer, darts, snooker and women, but not necessarily in that order. Les was an older version of his young brother but without the freckles and he liked the girls, so with most of them reciprocating, he reckoned life was pretty good. He worked hard and he worked regularly so he earned enough to be able to buy his beer, his Woodbines, make sure his mother had money for his keep every Friday and have enough left to take a girl to the pictures. After a few pints one night, he had taken Billy by the shoulders, given him a wink, before launching into one of his favourite philosophical quotes.

"Now then, thee listen to me, our Billy, here's a bit of good advice for thi, are you ready?" Billy nodded that he was paying attention.

"Tha wants to hear all, see all, say nowt ... Eat all, sup all, pay nowt ... And if tha ever does owt for nowt ... Allus do it for thisen."

He then gave Billy another big wink before tapping the side of his nose with his forefinger.

"Has tha got that?"

Billy laughingly replied, "Right Les, I'll remember."

He now scanned 'The Grips' and noticed the three men were about halfway across so he called back to his mother before running to meet them.

"Hello, Dad; hey up, Les; how do, Stan." His father gave him a gentle cuff round the ear and replied "Billy." That's all he said but his tone was warm. Billy fell into step beside his brother, knowing full well what to expect.

"Gimme that cap, you young bugger." Les swept Billy's cap from his head and threw it into the air for his workmate to catch. Billy jumped, trying to retrieve it but it was to no avail, the two men were much too tall and Billy would only get his cap back when their little game was over.

"Leave lad alone, that's his school cap." The words were delivered with a pretence at severity but the two participants knew they had a licence to carry on, otherwise a very different tone of voice would have left them in no doubt that they were to discontinue and none of the boys argued with 'the old man' as he was affectionately called. The cap was indeed a school uniform cap, dark green with yellow cord piping and sporting a badge depicting the school motto 'Summum Petite'.

"It's Latin," Billy had informed the family. "It means 'Aim for the Highest' and that's what I want to do." He had surprised everyone, except his teachers, by winning a scholarship to Woodhouse Grammar School and he was near the end of his first year.

"I'll treat him to a new 'un for next term," promised Les, holding out the cap to Billy, "if he can catch this 'un mind, here you are." Again, Billy leapt into the air but the flying cap sailed too high and was deftly caught by Stan Norbury, their next door neighbour.

"Does tha know, Les, I reckon we ought to have gone to that big school; I fancy one of these missen." And with that, Stan placed the cap on his own head at a jaunty angle. "What do you reckon?"

Les studied the effect before giving Stan a quizzical look. "Aye, I have to admit it suits thi Stan, but I think you need to have a few brains or plenty of money to get to Woodhouse; better let Professor have it back."

With a laugh, he redeemed the cap from Stan to jam it on Billy's head so that his eyes were completely covered.

"There you are, young Billy, it suits thi like that."

An arm was placed round his young brother's shoulder, their little game over, until next time. So he addressed his companion, "I wonder what the news is from Dunkirk? They're still getting the poor buggers away and we haven't heard from our Jack for weeks."

Jack was the eldest of three sons and he had enlisted at the outbreak of war to join up in the King's Own Yorkshire Light Infantry. However, his letters home had ceased several weeks earlier when France was being overrun by the German army. Les continued in a grave tone.

"The last news we had was that our Jack's company was making its way to the northern coast, but other than that we don't know."

Stan shook his head before replying "Aye, it's a shambles alright, somebody's made a cock-up." Billy looked towards the tall figure in front; he could see his dad's jaw tighten and without a backward glance, John spoke sharply.

"Don't thee fret about our Jack, he'll get home even if he has to swim that English channel wi' a full pack on his back, he'll not let a strip of watter stop him." He jabbed the air forcefully with his finger to give emphasis to his words.

The three looked at each other and they instinctively felt better, and Les gave his young brother's shoulder a squeeze. By now they had passed through 'The Grips' and had reached the start of the two avenues of houses. The only features that differentiated one house from another were their doors and windows. Dark green, dark blue, dark red, dark brown, throughout all two hundred or so dwellings. Some had gates fitted to the yard entrance, but most just had an opening in the brick wall that led directly onto a strip of concrete separating the backs of the houses. It was on to this concrete that the four strode, the men's studded boots clattering on its hard surface until coming opposite a yard with a khaki army bicycle still leaning against the wall. Billy gave a sideways glance towards the back door and at the same time his brother gave Stan a nudge.

"I see Bean Pole is paying Brenda another visit; I've a good mind to let his tyres down, but then, the poor sod's a long way from Poland and you've got to have some home comforts." Stan grinned before answering. "I bet he's getting more home comforts that thee just lately, they do say Brenda is a very generous woman!"

They both laughed but a voice in front called out, "That'll do," and they fell silent before wheeling into a yard with identical brick coalhouses, identical outside toilets and identical back doors. If one was to go round to the front then they too would be found to be identical except for the curtains up in the windows and the numbers screwed to the doors: numbers 14 and 16, with the Fosters occupying number 16.

When the four reached their respective back doors, Stan turned left and stepped into his kitchen, giving a whistle as he did so.

"Anyone in and if not, why not?"

There was the sound of a woman's step.

"Hello, luv, your dinner is almost ready."

The door closed but not before the sound of lips creating a distinctly audible kiss of welcome was heard; it probably carried up to the sparrows, once again perching on their ridge tiles. Billy waited while his father and brother discarded their jackets and mufflers, then as they hung them in the passage he also entered and heard the sound of tea being poured. In the living room, his father was just appreciating his first sip of steaming brew.

"Ah, that's better, lass," and as John sat in his chair he gave Annie a gentle slap on the bottom. She didn't reply but her face mirrored her feelings 'she still loved her John.'

Les too was now seated after taking his first noisy mouthful, and as his head was tilted back and his eyes were closed, he spoke softly, "Thanks, Ma, best drink I've had all day."

"Get on with you," replied his mother. "You'll say exactly the same tonight when you have your first pint." She waved her arm to those present. "Meat and potato pie on the table in five minutes; your hands clean, our Billy?"

Billy looked down at his hands but he didn't reply because he knew he would have to wash them come what may, so he made his way into the kitchen and ran his hands under the tap. It was cold water, for any hot water had to be ladled from the fireside boiler before being carried through to the kitchen, except on wash days. On these days the large copper in the corner of the kitchen would be filled with water and its fire lit, resulting in steam filling the room and only escaping through the open door or window. But not today – that unwavering routine only took place on a Monday come rain or shine, so today the large copper had its wooden cover in place and its grate cold and empty.

Billy called from the kitchen, "Mam, our Les says he's going to buy me a new school cap ... For next year, that is."

"Oh aye," replied Annie, "he'll have to go to Sheffield then; you want proper thing and you can only get them in Sheffield, does he know that? Besides, if you didn't play in your school cap you shouldn't need one, not yet; what's wrong with it anyway?"

At this point, Les opened an eye. "I said I'd buy him a new one, Ma, and he can keep it just for school. We don't want doctors' and lawyers' sons thinking we're hand to mouth just because his dad works down pit and I've an idea where shop is in Sheffield so that's no problem."

Annie shrugged her shoulders, "It's your money, lad." She nodded to the table. "Come on, let's sit down and put wireless on, Billy luv; news will be on soon and that reminds me, we need a fresh accumulator. Better slip to Townsends this afternoon and take old 'un for charging; mind he lets you have a decent one to bring back."

Billy walked over to the sideboard and turned a knob on the Bush wireless, a few seconds to warm up before the strains of a dance band playing 'Begin the Beguine' emanated from the speaker. Les rose from his chair and performed a few dance steps on his way to the table.

"How about that, our Billy, don't you wish you could dance like that?" Billy blew a raspberry but refrained from answering as he could see his mother shaking her head.

"Sit down, you great lump, I bet Fred Astaire is right worried." She then turned to John, "Come on luv, dinner's ready."

John still had his eyes closed but he was not asleep and

he too rose to take his place at the head of the table. Billy and Les sat on either side, with Annie at the other end. Large plates were in position with generous helpings of meat and potato pie being served out on them. A large jug of thick brown gravy was steaming away in the centre of the table and plates of freshly baked bread arranged either side of it. Annie was a good cook and they were all looking forward to the meal so they tucked in with gusto. After a few mouthfuls, Billy paused to broach a query directed at his father: "Dad, do you think I could have a bike soon? Jimmy's got one, racing handlebars, fixed wheel and it's got a bell."

Billy was about to continue but his father raised a finger to his lips to indicate for silence. The dance music had faded away and an announcer's voice was now coming from the wireless.

"This is the BBC Home Service and here is the three o'clock news." The eating at the table ceased while all four heads swivelled towards the wireless as if to look at whoever was speaking; the disembodied voice continued in its distinct, controlled tone.

"Reports are coming in that the British Expeditionary Force, now withdrawn to the beaches of Dunkirk is fighting a fierce rearguard action and evacuation is taking place as speedily as possible. All available ships and craft of the Royal Navy are in operation and by six o'clock this morning, more than 200,000 troops, 140,000 of them British, had been safely taken off. Meanwhile, under the command of

Admiral Ramsay, Flag Officer at Dover, dozens of small private craft, fishing smacks, pleasure boats, channel steamers, anything that will float and carry men is being manned and sailed across the channel to try and save as many of our boys from capture as possible. There are still thousands of troops awaiting evacuation and Winston Churchill in the House of Commons said, 'This is our darkest hour.' Fresh reports will be brought to you as they arrive at Broadcasting House. Now here is the rest of the news."

Annie gave a little sob and quickly reached over to turn off the wireless. As the illuminated dial went blank, the announcer's voice faded away.

Billy bit his lip, "Do you think our Jack will be alright, Dad?" he asked, his eyes moist.

John fed a forkful of meat and potato pie into his mouth and chewed for a while before answering.

"Listen," he proclaimed to everyone round the table, all looking forlornly down at their plates, "there's no German good enough to get the better of our Jack. They'll not shoot him and he'll not let 'em shove him into a camp for the duration. You mark my words, he'll get home some road, he'll get back."

John's hands gripped his knife and fork, huge knuckles showing white, before he relaxed and resumed doing justice to his wife's admirable meal.

"Nice bit of pie, lass, I'll have another slice and a spot more gravy, if you please."

Annie acknowledged with a little smile as she spooned

—19—

more pie on to John's plate, and she then addressed her two sons.

"Your dad's right, our Jack will get through, you'll see. Now come on, pass your plate, our Les, and you Billy. I know this is one of your favourites so you might as well finish it off."

They both passed their plates and the meal progressed in silence as everyone tried to force all thoughts of foreboding from their minds. Annie gave a little sigh as she contemplated the two empty chairs on either side of the table. The one next to her would be occupied at teatime when her daughter came home from work, because Susan was a counter assistant at Woolworth's in Worksop. The other chair would remain empty for a while, 'but still,' reflected Annie, 'I am lucky compared to some mothers, some have more than one empty place at their table,' and with that small consolation she offered a little prayer of thanks.

When the meal was finished, Annie mashed a fresh pot of tea and they all helped themselves to sugar.

"Remind me to let Mrs Next-door-but-one have this sugar back when the groceries come; don't let me forget."

Billy nodded. "I'll take it back, Mam," but he didn't mention where the sugar was really from. If he played his cards right, no one would be any the wiser and consequently no awkward questions would be asked.

Billy closed his eyes, recalling once again the graphic scenes he had surreptitiously witnessed taking place on

Mrs Barlow's stairs, and which in due course, he would relate to Jimmy Keats. He gulped down his tea. "Can I leave the table? I'm just going to see if Jimmy is in, won't be long."

He looked enquiringly at his mother and then to his father; John nodded. "Aye, off you go but don't forget that accumulator needs changing." He leaned back, draining his pint mug before addressing his wife, "Just off to pigeons, Annie, you'll let me know if we get any word about our Jack."

Annie nodded, "I will," she said.

She too rose from her seat and began to gather the dinner plates; Les finished off his tea and began to collect the empty cups and mugs but his mother took them from his hands and nodded towards an armchair.

"Go on with you, I know you like five minutes when you're on days, I'll see to these."

Les sank down, gratefully closing his eyes; 'morning shifts were alright, but it meant an early rise. How did his father do it?'

"Do you reckon Dad has a kip down at the pigeons, Ma?"

A voice floated back from the kitchen. "Wouldn't be surprised lad, your dad can sleep on a clothes line and I know he's got an old deckchair down there."

Les fell asleep to the sound of washing up.

CHAPTER TWO

Jack Gets Home

Around four o'clock that afternoon, Billy went running home with a satisfied look on his face.

"I'll take accumulator now, if you like, Mam," the offer was made as he swept into the living room.

"Go on then but be careful with it; did you see Jimmy?" Billy nodded as his mother continued.

"You look pleased with yourself, what you been up to? Not up to any mischief?"

Billy looked at his mother, big brown eyes amidst a mass of freckles. "No, Mam, just been talking, that's all."

Annie gave a little grunt. "I'm sure you have, but I know you when you've got that look on your face."

A slight pause before she continued. "Go on then, uncouple the battery and don't ... drop ... it!"

Billy unscrewed two connectors, carefully lifting the accumulator from its position in the rear of the wireless, but as he did so he gave a loud gasp. "Oh, nearly went that time, Mam."

He raised his shoulders and grimaced but the battery was never in danger. Annie looked across in alarm before realising she was being teased. "You little devil, our Billy, you'll try my patience one of these days."

Billy wagged a finger, "Dad says you shouldn't swear."

"Your dad isn't here and I didn't swear, so be off with you and be careful."

She lent some significance to her words by leading him outside by his coat collar. "And don't be all day."

Billy set off on his errand; he had just spent the last hour enthralling his friend Jimmy with a greatly exaggerated version of the brief glimpses he had caught of Stefan and Mrs Barlow.

Everything he had gleaned from school chit-chat and cheap novels had been included and interwoven into his vivid narrating of the happenings at number 12, so there was a definite nimbleness in his step as he hurried towards Townsend's electrical shop.

Billy reached the double fronted building and went inside. As a bell rang in the rear room an elderly figure appeared through the connecting doorway. It was the figure of a rather frail looking gentleman but he smiled when he saw who his customer was and he greeted Billy warmly.

"'Ey up, sunshine, accumulator flat again? When are they going to put electricity into them houses down there; any news of your Jack?"

Billy placed the battery on the counter. "No, we haven't heard owt yet but my Dad says there's no Jerry can get the better of our Jack, and he reckons he'll swim back home if he has to."

The white-haired figure nodded in agreement before running fingers through his snowy locks.

"Aye, I reckon your Jack can take care of himself. Now then, do you want to go through and see to this battery for me? It'll save my old legs."

Mr Townsend liked Billy; he knew he was a bright lad and some time ago he had instructed him on the workings of lead acid batteries and how to recharge and maintain them. He missed his own son who was in the Royal Air Force so Billy was happy to oblige.

"Right, Mr Townsend, I'll see to it."

He disappeared through the connecting doorway, made his way through a back room then outside towards a brick lean-to. Inside, shelves were fitted to three of the walls all groaning under the weight of discarded electrical paraphernalia. Old wireless sets, partly dismantled vacuum cleaners, irons, lengths of cable, light fittings, and old electric motors. However, the rear wall accommodated a large wooden bench and it was here that accumulators were recharged. Half a dozen were already connected as indicated by the occasional surge of bubbles rising within their electrolyte. Billy carefully coupled his battery to the charger and began to recall Mr Townsend's explicit instructions. No naked lights, release the filler caps, check the level of electrolyte and top up if necessary, check for correct polarity of the leads, then switch on the trickle charger. Billy stood back, watching as the plates started to gas freely, indicating recharging was underway; now for a replacement to take home. He selected the largest of three on the 'charged' section and made his way back to the shop. Mr Townsend was serving a customer with a light bulb and when he was through, he turned to Billy.

"Okay, Billy?"

Billy nodded before replying. "Yes thanks, Mr Townsend, I've got this one for a loan." Billy held up the charged accumulator and Mr Townsend smiled.

"Good lad, tell your dad yours will be ready in a couple of days, give him my best and your mam."

Billy raised his free hand in acknowledgement, confirming that he would pass on the message before stepping outside and heading for home. When he arrived, he found his brother and next door neighbour sitting outside enjoying the late afternoon sun. It was just after five o'clock and Billy knew his sister Susan would soon be home; they got on well together most of the time so he was always glad when she got home from work, especially if he had any problems with his English homework.

A cheer went up from Les as Billy turned into the street carrying the accumulator.

"Come on Billy, I want to listen to Victor Sylvester's dance lessons at half five; got to keep up with all them new steps so I can impress the young ladies on a Saturday night."

With that, Les took hold of an imaginary partner and twirled round the yard until his foot caught the edge of a manhole cover to bring his terpsichorean demonstration to an end rather sooner than he intended and certainly less gracefully. Stan raised his eyes to the heavens.

"What do you reckon, Billy?"

Billy shrugged his shoulders, "Mam says that Fred Astaire has nowt to worry about."

They both laughed unsympathetically as Les sat down, tenderly feeling an abused toe. Billy went indoors to couple the battery into the wireless and switched on to hear a voice explaining to the nation how to make the most of dried fruit, so he quickly switched off again. He received a nod of approval from Annie.

"Thanks, luv, now we can have tea as soon as Susan gets in; slip and tell your dad what time it is and say that tea will be ready in about a quarter of an hour. If he asks about our Jack, say we haven't heard a thing."

Billy said "Okay" before going outside to find his brother still nursing his toe.

"Hey, Les, this is how you do it," remarked Billy mockingly while performing a few impromptu steps of his own. But he too made a less than elegant exit, much to the delight of the two onlookers, especially Les who gave a disdainful hoot accompanied by a slow handclap. Billy recovered himself to race off in the direction of the old waste tip until he heard his father calling to his pigeons. He could see the birds circling over the loft so he decided to keep his distance, for he knew his presence might avert the birds from landing. His father was rattling a tin containing a few pebbles and inviting the pigeons to settle.

"Come on then, kup, kup, kup, come on my little beauties, come on in."

Billy called when he saw that his father had noticed him. "Mam says tea in about five minutes, Dad."

John waved, so Billy retraced his steps and back home he found Susan just about to take her coat off. She was a pretty girl with a good figure and a nice smile, only there were times when she could display her mother's fiery disposition, but not today. As Billy entered, she ruffled his already dishevelled tresses.

"I hear you've been showing our Les how to dance, until you nearly fell on your face."

"I just slipped, that's all," replied Billy with a cheeky laugh. He tried to thumb his nose at his brother without being observed but wasn't successful. A towel was skilfully flicked, catching him unerringly behind his ear.

"We can do without that, thank you. Did you tell your dad a quarter of an hour?"

Billy ruefully rubbed his ear before nodding in reply.

"Right then, everybody get ready for tea, as soon as your dad gets in we can sit down." She looked at Billy, "Hands, off you go."

This command was accompanied by a nod towards the kitchen. Billy sighed, but Susan ruffled his hair a second time and gave him a gentle shove.

"Go on, I'll bring some hot water, it will do for the both of us."

"Thanks, Sue," said Billy gratefully. He made his way to

the large white ceramic sink under the window, fitted a waste plug then waited for Susan.

As she came through the passage carrying a pan of hot water, John came back from attending to his pigeons.

"'Ow do, lass, alright?"

"Hello, Dad," Susan replied warmly, "no word of our Jack then?" John shook his head. "No, not if your mam hasn't heard owt." He then waved a huge hand towards the pan Susan was carrying.

"Save that hot water when you've finished, I might as well use it." He walked into the living room to speak to Annie. "You haven't heard owt yet then?"

Annie knew that he was referring to news of Jack and answered softly, "No, John, I would have sent word down, you know that." She then raised her voice to address everyone. "Right, I've got some spam, I've got some pork dripping or you can have raspberry jam, what's it to be?"

She turned to John. "What do you fancy, love?"

John settled for the raspberry jam so Annie called through to the kitchen. "What about you Susan?"

"Oh, no spam for me thanks, I had that in the canteen at dinner time, I think I'll have some of that dripping."

Billy was drying his hands but he paused in order to specify his preference.

"Can I have dripping too, Mam?... On toast ...With some of that 'brown stuff' from the bottom of the basin."

That 'brown stuff' he was referring to, was gravy that had been poured into the basin with the dripping while it was still hot, then it had settled in the bottom to solidify into a tasty brown jelly.

"Alright, I knew you were going to say that," his mother answered before finally turning to Les. "Jam for you, Mr Astaire?" Les grinned in agreement, "Aye, that'll be fine, Ma, but I think I'm more of a Gene Kelly, only better looking."

Annie shook her head in feigned disbelief before hurrying to collect things from the pantry.

"Mash tea, Susan please, the kettle is on the boil."

She gave the instructions as they passed in the passage and by the time the task was completed, everyone was in their seats.

"Do you want wireless on, Dad?" Billy asked and John pondered for a short while before answering.

"No thanks, Billy, I'll catch the nine o'clock news. It'll be Alvar Lidell and they give more details at nine."

Susan spoke up at that juncture, "Talking of news, Joyce at work said she went to the pictures last night and it showed Dunkirk on the Pathé Newsreel. She said it showed thousands of soldiers on the beach and some were up to their necks in water as they waded out to climb aboard boats."

"Did she see our Jack?" asked Billy hopefully.

"She doesn't know our Jack so she wouldn't have recognized him even if she had seen him, and I don't suppose the cameras would get all that close, would they?" Susan looked round the table. "Anyway, I'm going to The Regal on Saturday so I shall have a good look for our Jack."

When she had finished speaking, Annie put her half-finished cup of tea back on the table and placed the tips of her fingers to her brow, as if to help erase an unwanted vision.

"I couldn't bear to see our Jack on that beach, the only place I want to see him is sat there, safe and sound." She nodded towards the vacant place at the table then dropped her eyes to hide her sadness. John had sat silent up to that moment, enjoying his meal, but now he spoke up.

"Now come on, Annie lass," he said firmly, "I've said our Jack is going to be alreet and he will. He'll be sat in yon chair before you can say Jack Robinson, so don't fret thisen over some newsreel; for all we know he could be back in Blighty. They don't let on, but I've heard that they've been pulling our lads off Dunkirk for some days."

Annie wiped an eye with her apron. "Do you really think so, John?"

John gave her a reassuring look. "You'll see, lass."

Annie knew John was only trying to make her feel better, but it did perk her up and they finished tea without any further mention of Dunkirk.

June 2nd came and still no news of Jack. Troops were still being evacuated from the beaches but the German blitzkrieg was proving to be an awesome power, and it could only be a matter of days before the whole area was in enemy hands. Annie listened anxiously to news bulletins, but the British Government were reluctant to give too much information to the general public for morale reasons.

Hitler's panzers had swept through Denmark, Norway, the Netherlands, Belgium and Luxembourg and now France was on the verge of collapse, so the Ministry of Information wasn't keen to give too much away.

Germany, however, was only too eager to spread the word, and they did so through the infamous William Joyce, broadcasting from Radio Hamburg. He was better known as Lord Haw-Haw and his news bulletins always began with the call sign "Germany Calling, Germany Calling", but which sounded like "Jairmany Calling, Jairmany Calling". According to Joyce, the beaches at Dunkirk were littered with thousands of dead troops and hundreds of boats were sunk in the sea as they tried to evacuate the encircled soldiers. However, this kind of news was taken with a pinch of salt by a wary British public, wise to his mocking lies, therefore little or no credibility was given to any of it. Billy had Lord Haw-Haw's intonations off to a T. "Jairmany Calling, Jairmany Calling" he would chant until his mother silenced him, so he sometimes practiced in his room before falling asleep, and this particular night he slept with his window wide open for it had been hot for days. About 3 a.m. he awoke to the sound of studded boots reverberating on the concrete road between the houses. He had no clock or watch but instinct told him it was too early for the miners' night shift to be coming home or for the morning shift to be going to work. His heart leapt as he sprang out of bed and towards the open window. It was positioned above the coalhouse and toilet, so it faced on to the dividing concrete road. He craned his neck through the aperture and could just make out a dim figure striding purposefully forward; it wasn't a miner, this figure had a large sack on one shoulder and something slung from the other. That something was a Lee-Enfield rifle and a gas mask while the large sack was a kitbag, but Billy had no need to know the particularity of the items because even at a distance, he knew who the person was. A cry of joy accompanied his call to the household.

"It's Jack! It's Jack, Mam! It's our Jack!"

He knew the back door would not be locked but that route would take too long; he couldn't waste time going down the stairs. With a bound he was straddling the window ledge then out on to the slate roof of the coalhouse and toilet. Gingerly he negotiated the slope of the roof until he neared its edge, and from there he could dangle his body until an extended bare foot reached the top of a wooden fence separating their yard from a neighbour's yard. After that it was an easy leap onto the concrete where small lumps of coal and pieces of gravel stung the soles of his feet, but they were ignored.

Clad only in his pyjama bottoms, Billy raced through the yard's entrance towards the advancing figure; a few more fleeting steps and he was throwing eager arms around the advancing soldier's neck.

"Jack, Jack!" he gasped. "Dad said you would get home some road." The soldier dropped his kitbag and hugged the boy tight; he looked fit but his eyes were tired except for a brief few moments when he answered.

"Aye, Billy, Father were right an' all; we can't let the buggers get us down, can we? Come on, I could murder a mug of tea."

With that, he bent down and hoisted the kitbag back on his shoulder; he still held Billy and the sound of boots once again echoed between the houses as he hurried towards number 16. They turned into the yard to be greeted by a small figure in a coat, her hair in curlers.

"Hello, Ma, fine time to be coming home in't it, any chance of a brew?" Annie didn't answer, she just held out her arms to embrace her two sons, a kitbag, a gasmask and a rifle. Her heart felt too large for her breast, it was full of joy. They all made their way inside to be greeted by a tearful Susan, a hugely grinning Les, and John who, having just lit the gas mantle was standing with his back to the fireplace. Billy was now holding the rifle and standing looking up at his brother.

"Shall I tek it upstairs, Jack?" he enquired.

"Aye, good lad, put it under my bed."

They all looked at each other and burst out laughing. Susan flung her arms round her brother's neck, laughing and crying simultaneously and after giving him a big kiss on the cheek, she went to hug her mother.

"There you are, Mam, Dad was right, wasn't he?"

Annie nodded, her eyes wet but shining like diamonds as she gripped Susan's hand. Les stepped forward to pump his brother's arm and slap him vigorously on the back.

"Good to see yer Jack, I don't relish having to listen to you snore again but welcome home, brother." A bear hug completed the greeting before he stepped back and Jack turned towards his father. They stood a few feet apart looking intently at each other and for nearly half a minute neither of them spoke or moved, they just stood earnestly regarding the face of the one opposite. Slowly, a huge hand was extended and Jack clasped it within both of his. He spoke first.

"'Ow you doing, Father?" He asked, with a wry smile.

John made a slight sideways inclination with his head before answering.

"I'm alright now, lad, now I can see tha's safe and sound but I knew tha'd make it. I told your ma so and maybe she'll get a good night's sleep now, but any road, come on, sit you down. I reckon we'll all have a cup of tea."

Annie and Susan bustled with kettle, teapot, mugs and cups while Billy slipped upstairs with the Lee-Enfield. The two older boys shared a front room and Jack's bed was always made up in case he could get home for a spot of leave, but since being posted to France that had not been possible. For the next ten days, however, the bed would be comfort to a weary soldier and the rifle was safely ensconced out of view beneath it, but not before Billy had lined up an imaginary target through the sights and uttered the obligatory "Bang! Bang!" When he returned downstairs, everyone was seated and chattering away waiting for the kettle to boil. The fire had been stirred with the poker, for although the weather was warm it hardly ever went out in order to ensure a ready supply of hot water and for cooking.

Billy knelt beside Jack's chair just as the kettle started to sing, so he did the honours and mashed a full pot of tea, then as he returned to be near Jack he looked at all the happy faces about him. It reminded him of Christmas times and the occasions when the last shift had been worked at the colliery prior to its annual holiday. Everyone was talking away but no mention was made of Dunkirk or the war, then it was time to fill cups and mugs and pass them round the circle of six. Jack savoured the steaming contents of his own mug and was about to comment when Annie interrupted him.

"Don't tell me, it's the best drink you've had all day."

Jack and Les looked at each other and burst out laughing.

After an hour or so, the spontaneity of the banter moderated and Susan expressed a need to return to bed; she gave Jack another kiss before going upstairs. John and Les decided it was too near their shift time so they opted to get dressed and prepare their snap tins ready for work. Billy received a gentle tap on his head from Annie with a behest for him to return to bed also, while she would empty Jack's kitbag and wash whatever needed washing after its immersion in the English Channel. Jack's eyelids were drooping by now so Annie nodded in the direction of the door leading to the stairs.

"You go and get your head down, son, you look all in," she entreated. "Don't get up until you feel like it and if you drop your clothes outside your door I can get them washed; go on, there's a luv."

Jack gave his mother a weary smile, "I've nearly forgotten what a bed feels like, thanks, Ma."

He rose to go upstairs but paused to give Billy a playful right hook. "Here, I reckon you've got a lot more freckles than when I saw you last, you been kissing all them girls at grammar school? It's that what causes them to show up, you know." He gave Billy a wink, "I had a lot when I was your age."

They climbed the stairs together and at the top, Billy slapped his big brother on the back before turning into his little room overlooking the back yard. The sky was beginning to lighten in the east to herald another fine day.

Billy mused on the anxiety and apprehension they had all felt over the last few days, 'Why can't it always be like it was downstairs just a short while ago, instead of people trying to kill each other? Still, our Jack is safe now,' and with that thought uppermost in his mind he fell asleep, remembering the sound of the boots on the concrete below his window.

CHAPTER THREE

A Drink in the Red Lion

Friday afternoon and the ambience in the living room at number 16 was very different from that prevailing twenty-four hours earlier. A tablecloth, which usually only made an appearance on Sundays, covered the table so it was fairly easy to imagine that here was a family fairly satisfied with their lot. Even though Germany was expected to invade and happiness could be transient, the Wehrmacht was not yet on English soil so why agonise over such trivialities? Let the War Office do that and besides, it was pay day. John and Les had walked home from the mine, each with a wage packet tucked into his back pocket and fairly satisfied that their endeavours had been rewarded. Susan too was feeling good even though her pay day was not until Saturday, but she did have a night at the pictures to look forward to so she allowed her imagination free reign. For a couple of hours she could imagine Clark Gable sweeping her into his arms, enabling a close acquaintance with that famous moustache. But that was only make believe, best to stick to reality. What if that Canadian airman she had served last week were to call into the store again and ask to take her out? He had seemed to fancy her and he did have a moustache, only he

—37—

didn't look much like Clark Gable. Susan discontinued her daydreaming to ask her mother if there was anything else she could do to help prepare tea.

"Just milk and sugar to put on the table, and that reminds me, I must let our Billy take that sugar back to Mrs Next-door-but-one." Annie hummed to herself as she filled the big black kettle with water.

"Jack looks better; he had a good sleep and a wash and a shave so you can give him a call in a minute; our Billy too, he's doing some homework."

Billy, upstairs in his room, was trying to catch up on some neglected French homework for it had to be ready for the first two lessons Monday morning; he groaned at the consequences of his procrastination.

'Must sort out these verbs: être to be, avoir to have, travailler to work, now let's see. Je suis, tu est, il est, elle est, nous? Strewth, why can't everyone speak English?'

A call from Susan to say that tea was ready saved him from further anguished cogitation. Jack too heard the summons from below and emerged from his room dressed in mufti; the khaki uniform had been replaced by grey flannel trousers and a white open-necked shirt which helped to enhance his tan. After his sleep he certainly looked a different person, and at the foot of the stairs he was greeted with a whistle from Susan.

"Well, well," she purred, "I take it you won't be staying in tonight, out on the razzle-dazzle by the looks of you." Jack gave a satisfied grin.

"Well, first of all I'm going to take my no good brother for a pint; I haven't had a decent one since I left Yorkshire. Then after that, who knows? Some rich widow might invite me to spend the weekend at her country place or … Betty Grable could fly over from Hollywood to see what I'm doing next week, although I would have to think seriously about that because I promised Bing I would have a round of golf with him, so …"

The verbal meandering ceased at that point when Jack caught sight of his mother shaking her head.

"I don't know who's the worse, you or our Les, and no doubt this one will get just as bad." Annie nodded towards Billy. "But what can you expect with you and our Les to teach him?"

Jack gave his mother a hug, "Now, Ma, you know you wouldn't swap us; we're little angels really."

Annie gave a snort but she didn't disagree; instead she addressed Billy. "Go and fetch your dad, he's on the yard talking to Stan; tell him tea's ready." When he had gone, Annie turned to Jack. "You must be hungry, we've all had a cooked meal but you; is there anything you fancy? Groceries have been delivered."

Jack pondered for a few seconds, "Well, a little bit of smoked salmon would be nice, or a T-bone steak with a salad on the side; do you have the wine list?"

Annie looked round at the grinning faces. "It's true," she said, "they say the older you get, the dafter you get; no wonder my hair's starting to turn grey." Her gaze of mock derision was again directed to Jack.

"Now, you soft ha'porth, we'll start again: is there anything you fancy for tea?"

Jack placed his hands on his mother's shoulders. "Ma, I could eat owt but I'll tell you what, have you got a few sausages? I could enjoy them."

Annie nodded, "You can have some sausage and you can have an egg with some fried bread, how's that?"

"Smashing, I'm starved."

They had just finished sorting out Jack's menu when his father walked in and immediately gave Jack a close scrutiny.

"Well I must say tha's looking a hundred per cent better; sleep alright?"

"Like a log, thanks, I were ready for a good kip and now I'm being treated to a bit of Ma's home cooking."

Annie was busy laying sausages into a big frying pan but she spoke over her shoulder as she settled it on the fire.

"It won't take me long to see to our Jack; everything is on the table so help yourselves, I'll only be a minute."

In no time at all, a full loaf of bread had disappeared along with some corned beef that John and Les had chosen to have, cheese for Susan and Billy, who called it 'mousetrap food', while Jack tucked into his sausage, egg and fried bread. Annie tried some new Heinz sandwich spread which, according to the man behind the counter at Melia's grocery store, had come all the way from America.

"Lend-Lease apparently. Also this week we have had some cartons of dried eggs delivered and more 'Spam';

stands for Supply Pressed American Meat, did you know that?"

Annie had shaken her head in ignorance but when home she found the sandwich spread wasn't bad, and as she watched everyone enjoying the food she forced all thoughts of ration books and coupons from her mind.

At the end of the meal, John went to attend to his pigeons while Annie cleared the table before taking a stool outside to do some darning. The rest remained seated still chatting away but eventually Jack decided it was time to arrange entertainment for the evening.

"Do you fancy a pint tonight then, dear brother?"

"I reckon I could force one down," replied Les. "Red Lion?"

Jack nodded, "The Red Lion will do fine; what's the place like these days?"

Les chuckled, "About the same; we had a good laugh there a few weeks ago."

Susan interrupted, "If you're going to talk about the Red Lion I'm off; I've heard enough about that place."

Les held up his hand, "It's alright, Sue, it's nothing mucky, not really, honest."

Susan gave him a sideways look but she remained seated. Billy on the other hand was all ears as Les started to relate his story.

"You haven't been in the Red Lion have you, Susan? Well, it's a big pub, lots of rooms and one of these is called the parrot room."

Again, Susan interjected. "I've also heard all about the parrot room; some of the girls at Woollies have been in and they didn't stay very long."

Les laughed. "Alright, alright, let me explain how it came about. Some years back, the old landlord, not the present one, bought this parrot, complete with its cage, because he thought it would be a good gimmick and he put it in the main bar just inside the entrance. Well it was a great attraction but it had one drawback: it swore like a trooper and whenever a woman walked past it would let out a loud wolf whistle and then say, as clear as anything, 'Look at the arse on that,' followed by more wolf whistles and stomping up and down on its perch."

Les had to pause at that point because Billy broke into fits of laughter as he conjured up the scene in his mind's eye. Susan however, shook her head but she remained seated and Les was able to continue, accompanied by chortles from Billy.

"Right, well as you can imagine it was a bit too much so the parrot was transferred to a side room and it is still in there, still swearing and still accosting females when it gets the chance, but some of the women who drink at the Red Lion go into the parrot room on purpose just to get noticed. That's been going on for ages, but what I'm getting at happened about two weeks ago when the Jenkins from across the road had some friends down from Scotland for a few days. The old boy used to go out at night dressed in the full regalia, tam-o'-shanter, short jacket, kilt, sporran, the whole lot. Anyway, one night, Arthur decided to take Jock for a drink in the Red Lion, the bar was a bit crowded so they went into the parrot room. I was in there with Stan and as soon as Jock walked through the door, up started the parrot with the whistles, the 'look at the arse on that', the swearing, etcetera, etcetera and this went on all night. Every time poor old Jock stood up to go to the bar or the gents, the parrot gave him the full routine. Anyway, just before time was called, Jock turned round on his stool and gave the parrot a long hard look. The parrot cocked its head to one side, muttered a swear word or two and looked back out of one beady eye, real mean like, so that was enough for Jock. He picked up his pint, got up, then walked slowly over to the cage, which prompted the bird to become even more strident. It was still stomping on its perch when Jock, in a real Scottish accent said, 'Reet then, yer miserable, overdressed apology for a bird, tek a hold of this little lot.'

"First of all he took a good draw on a cigarette and blew the smoke right up the parrot's beak. He then filled his mouth with beer and spurted it all over the parrot's head. It went mad, screeching and squawking for a good five minutes and we were still laughing our heads off when Fred shouted 'time'. Jock was back in his chair by then but when he did get up to leave, the bird stayed quiet. I haven't been in since to see if the hush is permanent but the parrot was silenced good and proper that night."

Billy was still laughing but he paused long enough to acclaim his approval.

"That was great, Les, can I tell you of something that happened when I was going to school a couple of weeks ago?"

Jack was leaning back on his chair, thoroughly enjoying the raillery and he nodded agreement. "Might as well tell us while we're all together, go on." He placed his hands behind his head and settled back.

Billy looked round the table with a grin on his face before glancing over his shoulder to ensure his mother was still outside. "It isn't as funny as our Les's tale but it gave Tommy and me a good laugh. First I have to explain that I have a French pen pal – we all have one at school. Mine is called Pierre and he lives at 10 rue de la Machine, Paris. Anyway, you know I have to catch a train to Woodhouse? Well me and Tommy Platt travel to school together and we..."

The words trailed away as Susan held up her hand.

"That should be 'Tommy Platt and I'," rebuked Susan. "You know that, but go on."

Billy grimaced, "Yes sorry, but as I was saying, we always try and get into a carriage with other kids who are already on the train. Anyway, this particular morning, we had to rush on to the platform and we could only get into a carriage with business people going to Sheffield. There was no corridor so we were stuck in this carriage all the way to Woodhouse with me sitting on one side and Tommy on the other. Nobody was talking; they were all reading their papers and I was trying to think of something to pass the time, then I had an idea. I opened my satchel, but before I realized what I was saying I remarked in a loud voice, 'Here, Tommy, would you like to see some French letters?' You should have seen their faces, all the newspapers went down and eight pairs of eyes looked at me. I didn't twig at first then it dawned on me, so I slowly took two letters from Pierre out of my bag and Tommy and me burst out laughing. A bit later, I heard some of them having a little chuckle behind their papers but they still didn't speak to each other, it was really funny."

Susan tried to look disapproving, but she had to smile. "You cheeky little devil you, how do you know about such things?"

Billy grinned back, "A lad brought one to school a bit back and we blew it up."

Les shook his head in mock alarm, "Hey, I thought you went to that grammar to learn Latin and physics and such like. I don't know what things are coming to, what do you think to him, Jack?"

Jack looked at his younger brother then laughed; at least he was helping him to forget that only a matter of hours ago he was having a hard time just trying to stay alive. He had wondered if he would ever be with them again yet here he was, laughing and joking, sitting in his chair safe and sound. Suddenly a serious expression eclipsed the humour on his face and he gave a deep sigh.

"Nay, Les, I don't know what things are coming to, but it's a pity they are nowt more serious than what our Billy gets up to; the world would be a better place I can tell yer."

He leaned forward and placed both hands flat on the table; he had nine days leave left, nine days to forget the war and enjoy himself: the smile returned to his face.

"Right, I'm just going to have a word with Ma, then when my brother here has made himself presentable, we can go and see what the Red Lion has to offer."

Jack hoisted himself upright but before pushing back his chair he wagged a finger at Billy.

"Haven't you some homework to finish? Some French letters to write perhaps?"

Billy pulled a face, "Yeah, but I'd rather sit here and listen to some more stories." However, he made his way upstairs muttering to himself, "Je suis, tu est, il est, elle est, oh roll on summer holidays, nous what's it, vous how's your father, di da, di da, di da."

Les shook his head and as Billy reluctantly climbed the stairs he stretched himself and stifled a yawn. "I don't mind the day shift but I'm no early bird, I like my bed." He rubbed his chin. "I'd better go and get ready then I'll feel better. After a couple of pints I'll be on top of the world." He paused for a moment, contemplating what to wear.

"Right, let's see, a wash, a shave, then I think the grey assemble along with an eye catching tie and brown shoes."

Susan interrupted him. "I think you mean ensemble; ask our Billy, it's French."

Les shrugged his shoulders, "Assemble, ensemble, what's it matter? I'll still end up looking like a million dollars."

With that he started to strip to the waist but again Susan interrupted.

"You can hang on, brother dear, because the sink is full of pots. I told Mum I would help with the washing up, unless *you* feel like giving me a hand."

Les pulled a face but he agreed, before remarking, "Do you reckon our Jack is alright? I know he looks fine but, well ... like a few minutes ago when he went all serious, did you notice his eyes?"

Susan shook her head, "Oh I don't know, Les, we can't possibly realize what it was like on that beach, can we? I dare say he'll be alright after he's been home a few days."

"Yes, I suppose," Les agreed. "It'll take him a while to get sorted."

Thirty minutes later, Les was washed, shaved and sporting his grey flannel assemble, as he called it. Just one final touch was needed to complete his grooming so he called to his brother still outside talking.

"Jack, have you any Brilliantine or Brylcreem?" The daily showering at the pit baths meant that his hair was a bit unruly, to say the least, so no amount of combing kept it in place for very long.

Jack walked indoors before answering and he stood in front of Les with arms outstretched, the palms of his hands uppermost. "Now why should I need Brilliantine?"

Les observed Jack's closely cropped hair. "Aye, fair enough, I see what you mean." This was followed by a few seconds of serious thought before he exclaimed triumphantly, "Lard, that'll do nicely."

Jack looked askance at his younger brother. "Lard?" The word was spoken with extreme dubiety. "Lard?" he repeated.

Les nodded. "Yes, that'll do it, is Ma still outside?"

Jack confirmed that she was then watched as Les tiptoed into the pantry to stick a digit into a packet of lard and to reappear with a blob of it on the end of his forefinger, a huge smirk across his face. The lard was quickly rubbed between the palms of his hands before being smoothed on to his head to transform tussled tresses into a dark glossy mane with an arrow-straight parting positioned precisely over his left eye. His hair was then combed back in a natural kink, shining like polished silverware.

"There you are, Jack, how about that?"

Jack didn't answer straight away but stood scratching his own head, until eventually commenting in a dry tone. "Well, you won't be troubled with flies landing on yer brainbox, they'll never keep their footing, and for goodness sake be careful when you light your fags, you could go up like a roman candle."

Les grinned, ignoring the caustic remarks.

"I knew you'd like the effect – a bit like Tyrone Power, don't you think?"

Jack let out a huge sigh before pointing to the door. "Out, Tyrone, the first pints are on you; let's say cheerio to Ma."

Just then, Billy came dashing down the stairs, "Nearly

forgot, must take that sugar back to Mrs Next-door-but-one – where's Mam?" He ran outside, calling for his mother.

Jack and Les looked at each other, shrugged their shoulders but made no comment, before they too made their way outside where they found Billy reminding his mother about the borrowed sugar. He didn't want anyone else returning it and he couldn't take it back while his mother was still outside so he had to be a bit crafty. He would get the sugar ready then slip across to Mrs Carter's when the first opportunity arose – that would save any awkward questions. Meanwhile, Jack and Les had said "Cheerio" and were now striding up the avenue. It was a good 250 yards to the top and as they neared the end, Jack nodded to one of the houses on his left.

"How's Val doing these days; her and Cliff alright are they?"

Les glanced at his brother before he answered. "Why? Do you wish you had gone and married her then?"

"No!" replied Jack sharply. "I just wondered if they were alright, them and the little lass."

About three years ago, Jack and Valerie had been very close and most of their friends had expected them to get married, including Valerie herself, but Jack hadn't been ready to settle down and they broke off the relationship. Several months later, Valerie had married Cliff Burgess and they now had an eighteen-month-old daughter.

"Yes, they seem fine," answered Les. "Val still looks a smasher and the little girl must be a year and a half old now.

You'll have to give 'em a call while you're on leave; I know Cliff is on nights this week and he'll be on days next week, or you could catch him in the Comrades for a pint if you wanted."

Jack gave a grunt, "Aye, we'll see."

They had now reached the bottom of the main street and their steps took them past several shops, the local dance hall, a cinema, and past an open-air market with some of the stalls still trading with it being Friday and pay day. Past the Comrades Arms Club, more shops then up a slight incline leading to a large square. On one side stood a stone-built church, while the facing side represented the boundary of a farm with its high stone walls and farm buildings. A further segment of the perimeter housed the entrance to a park and footpath, while the remaining side accommodated a large red brick building, towards which Jack and Les now strode. Large double doors were swung open and above these was hung a sign depicting an obligatory rampant red lion with the words 'Free House' written in gold lettering beneath the majestic beast.

In the centre of the square stood a recently built bus shelter, for this was the turning point and main bus stop for all of the public transport journeying to and from Worksop, Sheffield, Rotherham, Retford and Doncaster. However, in sharp contrast to the modern bus shelter and as if to serve as a reminder of days gone by, the forecourt of the Red Lion displayed an elevated granite slab complete with stone steps. In the old days this had allowed the gentry to acquire the necessary height to bestride their horses if the customary manner of mounting had proved too demanding after quaffing the ale or whatever their tipple had been. For donkey's years it had stood there and it looked good for a considerable few more, unless a stray bomb removed it. Jack and Les were now level with the ancient reminder of bygone days so as they passed, Les gave a nod in its direction.

"Remember when you tried to jump that after eight pints?"

Jack gave a wry grin. "Nearly broke my damn neck, and later, you and Nobby helped me home then quickly scarpered.

Les threw back his head and gave a loud guffaw.

"We took you home, stood you up outside the back door, knocked, then left you to it; I could hear Ma ranting at you six houses away. I didn't go in until half an hour later and she was still on; I told her I hadn't seen you all night, otherwise she would have started on me."

They were now through the inner doors of the pub leading to the main bar which served all the other rooms radiating from it, and although it was the kind of place that was just one step above having sawdust on the floor it suited the locals admirably. It sold the best pint for miles and the miners had their own priorities when it came to choosing where they bought their beer. Number one was the quality of the pint, number two was its price, number three assessed the landlord and staff, number four appraised the entertainment facilities which meant, was there a piano? And way down the list would be the pub decor. Well, Jack and Les were well satisfied with the beer, the price was right, the landlord was amenable, as were his wife and barmaid, and there was also a piano and stage. Greetings came from some of the regulars as the two young men breasted up to the long bar and a bearded innkeeper stepped forward to thrust a ham-sized arm over the polished top to shake Jack warmly by the hand.

"Glad to see you back home, Jack, I've kept asking after you from Les here; the lad's been right worried but it never put him off his beer mind. You alright, eh?"

Jack appreciated the warm welcome and spread his arms wide as if to prove he was alright. "Yes, fine thanks, Fred, and I'll be even better after a pint of your best bitter, one for this rapscallion as well. What do you reckon to his hairstyle?"

Jack had tried to ruffle his brother's hair but Les was too quick for him. Fred looked up from pulling a pint and paused before answering.

"Very smart, reminds me of one of those Denis Compton ads; have you varnished it, Les?"

Jack interrupted with a sharp intake of breath. "It's not varnish, no, it's a top secret formula, is that." He then turned to his brother, "Am I right, youth?"

Les pulled himself tall and adjusted his tie. He knew Jack wasn't being derogatory by calling him 'youth' for it was a common term between brothers and close friends, but he did know he was being teased so he responded accordingly.

"Look, for you unfortunates who don't have much luck with the women, I have to inform you that a man needs to be smooth, sophisticated and also well groomed, know what I mean?"

He received blank looks from Jack and Fred, so he continued.

"Some nights I have to fight the women off, it's called charisma, or at least I think that's what it is. Listen, I'll show you what I mean." He raised a finger and called to the barmaid at the far end of the bar. "Hey, Gloria, do you still love me?"

The girl continued with her chores without looking up but replied in a nonchalant and rather less than enthusiastic tone.

"Oh aye, Les, I'm crazy about you, can't get to sleep at night," and in virtually the same breath, she spoke to the customer she was serving, "That'll be two and fourpence please."

Les grinned and raised his shoulders, "There you are, more or less putty in my hands."

Fred had now finished pulling the pints and after placing them on the bar, he raised his hand as Jack offered a ten shilling note. "These two are on me." He then gave Jack a wink, "Must be a big strain to have a Don Juan in the family?"

Jack thanked Fred before answering. "Oh, you don't

know the half of it, one minute he's Fred Astaire, the next he's Tyrone Power and I'll tell you what, if that piano of yours gets going later, he'll be Bing Crosby as well, you mark my words."

Les grinned before taking a gulp of his pint. "Funny you should say that but I've been told I'm a pretty good crooner, listen." He struck a casual pose and started to sing:

"Where the blue of the night meets the gold of the day, someone waits for me…"

At that juncture his voice was stifled as Jack clamped a hand over his mouth and led him briskly away to a large side room boasting a stage, a piano, a set of drums and a microphone that didn't work.

This was the concert room and Les was led to one of its many round tables then firmly seated. "Sit," said Jack, "I'll go and fetch the beer." While he was gone, a couple of fellow miners joined Les to enquire about his brother but before he had the need to elucidate, Jack was back and handshakes were being exchanged. Jack rubbed his hands together and invited the two men to join Les and himself.

"Bring yer beer over lads, I've bin looking forward to this."

He picked up his pint, held it up to the light to examine its colour, closed his eyes and with a smoothness perfected through years of practice, downed three quarters of the amber liquid.

Jack slowly shook his head. "You can't get nowt like this bugger in France." The remaining nectar vanished just as swiftly to be followed by a loud burp.

"Pardon, better out than in," he beckoned to his companions. "Come on lads, it's my shout."

When the glasses were drained of their contents Jack collected them to retrace his steps to the bar, causing Fred to smile as Jack walked towards him carrying the four empty jars.

"Didn't waste much time with that first one; I guess you enjoyed it?"

Jack agreed, confirming the landlord's sound observation. "Never touched the sides Fred, so I'd better have a refill, along with these three as well, please."

At that moment, there was a clatter of boots on the wooden floor as a couple of young men in khaki uniforms entered through the open doors. From their gait it was obvious that the Red Lion was not their first port of call that evening. The shoulder flashes on their tunics proclaimed they were in the Guards and Jack surmised they were not long out of basic training.

"Two pints, barman," they chorused, even before they were half way to the counter.

Fred raised a hand. "Just a minute, lads, not catching a bus are yer? I'll see to you just as I've served this gentleman, and it's landlord, not barman."

The young soldiers looked at one another, tittering as they straightened their uniforms. The more obstreperous of the pair then swayed forward, jingling change in his pocket as he remarked in a sarcastic voice, "Right you are, landlord," putting deliberate emphasis on the word 'landlord'. "When you can spare a minute, we'll have two pints but don't dawdle cos we're very busy men; there's a war on, you know."

Fred nodded, "Aye, I've heard, are you two going to win it for us then?"

The pair looked at each other and again it was the stroppy one who spoke, this time placing his hands on the bar and tapping it with his finger.

"Just leave it to us pal and I'm going to tell you something for nowt, we won't come running back from France like the lot who were over there cos we're the cream, we are."

Jack sighed but kept quiet, looking down at the floor while Fred finished pulling the four pints, "There you are, Jack, I'll get you a tray for this little lot; why should England tremble, eh?"

Jack didn't answer but paid for the drinks and turned to make his way back to the concert room just as one of the soldiers remarked mockingly, "I bet they need the first couple of pints just to wash the coal dust down."

Jack shook his head at the fatuous bravado. 'Daft young buggers,' he thought.

Back in the concert room he set the tray down and Les gave him a hard look.

"You alright, Jack?"

Jack nodded before explaining. "Aye, I'm alright, but there's a couple of young recruits at the bar shouting the odds and if I'm not mistaken, the barmy sods are only just out of training. Aldershot most likely and they're full of it, just can't wait to start on Jerry. Christ, if only the silly buggers knew."

Les didn't wait for Jack to continue any further; he wanted this first night out to be a good one, so he picked up his glass.

"Come on, Jack, sod 'em all, eh? Let's get sozzled." He took a generous sip from his pint before looking round the room.

"Here, how do you fancy the big blonde in the red blouse? I reckon I stand a good chance with her mate, so what do you think?" Another swallow of beer but this time he addressed their companions. "Aren't they sisters off the Carver Estate?" The two men confirmed that they were. "Aye, that's two of them, there's four altogether and the mother is red hot too from what I've heard; you thinking of lusting after big Joyce, then?"

With tongue in cheek he directed the last remark towards Jack, who turned on his stool to glance at the two girls. The blonde was chewing gum and a cigarette was curling smoke from between her fingers. She placed the glowing cylinder between red lips and took a deep draw that hollowed her cheeks as if they had been pinched. A second later she gave a good impersonation of a dragon as twin jets of smoke were expelled from her nostrils. Jack shook his head and turned back to let out a deep breath, feigning indecision before answering.

"Oh, I don't know lads, ask me again just before

throwing out time; my eyesight won't be so good then." This provoked chuckles and the tone was set for the evening. Ten minutes later, a plump middle aged woman made her way to the stage, and amid loud applause she sat down at the piano, for the room was now nearly full so it wasn't long before everyone was accompanying her playing with raucous gusto. Jack and his mates threw back their heads and joined in as all the favourite songs of the day were belted out one after the other and with not a sheet of music in sight. 'Roll out the Barrel', 'Underneath the Arches', 'Paper Doll' – the room came alive as drinks flowed. The miners forgot all about the pit and their daily toil, while some wives and girlfriends tried to ease the sorrow of absent loved ones by briefly living in a world that was not torn asunder by war and its heartaches. Tomorrow they would face them again but just for a short while they would be put aside as inhibitions were suppressed and would-be vocalists displayed assorted levels of talent to give impromptu renderings of their particular favourite. But whatever request was asked of the piano player she delivered it without hesitation, albeit after having to find a key that suited the artiste, therefore requiring considerable musical ability. After a while, a shout went up, directed towards Les.

"Come on, Leslie, let's have one, how about 'Coming round the Mountain'?" Les, with three pints under his belt didn't need a lot of persuading, so he loosened his tie and jumped up on the stage to sing this request. It was particularly popular because the audience could accompany the performer at the appropriate junctures with their own rude versions of the lyrics. After his performance, Les, rewarded by loud clapping and whistles, returned to his seat grinning like a Cheshire cat.

"That were good; might just give 'em a bit of the old crooning near drinking-up time because there's a nice looking girl just come in that I fancy. 'See you in my Dreams'; now that's always a good 'un. What you do is, you pick out this one bird in the audience you've taken a shine to then sing straight at her; Sinatra does it all the time." Les looked round the table for some sign of approval.

Jack pursed his lips; he didn't want to stifle the lad's enthusiasm but he couldn't help a surreptitious wink to the other two.

"Tell you what, Les, you swoon 'em and we'll catch 'em, how's that?"

Les realized he was having his leg pulled but he was beyond caring.

"Alright, alright, maybe I'm not quite as good as Frank, but you have to admit, I'm not bad. Tell you what: say you agree with me and I'll get another round in."

They all laughed and drained their glasses but Jack tapped the table as he slid his empty towards Les.

"We don't have to, little brother, it happens to be your shout anyway so, on yer bike."

Les made his way to the other room and as he did so the pianist decided to have a break, but that didn't stop the singing near the bar. As Les approached he had to perform a neat sidestep to avoid the two soldiers who, with pints in their hands, swayed to their own music making. It was a barrack room ditty and not for the ears of anyone prim and proper, but nothing the clientele of the Red Lion couldn't handle, so Fred did not intervene.

Les nodded in their direction as he ordered the beer. "They seem to be getting a right skinful; I hope they're used to this Yorkshire bitter."

Fred gave a wry laugh as he replenished the four glasses. "Oh, I think they're northern lads but they haven't done a great deal of supping; they just need to grow up a bit so let's hope they get the chance."

He placed the refilled glasses on the bar. "How's your Jack doing in there? I reckon I could hear him singing." Les confirmed that Jack was indeed enjoying himself.

"I tried to get him fixed up with one of them sisters, the blonde one, Joyce, but he didn't seem all that keen; must be getting a bit fussy in his old age."

Fred gave a low whistle, "Hey, there's four of them tha knows and any one of 'em could eat you for breakfast."

He nodded his head towards the two guardsmen.

"I wish these two buggers would get interested, that'd quiet 'em down for a spell."

Les glanced down the bar; the soldiers had finished their song and were again loudly congratulating each other on becoming fully fledged members of His Majesty's Forces and what they intended to do with the German army.

"Our Jack was right then, they have only just finished

their training." He paid for the beer and had to move pretty smartly to avoid having the tray jolted but he returned to the concert room and reached it without any mishap. He set the tray down just as the music resumed, only this time the piano playing was accompanied by someone playing the drums. The room reverberated to a turbulent rendering of 'Kiss me Goodnight, Sergeant Major', followed by 'Bless 'em all'.

Jack was halfway down his pint when he looked at his watch and almost had to shout in order to be heard above the singing.

"Look, there's no need to drink up, but Fred will be calling time any minute so I'm going to get the last round in; I'll get fresh glasses."

He made his way through a haze of cigarette smoke but as he neared the bar one of the young swaddies gave a demonstration of 'right about turn' which sent Jack reeling into a young couple, quietly drinking a few feet away. Jack apologized and turned, expecting the same from the soldier but none was forthcoming, for instead he received an angry glare and abuse.

"Hey, pal, tha needs to be more careful, I'm valuable government property I am, got an important job to do, ain't that right, Terry?" He swayed tipsily and turned to point to his mate before continuing.

"We," and this time he repeatedly indicated with a forefinger to his partner then back to himself, "me and my mate might have to go and do what them other silly sods should have done when they were already in France, but what happened? I'll tell you what happened." He took a swig from his pint pot. "They comes running back like scalded cats, that's what happened; ought to be in t' Salvation Army, not British Army." A drunken finger was poked at his shoulder flash. "Here, look, that's what you need to get the job done proper – the Guards, the bloody Guards." He wiped a dribble of beer from his lips before giving Jack a lopsided grin. Fred had been keeping a careful eye on the situation and winked as Jack moved up to the bar gritting his teeth.

"Keep yer hair on, Jack, he don't know any better, the daft sod." Jack exhaled noisily before placing both hands on the bar. "Better give me four pints quick, please Fred, so I can get back to the concert room."

But the soldier had other ideas and he leaned towards Jack with a noisy belch. "Do yer need all that beer to wash coal dust down?" Turning to his mate, he continued in a loud voice, "Does tha know, Terry, I just can't understand why a man would want to go down a pit instead of in the army.

Jack stared at a row of bottles behind the bar trying hard to ignore the ramblings as the sarcastic tone continued.

"Can you imagine it, Terry, eh, preferring to go working down a pit instead of in the forces? Why, three months at Aldershot would do 'em the world of good, don't you reckon?"

Jack looked at Fred but remained silent, breathing hard as he paid for the beer and picked up the tray to return to the concert room but it was not to be. As he turned, with the tray nicely balanced, the young soldier leaned forward once more to mockingly enquire.

"Wouldn't tha like to be in t' army instead of down pit?"

Jack ignored the question and tried to go on his way, but that was not good enough for his bellicose antagonist who extended his left arm intending to hold Jack and solicit a reply. His aim was poor however and all he succeeded in doing was to jog the tray and send a couple of glasses crashing to the floor amidst a shower of beer; simultaneously he unconsciously clenched his right fist and that was enough for Jack. Virtually throwing the tray and remaining beer on to the bar, he gripped the front of the soldier's tunic then let fly with a full-blooded punch into the lad's face. The blow put him on his back and he slid three or four yards across the bare wooden floor with blood spurting from his nose, now split like a ripe tomato. His mate Terry squared up to Jack ready to do battle, but a loud voice from behind the bar stopped him in his tracks – it was Fred.

"That'd not be a very clever move, young man." Fred's voice was full of intensity as he pointed to Jack. "This chap has only just got back from being bombed, shelled, shot at and being half-drowned at Dunkirk. He also happens to be his platoon's boxing champion, so I reckon it would be a good idea to see to your mate, don't you?"

Terry's shoulders eased and he blew hard. "Oh, Christ!" he said, before turning to his friend, still floundering on his back mumbling away to himself.

"I'll kill the bastard, I will, I'll kill him!"

Terry stepped forward, suddenly sobering as he called over his shoulder, "Sorry, mate, we got a bit carried away." He then knelt down and addressed his blood spattered partner.

"That's enough, John, we were out of order, come on, stand up. I'll help you through to the bog; it's over, pal, settle down."

Les had heard the commotion and by this time was standing beside Jack.

"What the hell happened? You okay?"

Jack turned to his brother, his jaw tight. "Aye, nowt to mek a fuss over, I'm alright." But his fists were still clenched and he felt uneasy because he had enjoyed hurting that soldier; he was even sorry the lad hadn't got up to continue and felt resentful that Fred had intervened to stop his mate having a go. Putting both of them on their backs would have suited him fine. Some of the frustration and opprobrium that had built up by days of having to retreat out of France had found release when he had struck that blow.

Jack was a well-trained, disciplined soldier and his pride had been sorely wounded as he had been forced to backtrack mile after mile, day after day, the only place left to go being the coast and defeat. He had hated it, hated the humiliation of holing up on the beach, of being shelled, dive-bombed, machine-gunned and unable to fight back. Then to wade out to the sea, up to his neck in water, only to see the ship, sent to repatriate him, sunk before his eyes.

Jack was not used to yielding or losing, it wasn't in his nature and Dunkirk had made him bitter. He was still angry, deep inside it was still gnawing away at his gut, only just now a little bit of that bitterness had escaped when he had landed that blow. Some of the ire had been released through his fist and it had felt good. 'Why the hell had Fred butted in? I could have taken both of them.' He glanced at his brother, ran strong fingers through his short hair then almost snarled, "Look, I'm off, there's what's left of a couple of pints on the bar and the rest is down there."

He pointed to the broken glass and beer on the floor now being swept up by Gloria. "I've had enough, see you later." He made his way swiftly towards the door with Les calling after him to return to the concert room but he was in no mood to heed the supplication. Once outside, he took a deep breath of the warm evening air and tilted his head back to gaze skywards. It was now dusk and due to the blackout there were no street lights, no shop windows lit to display their merchandise, just indistinct outlines and shadow. In that semi-gloom, Jack could just make out the shape of the old upping stocks, the well-worn steps and the slab of hewn stone from where the farmers and squires had mounted their horses in the distant past. He sized up the antiquated stone slab and in his present state of mind it represented a challenge, one more means of gratifying his bruised ego. His last attempt to jump it had been less than celebratory, so success was all important, especially so after the last few weeks. He drew in his breath and tensed his muscles. 'Right you bugger, here I come.'

With pounding feet he raced towards his objective before launching himself upwards, arms extended wing-like as if to soar into the night sky. Not enough height and his shoes would catch the leading edge and he would be counting his bruises. One heel did scrape the stone surface but he was safely over and landing with a grunt as air was expelled by the force of his descent. Jack steadied himself, gritting his teeth as he turned to look back in triumph, a wicked grin spreading across his tanned face.

"I did it," he announced in loud jubilant satisfaction before cheekily mocking the ancient stonework by raising his right arm, extending his fist towards the upping stocks and striking the fold of that arm with his left hand so that the fist was raised in disdainful contempt. A scornful chortle emphasized the action prior to turning for home and casting one last glance over his shoulder before the wall of the churchyard hid the dim outline of the Red Lion from view. Very few vehicles were on the road but a service bus passed as he walked swiftly down the main street. Its headlights were hooded and the internal passenger lighting was virtually non-existent, while a dimly lit destination sign read "Worksop – Retford". Jack gave the bus a cursory glance as he concentrated on negotiating the dark thoroughfare until he eventually turned into the avenues. As he approached the first block of houses he became aware of activity in one of the yards, the dim light allowing him to discern a female figure busy filling a bucket with coal. He knew at once it was Valerie so he stopped and stood for a second or two, remembering how it had been between them almost three years ago, for he knew he could now be looking at Mrs Foster, Mrs Jack Foster.

As the scraping and bucket filling continued, he quietly retraced his steps some twenty yards or so before again walking forward, only this time he ensured his line of travel would take him close to the wall of the yard. He whistled a tune as she came into view, but now the bucket was obviously full for she was latching the coalhouse door and she turned as he drew near. Jack stopped in his tracks, the tune fading away to be replaced with an affected note of surprise.

"Valerie? That you, Val?"

There was a faint gasp as the young woman realized who was calling her name. "Jack! I heard someone whistling and I wondered who it was, how are you?"

She walked over to the wall, a pretty lass with shoulder length, dark brown hair and nearly as tall as Jack. In the dim light the genuine warmth of her smile emphasized and complemented the luminosity of a pair of eyes that were large and wide-set. Jack gazed into them as she leaned over the wall and he detected the familiar fragrance of her perfume, vividly recalling her warmth and the fullness of her mouth now so close to his. He gave a little cough before answering, "Oh I'm fine, you know me, just like Hovis bread, I never vary much."

Valerie gave a soft chuckle; "No, you're one of life's survivors, that's for sure." She could just make out the strong clean-cut features she had once kissed so passionately and she felt a little short of breath. After a few pleasantries they fell silent, peering at each other in the dark until Valerie laughed. "What are we standing out here in the blackout for? Do you fancy a cup of tea?"

Jack didn't fancy a cup of tea but he accepted the offer instantly so Valerie turned to pick up the bucket, but Jack was over the wall in a flash and taking the handle from her hand.

"Here, let me do that, Val," he said softly and again his pulse gave a little skip as he momentarily held her fingers in his. He tried to see if there was any reaction from Valerie but it was too dark and she was already walking towards the back door. Jack picked up the bucket and followed her into the kitchen where, at Valerie's request, he deposited the coal then continued through into the living room. It was nicely decorated and fitted out with modern furniture and obviously well cared for; Jack looked round approvingly.

"You've got this looking nice, Val. Cliff's a very lucky man, is he at club?"

He knew Cliff was not at any club but he was curious to hear Valerie's answer. She was settling a kettle on the fire and turned when it was safely in position, she then looked around the room before answering. "Yes," she said with a nod of her head, "I'm quite pleased with it, surprising what you can do with these houses." She looked back to the fire before continuing. "Cliff? No, he's not at the Comrades tonight but he'll want to have a drink with you before you go back." She collected cups and saucers from a sideboard cupboard, along with a sugar bowl and spoons and placed them on the table.

"Come on, sit down, Jack, I'll just get some milk, kettle won't be long." Her summer dress swung about her long legs as she turned to collect milk from the pantry but before going she placed her hands on Jack's shoulders backing him towards an easy chair. "There, make yourself comfy."

Jack sat down, pursing his lips and blowing hard when he was sure Valerie was out of sight. 'Ruddy heck,' he declared to himself, 'she certainly hasn't lost her looks, in fact I think her figure is even better, now she's filled out a bit.'

When Valerie returned with the milk, the kettle was starting to whistle so she sat on the edge of a chair near the fire and spooned tea into a teapot on the hearth. Carefully crossing her legs she looked hard at her visitor before asking coquettishly, "You didn't go and get married to one of those French girls while you were over there, then?"

Jack put on a boyish grin; "Married? ... Me?" He shook his head slowly from side to side. "We were too busy trying not to get caught by Jerry to have any time for fraternising." He wagged a finger in Valerie's direction. "Hey, tha knows very well that if I'd been thinking along them lines I would've married you long ago."

"Oh, aye," retorted Valerie, her eyes opening wide. "Just

what makes you think I might have wanted to marry you then?"

She smoothed her dress over her knee, before allowing her tongue to protrude ever so slightly as she moistened full red lips. Jack tightened his jaw.

'The bugger is teasing me,' he said to himself, then thought back to what would have happened three years ago if she had teased him, but any further reflections were brought to an end as the kettle started to spit. Jack swung his gaze to the grate and automatically reached for his handkerchief but Valerie beat him to it by picking up the teapot in one hand and grabbing an oven cloth with the other.

"Right, Jack, I'll see to it." In one smooth operation she lifted the kettle from the fire to pour boiling water into the teapot which was then placed on the hearth to allow the ingredients to brew. She now rose, leaned forward and placed both hands on the arms of Jack's chair with the result that her brassiere was no longer fulfilling the task for which it was designed. When she spoke, her voice was low, vibrant.

"Let me get you a biscuit, eh?"

Jack gave a silent groan as he surveyed her cleavage but managed to stop himself from saying 'Well at the moment, Val, you can stuff the biscuits but I wouldn't mind a bit of crumpet and I don't mean toasted.' Instead he held up his hand to decline the offer. "Er, no thanks, Val, just the tea will be fine."

He raised his eyes to meet Valerie's and she allowed a little smile to turn the corners of her mouth so she sat down again to pour out two cups of tea. Jack took a sip, feigning appreciation, but his mind was working overtime. What if he came straight out and told her he still fancied her? What if she still fancied him? Why hadn't she said that Cliff was at work? Les had said he was on nights.

He gazed at her intently as she sat there, her legs were again crossed, but this time she hadn't been so careful in arranging her dress. Quite a bit of knee was on display causing Jack's nether region to become active so he pretended to need his handkerchief. When he replaced it in his pocket he surreptitiously adjusted himself in order to hide what was becoming perceptible.

If Valerie had noticed she gave no sign of having done so, but as she chatted on about life and things in general she uncrossed her legs and stretched them out towards the fire. Her knees were not wide apart, just enough to be provocative and Jack sat there suffering, sipping his tea and contemplating the situation. 'Hellfire,' he reflected angrily, 'what happened three years ago is gone, finished, it's over. Val is a married woman with a two, or nearly two, year old kid asleep upstairs and I'm sat here getting all worked up over a bit of leg. Mind you she must know what she's doing sitting like that.' Jack half closed his eyes, as if shutting out the temptation would lessen the desire, but it didn't work, his imagination took over instead. 'Sod it, I'd better go,' he clenched his hands, 'otherwise, as sure as God made little apples, madam there is going to end up on the rug with her frock around her neck and both of us with a guilty conscience in the morning.'

He finished off his tea, tried to ignore the throb in his loins and gave a good pretence of appreciation.

"Thanks, Val, that was fine; look, I'd better be off, I feel shattered, perhaps I need to catch up on all that sleep I've lost. Tell Cliff I'll see him before I go back, probably in the Comrades."

He rose from his chair to place his cup and saucer on the hearth. "Don't get up," the request was spoken softly as he stooped to kiss Valerie on the cheek. She closed her eyes and her bosom soared as she arched her back to raise her face to his lips; her hands gripped the arms of the chair but she remained silent. Jack stood for a second, looking down at her lovely face, but he turned and made his way through the passage to the back door and raised its latch. As it clicked, Valerie called from the living room, her voice hesitant, tentative, "Jack?" There was a slight pause before she continued, "Jack, Cliff is at work, he's on nights."

Jack froze as the implication of those few words sank in, his breathing quickened and the latch was allowed to fall back into place. For a second or two he stood motionless before retracing his steps and was once again standing beside her chair. She hadn't moved, her eyes were still closed, her hands still gripped the arms of the chair and she again arched her back until the fabric of her dress was strained taut. It was obvious she wanted Jack to kiss her but he resisted as his urgency increased, instead he turned to reach up for the chain that regulated the flow of gas to the living room light.

As the chain was drawn downwards the gentle hiss of the gas ceased, replaced by a plopping sound that reduced the hot mantle to a small white dome, bereft of its glowing incandescence. The room was now illuminated only by the flickering flames from the fire but Jack could see Valerie moisten her lips as he bodily picked her out of the chair, walked to the table and positioned her on its edge. She half opened her eyes, her throat dry as she protested with a quiet gasp, "Jack! We shouldn't!" but her demur was less than convincing and Jack was deaf to anything that might stand in the way of his gratification now, he roughly hoisted her dress around her waist.

"I see you still wear French knickers," his tone was animated, excited, he gritted the words through clenched teeth.

Valerie drew in her breath as Jack hooked a finger into the elastic waistband and deftly removed them along with her shoes, which were thrown into the vacated chair.

She placed a hand against his chest. "Jack, what if Kathy comes down?"

Jack was removing his shirt, "Does she usually come down once she's in bed?"

Valerie shook her head, "No ... but."

Jack cut her short, "Well then, why should she come down tonight? Should I put a chair against the door?" He didn't wait for an answer but used a chair from beside the dining table.

Valerie swallowed hard, putting a hand to her mouth, "Somebody might come in, Jack."

Jack looked up from unbuckling his belt, "You expecting anybody at this time of night?" He demanded, almost angrily. "Alright, I'll go and lock the bloody door, what about the windows? Do you want me to bar them while I'm at it?" Now the tone was sarcastic but two seconds later, he was back facing Valerie. "Owt else?"

Valerie bit her lip; "What about Cliff?"

Jack exhaled noisily; "For God's sake, Val; I've seen to the stairs so Kathy can't come down, nobody is going to walk in on us and be honest, you want it as much as I do. Cliff isn't going to miss a slice off a cut loaf and right now my need is greater than his." By the time he had finished speaking, his voice was almost hoarse and his trousers were now around his ankles, revealing quite plainly that his need was undeniably urgent.

Valerie closed her eyes and gave a faint gasp as Jack placed both hands between her knees and drew them apart, he was breathing deeply as he searched her face, but the signs of love that used to be there were no longer present. There were no kisses, no softly spoken words, no caresses, only an urgency that compelled his action to be swift, savage almost, then he set about his mission with fervour and a passion that had them both gasping for breath. His release was accompanied by a stifled moan as his fingers dug into Valerie's buttocks before he allowed his head to sink on to her shoulder. They clung to each other breathing heavily. A full two minutes passed with only the flickering flames of the fire making any sound or movement until Jack took a small backward step and adjusted his attire. Valerie remained on the edge of the table, her hands gripping the rim and her head bowed as if she was deep in thought.

"Don't light the gas," she said softly as Jack made a movement to reach for the chain, his hand fell back to his side and he pressed his lips together as she looked up.

"Could you get me a drink of water?"

Jack nodded and picked up her cup from the hearth, "I could mash another cup of tea if you like."

"No, just a drink of water, please."

He made his way to the kitchen; it was dark but the sink wasn't difficult to locate and he was soon returning with the cup half filled with water.

Valerie was now standing in front of the fire smoothing her dress. He offered her the cup.

"Thanks," she murmured with a deep sigh. "Look, Jack, this must never happen again, I'm not trying to put all the blame on you because you were right, I did want you but I'm married and I've got Kathy to think about. Three years ago I loved you, I thought I had got over it; well maybe I haven't and I should've realized the consequences when I invited you in, so I'm just as much to blame as you."

Jack took hold of her by her shoulders, looking deep into her eyes. He wanted to take her in his arms, cover her mouth with his, but he felt that to do so would be more wrong than what had just taken place. He gave her shoulders a squeeze.

"Stop it, Val, don't feel guilty, I should have gone when I first meant to go then it wouldn't have happened. And I could say I'm sorry it did, but if the truth be known, I'm not." He closed his eyes as he recalled the transport that had overwhelmed him just a short while ago. "God knows I needed you, Val, I don't think you can realize just how much." He shook her gently, "I don't want you feeling responsible, do you hear me?"

Valerie nodded, "I think I knew how much it meant to you. I could sense it."

Jack glanced up to the ceiling. "Do you want me to light the gas?"

"No, it may as well be left off." Valerie shoved past Jack to stir the fire and the room brightened as the flames danced, casting strange shadows.

"Will you come and see us before you go back, back off leave?" Jack knew he wouldn't but he was reluctant to say so. "I'll try and slip in to say cheerio sometime before next weekend." He stepped towards Valerie but she moved away.

"Don't kiss me, Jack."

"Okay, I'm off then." Jack made his way briskly through the passage and once again stood before the back door to lift the catch and turn the key, this time the door swung open and he stepped out into the blackness of the night. As he made his way between the rows of houses he clenched his fists, tilted his head and drew in copious draughts of air. It was as if he had recovered from an illness, or had a burden lifted from his shoulders. Dunkirk was a grim reality of war and needed to be forgotten. His step was lighter as he made his way home.

CHAPTER FOUR

A Visit to Aunt Vera's

A Saturday morning in the Foster household was always disorderly, with only Annie and Susan needing a set time for getting out of bed: Susan because she had to catch a bus to Worksop, and Annie because she was a mother and therefore needed to see that her daughter had a proper breakfast before going out to work. This Saturday was no exception and it was past 9.30 by the time Les and Billy had roused in order to partake of breakfast. Not that wartime rations enabled anyone to indulge all that freely but Annie did get the extra egg from time to time so they were favourite to be on the menu. Available boiled, fried, poached or scrambled and with dry, toasted or fried bread, depending on your fancy. Today Billy was in luck: he had opted for his particular speciality and it had been granted. A thick slice of bread with a circular hole cut in its centre before being placed in a frying pan and an egg broken into the hole. After being fried it was served piping hot and Billy loved it. He sat at the table opposite his brother who was enjoying his second cup of tea.

Billy nodded towards the stairs. "Our Jack not up?" But Les ignored the question, looked over his shoulder towards the kitchen where Annie could be heard at work, then leaned forward to speak in a hushed voice. "Here, Billy, how would you like a nice little job in a couple of weeks' time?" Billy looked up from munching his egg and fried bread. "Doing what, Les?"

Les again looked round to make sure Annie was still in the kitchen.

"A nice little job, right up your street."

Billy grimaced, "Oh no, if it's putting dubbin on your football boots, then no thanks."

Les shook his head with yet another glance towards the kitchen.

"No! No! Nothing like that and look, you're not to tell anybody."

Billy forked another piece of fried bread into his mouth before answering. "Okay, okay, but are you going to tell me what the job is or not? I'm not a mind reader."

Les hesitated and pointed a finger; "If you let on, I'll kick your arse." Billy shook his head: he was curious now. If Les didn't want his mother to know, it must be interesting so he nodded for Les to continue.

"Right, well listen, some of us at pit are getting a tossing ring set up shortly, probably near the old tip, and we'll need a lookout, maybe two. Somebody a bit nippy like, so they can scarper if they have to and they need a good pair of eyes. I reckon if somebody got up to the top of the old slag heap they'd be able to see right up Breck Lane towards Laughton and spot any cop car that might be on its way

—79—

down." Les paused for a moment, gave a further glance towards the kitchen then continued. "I said we might need two because it'd also be a good idea to have somebody at that far end to keep an eye on that track from the road leading to Todwick."

Billy was now all ears; this was right up his street. "When do you think it will be, Les?"

Les drummed the table, "Well you'll have to be home from school, so maybe on a Saturday and probably in a couple of weeks."

Billy's eyes lit up. "How much, if I do it?"

Les pursed his lips. "How about a tanner?"

Billy laughed out loud. "Come off it, Les, an important job like that, it has to be worth at least two bob. I'll tell you what, call it two bob and I'll climb up that old gantry on the top; if I do that, I bet I could see as far as Laughton Church."

Les placed a finger to his lips and made a shushing sound. "Quiet, you daft bugger, if Ma gets wind of this she'll go mad. Look, I'll tell you what, you can have a shilling, no more, okay?"

Billy pretended to ponder. "Can I tell Jimmy?"

Les stabbed a finger towards his young brother. "Not till I say you can, and I mean it, do you hear?"

Billy nodded agreement so Les continued. "There are enough miserable buggers at pit would get the law on us if they knew where and when, so it has to be kept dark."

At that point Annie came from the kitchen to collect

their pots, so any further discourse was interrupted. They fell silent.

"What are you two cooking up between you?" Annie asked. "Something you shouldn't be, I bet. By the way, our Billy, I don't want you running off this morning; we're going to see your Aunt Vera and the new baby so don't go away and don't get dirty."

Billy pulled a face, "Oh, Mam, do I have to go? I could always have a bit of dinner at Jimmy's."

"You're going with me, now slip upstairs and see if Jack's getting up. Ask him what he wants for breakfast, not that there's a lot of choice, so tell him not to get too choosy." Billy rose from the table but not before receiving a knowing look from his brother that could only have been interpreted as meaning, 'remember what I have just told you, or else.' Annie cleared the crockery while Les vacated his chair to go and preen himself in the mirror over the sideboard.

"Dad did a good job when he created me, don't you reckon so, Ma?"

"Oh, I don't suppose I may not've had a part in it, just a bit?"

Les screwed up his eyes as if in deep thought. "Well I suppose the good looks, the poise and the charm could have come from your side, but apart from that?"

He concluded by extending a hand, palm uppermost, as one does sometimes when asking a question. Annie however had lots to do so she avoided being drawn any further and instead gave Les a push towards the passage.

"Go on, clever clogs, make yourself useful – we need some more coal in. By the way, did our Jack enjoy himself last night? He's having a good lie-in; didn't get drunk, did he?"

Les affirmed that Jack had enjoyed himself and no, he hadn't got drunk. No mention was made of the disturbance at the bar or of Jack leaving the pub early, he would only comment on that if he received a direct question about the incident. However his own curiosity was aroused as to where Jack had mooched off to because he himself was home and in bed by the time Jack had returned.

At that point, Billy started downstairs to say that Jack was awake and getting dressed, so Les decided that after getting the coal in he would have five minutes in the armchair with maybe a chance to have his interest satisfied.

"Did you ask him about breakfast?" Annie inquired as Billy jumped the last two steps to land in a heap before answering.

"Oh yes," gasped Billy, "he said he'll have a boiled egg and a couple of slices of toast but he'll have a wash and a shave first, so to hang on a bit with the egg." Billy looked at his mother. "Do I have to go and see the new baby?"

Annie didn't answer; she had no need to. Billy only had to glance at her face to know he had no choice but to resign himself to the forthcoming bus ride, plus all the 'diddums' and 'coochie coos' that would accompany greeting the new offspring. 'What a palaver over a baby,' thought Billy, but Annie was looking forward to visiting her younger sister.

South Anston was only a short bus ride away and outings were a bit of a rarity so she liked to make the most of them, and anyway she wanted to see the baby. John would not be going but Billy would be company for her even though she knew he wasn't very enthusiastic; 'maybe she would treat him to something later.' All further thoughts of the trip were deferred as Jack pushed open the stairs door, bidding everyone "Good morning" before making his way into the kitchen.

As he went through he called over his shoulder, "Hey, Les, can you let me have your locker keys later? I'd like a shower at the pit baths."

Les agreed and reasoned that the loaning of the key would provide him with an ideal opportunity to find out where Jack had got to the previous night. So he decided to forego his five minutes in the armchair and instead take a steady stroll up the main street to the billiard hall and maybe win himself a bob or two if he was on form. He donned a sports jacket, bid everyone "Cheerio", but stopped to tickle Billy under the chin and whisper "Coochie coo" and "Don't forget to change its nappy." Billy pulled a face at the prospect and in due course, he too was being told to get ready and to ensure he had a clean handkerchief.

"What are your hands like?" Annie enquired, so Billy offered them up for inspection.

"Right, they'll do but your shoes could do with a polish." As she spoke she glanced at the clock and calculated that the ten minute walk to the bus stop would provide a few minutes before the bus was due but not if the bus was early.

"No time to start polishing shoes now, just give them a quick rub over with a cloth then find your cap."

Billy donned his school cap but it wasn't positioned to Annie's liking so it underwent some readjustment. She addressed Jack.

"If your Dad comes back while you're still here, tell him we should be home on the same bus as our Susan. Don't forget … please."

Jack was still seated at the table reading the newspaper but he assured his mother he would inform his father or leave a note if he should leave the house before John returned.

Farewells were again exchanged then mother and son set of at a brisk pace to catch their bus and it wasn't long before Billy's cap was again perched on the back of his head. As they neared the designated picking up point, Annie nodded in its direction.

"I see Mrs Repeat-herself is waiting for the bus as well, look."

Billy grinned at his Mother's remark as he recognized the woman who was already at the bus stop, for she also lived on the avenue but quite a few doors from the Fosters. For as long as Billy could remember he had been intrigued by her conversational quirk of reiterating the last few words of whatever she had just said and sometimes, what other people had said also. It was like standing in a room with an echo or listening to a record with a defect; Billy cocked his ears in expectation.

"Morning, Madge," Annie greeted her neighbour as she and Billy automatically formed a queue before looking round to see if the bus was in sight.

"Morning, Annie." Madge clutched a handbag to her chest and inspected Annie and Billy intently. "You and Billy going to Worksop, to Worksop?"

The extra 'Worksop' was spoken in a tone that trailed away and Billy looked swiftly down the road in order to hide his toothy grin. Annie however had more self-control and explained that they were just going as far as South Anston, to her sister's, to take a few baby clothes and to have a look at the new baby.

"Oh your Vera's had her first, has she? That'll be nice for her, nice for her." There was a thoughtful pause. "I'd've liked another one but it wasn't to be, wasn't to be."

Annie remarked that things happened for the best and received a "For the best" back from Madge. Further conversation was interrupted by the sound of an approaching vehicle and they all stepped back from the edge of the pavement.

"It's here, Mam," exclaimed Billy and a double-decker bus bearing the livery of Sheffield Transport trundled to a halt before them. They boarded the bus and while Annie and Madge made themselves comfortable on the lower deck, Billy bounded upstairs hoping that the front seat would be vacant. He favoured that particular one as it enabled him to simulate driving the huge swaying conveyance but today he was out of luck so he retraced his steps and took a seat behind his mother and Mrs Repeat-herself. The bus wound its way along streets and through the avenues that made up the mining village until eventually it arrived at the main bus terminal, in the square where Jack had performed his bit of hurdling the previous night. Two other buses were already parked in their respective spaces and Billy knew there would be a five minute stay to enable passengers to change coaches if their eventual destination required them to do so. Routes to Worksop, Retford, Mansfield, Chesterfield, Sheffield, Rotherham and Doncaster were all available if one was prepared to change buses at certain points on the journey. Billy passed the five minutes by inspecting the advertising hoardings fixed to the high boundary walls and farm buildings bordering one side of the square. One displayed a giant glass of beer with a smiling face etched in the froth and bearing the message, 'You've had something more than a drink when you've had a Guinness.' Another advertisement illustrated a very attractive woman with a question written alongside asking, 'How does she keep so slim and healthy?' The answer read, 'Each night she takes Bile Beans.' Billy pulled a face for he reckoned that didn't sound very nice, but the next poster had him thinking along very different lines. It showed a huge open mouth with a round chocolate sweet about to be popped in. Big bold letters underneath it proclaimed 'Maltesers for you, 2d a bag. Simply bags of nourishment.' Billy leaned forward to rest his arms on the back of the seat in front.

"Mam, can I have a bag of Maltesers when we get to Anston? They sell 'em at that shop near Chapel Walk."

Annie interrupted her conversation with her companion, to look back at Billy.

"We'll see, perhaps if you can keep out of mischief I might."

Billy licked his lips, directing his next question to Mrs Repeat-herself.

"Do you like Maltesers, Mrs Clark?" He leaned quickly forward in order to catch the echo but his Mother gave him a withering look. Madge meanwhile, clasped and unclasped her handbag before answering.

"Well I am partial to a bit of chocolate and they do seem good value, good value, yes."

Billy was eager to continue but his mother had other ideas, for she knew what he was up to. Holding his chin in one hand she pulled his cap forward with the other and gave the peak an extra tug to settle it firmly in what she deemed to be its correct position.

"Keep it on properly," she demanded, so Billy sank back into his seat but he knew if he trapped his cap between his head and the back of the seat he could manoeuvre it to any position he liked and still say he hadn't touched it. He was busy with his little plan of action when the bus roared into life, followed almost immediately by two rings of a bell and a cry of "Fares, please."

Billy finalized the rearranging of his cap to gaze once more out of the window in order to catch any unusual activity that might be of interest as they traversed the few miles to South Anston.

The bus turned left out of the square then a sharp right, to follow the contours of the park with its high iron railings enclosing its twenty or so acres. The railings however, were being dismantled and a cry came from two ladies.

"Oh look," exclaimed Madge, "they're taking all the railings away; well I never did, I never."

Annie nodded in agreement with Madge's observations. "I've heard they want all the scrap metal they can get, on t' wireless t' other day they said that they were coming round to collect all our old pots and pans to help make aeroplanes and such like. Well I've got one or two they can have and I'll tell you what, if it would end the war any quicker, they could have the whole ruddy lot."

"As far as that goes, they could have all mine an' all, that they could,' agreed Madge.

Billy leaned forward again, now that the conversation was getting interesting.

"Do you reckon they could mek a tank out of that lot, Mam?"

Annie regarded the workmen dismantling the ornate railings. "I don't know if they would mek a tank but every little helps. I know it's a shame to see 'em go, but if it aids the war effort then tek the whole lot I say."

"Aye, tek the whole lot," repeated Madge.

Billy's gaze was now drawn to three chestnut trees he was very familiar with, for in a few months with the railings no longer in place, it would make his annual raid on them a lot easier. Over the past few years he had been chased away at least twice every autumn in his search for a supreme conker. Jimmy Keats had the champion last year, but that was last year.

The bus was now nearing Pond Corner, so-called because of the regular collection of rainwater at the low end of the field near the road. In a really wet spell the water would rise high enough for it to spill over the boundary wall and accumulate on the tarmac to resemble a miniature lake. There was no water today however, but Billy looked with interest at a bomb-like crater in the middle of the field they were now passing and he allowed his imagination free rein:

A German bomber complete with aircrew, the bombardier with his hand on the release button waiting for their house to come into the bomb sights. On the ground, his mother is busy cooking dinner. Within the bomber the intercom crackles into life, "Achtung, Herr Kapitän, the Foster residence is only two kilometres away," rasps the navigator.

"Very good, Fritz, we have to make sure the bomb goes straight down the chimney – the Führer has ordered it; we will start the bombing run ..." His voice trails away then continues in a tone filled with fear. "Gott im Himmel, what is this? Achtung, it is Billy in his Spitfire; release the bomb now or we are all doomed!"

Down goes the bomb to explode harmlessly in the field.

Billy warms to his fantasizing and raises an arm to represent the nose of a fighter plane; a swastika comes into focus on his gun sights. "Ratatat-ratatat-ratatat," snarls his deadly machine guns as they spit fierce retribution from the wings of his plane. A billow of smoke spurts from the pride of the Luftwaffe and it goes into a helpless spin; Billy banks his plane and watches as the German crew bail out one by one so he raises a hand in salute. As the white parachutes float to earth, he heads towards Bennington to perform a victory roll over the four rows of houses, one of them now saved from destruction by the lone Spitfire. At the sound of the Rolls-Royce Merlin engine, a small figure in a blue wrap-over pinafore emerges from this particular house and waves. Billy waggles the wings of his plane then executes a perfect loop-the-loop before heading back to his airfield to have another swastika painted on the Spitfire's fuselage.

As the big double-decker jolted to a halt it brought Billy's daydream to an end and passengers alighted or boarded the vehicle. Annie looked over her shoulder, furrowing her brow as she observed the satisfied expression on Billy's face.

'The little devil is cooking something up, I'll be bound,' she thought, but she just nodded to his head and uttered one word, "Cap."

At the destination point, Annie rose to alight and to say

cheerio to her companion. "I hope you get what you want in Worksop."

Billy jumped off then Annie stepped down carrying the shopping bag and her handbag.

"Here you are, Billy, carry this for me" she requested, holding out the shopping bag.

"Oh, Mam, do I have to?" But he took hold of the bag nevertheless.

"It won't bite you; frightened of being seen carrying a shopping bag for your Mam, then?"

Billy swung the bag over his shoulder just in case any of his school chums should see him carrying it; he reckoned it would look more manly.

However, the action was not necessary as no one of any consequence was encountered as they covered the short distance from the church to number 2 South Street, an end house in a terrace of four. They were all neat and looked well cared for, with front doors that were just three paces from the pavement, and it was on the first of these doors that Annie now knocked before pushing it open.

"Cooee! Anybody home? It's only me." The call preceded her entrance as she stepped into a small hallway with a flight of stairs just inside the door. Dark red linoleum covered both the hall floor and the stairs which, on previous visits, Annie had deemed to be dangerous to have on stairs.

"Vera, it's me, can you hear me?" A door opened just as she was about to mount the first step.

"It's our Annie," a female voice said excitedly, before a young man appeared at the head of the stairs to beckon Annie up. "Is John with her?" inquired the voice again and this time the young man answered.

"Aye, it's your Annie and a smart looking young bloke wi' a school cap on; well I'll be blowed, it's Billy."

Beckoning again, the young man invited the two visitors to climb the stairs.

"Come on up, Annie, we're in t' front room. Thee an' all, Billy, come and have a look at thi new cousin; he's a reet bobby-dazzler."

Annie and Billy did as invited and followed the young man into a bedroom overlooking the street they had just walked down. Annie entered first and rushed over to her young sister propped up in the big double bed.

"Vera lass, how are you?"

A plump young woman held out her arms, laughing as they warmly embraced.

"Right as rain now, Annie, but I think I'm going to let Tim have the next one; only I don't think he's too keen on the idea."

This time they both had a giggle as the young man shuffled his feet.

"Wouldn't worry me none, and any road up I reckon we did a right good job wi' this first 'un, so we'll carry on as nature intended. Just have a look here, Annie and thee Billy, he'll be wanting to play football wi' thi in no time."

Tim waved his hand proudly before him as they all

headed towards a wooden cot with its little bundle safely ensconced, and Annie instantly let out a cry of delight.

"Oh the little treasure, isn't he a beauty? What ... a ... little ... smasher; look Billy, your new cousin."

Billy wrinkled his nose as he detected that characteristic odour one associates with small babies, especially when one enters the room for the first time. He looked down at the pink wrinkled face; 'not much to look at,' he thought, but as he glanced at Tim grinning like a Cheshire cat he knew he had to tread wary.

"Smashing, Uncle Tim, our Les reckoned he didn't think you had it in you but I'll tell him he were wrong, I will that."

Billy had hardly finished speaking before he received a clip round the proverbial from his mother.

"All right, clever clogs, that'll be enough of that; Les never said any such thing." She turned to Vera; "He's lovely, Vera, can I hold him for a minute?"

Vera was still laughing at Billy but she nodded.

"Course you can, Annie. He'll be waking up for a feed soon anyway; pick him up for us, Tim, please."

Tim leaned into the cot and gently picked up the white bundle to carefully hand to his wife; Vera then straightened the baby's clothes before passing him into Annie's outstretched arms.

Billy gazed at the ceiling, still rubbing his ear. 'Can't see what all the fuss is about,' he mused, but aloud he ventured to ask, "Hey, Mam, do you remember on t' bus you said I could have some Maltesers?"

"I said maybe, if you behaved yourself."

Meanwhile Vera took pity on Billy. "Is it alright if I buy him some Maltesers?" she asked.

Annie considered for a second or two before replying, "Well I suppose so but not that he deserves any mind, just look at his cap again. The times I've put it straight and he knows he shouldn't be wearing it, not in the house."

Vera gave Billy a wink. "How much are they?"

"Well they have boxes at just sixpence, or they might have some little packets with just a few in ..."

Annie interrupted before he could carry on to elaborate any further.

"They're tuppence, Vera, never mind about his big boxes and if they haven't any packets then it's hard lines."

Vera pointed to a dressing table. "Pass my purse, Tim, it's in that top drawer."

Tim however, put his hand in his pocket and jingled a few coins.

"Here thy are, Billy lad, tuppence did tha say? I reckon I can manage that." Billy deftly caught a couple of pennies as they were flipped in his direction.

"Aw thanks, Uncle Tim; thanks, Aunt Vera; can I go and get them, Mam?"

Annie nodded so Billy was down the stairs like a shot and racing towards Chapel Walk and the adjacent sweet shop.

Minutes later they heard the front door open and close then Billy came bounding up the stairs. "Got some," he announced, bursting triumphantly into the room to hold aloft his already partly depleted bag of Maltesers.

Annie and Tim went downstairs to make a drink so Billy settled himself on the end of the bed in anticipation of watching the baby getting his milk. He slowly introduced a Malteser into his mouth as he sat swinging his legs, all agog as an ample bosom was revealed and the crabby bairn hungrily attached himself to his lunch. The kicking and grizzling ceased miraculously.

"Noisy little devil, isn't he, Billy?"

Billy's eyes were like organ stops as two pouting pink lips suckled greedily in unison, a little fist clenching and unclenching as he did so.

"Yeah! Good job it's not beer, else he'd get like our Les sometimes does and not be able to see straight." Billy was thoroughly enjoying the spectacle. "Tell you what, he's making me feel thirsty."

His need was soon resolved, for Annie and Tim returned with a brew at which time the conversation turned to options for a meal. This gave Billy an opportunity to pay a quick visit to a nearby favourite play area while Tim detailed the available choices.

"Vera, could tha fancy some fish and chips, and the same for you, Annie?"

Both women looked at each other before nodding approval.

"That'll do me fine, also for our Billy," Annie remarked.

Vera acquiesced. "Just a fish for me, but I know Billy likes scallops so get him scallops with some batter bits, then whatever you fancy for yourself.

Tim departed and it wasn't long before hot fish and chips were being turned out onto respective individual plates, just as Billy came in, sniffing appreciatively.

"Smells good, Uncle Tim, did you get me any scallops?"

"Aye, and some batter bits."

"Oh great, I can mek scallop sandwiches. My all-time favourite they are, next to steamed jam roly-poly pudding; thanks, Uncle Tim."

Without any prompting he went to the sink to wash his hands.

'Well, well, that makes a change,' thought Annie, 'perhaps he's sickening for something.' Out loud however, "you feeling alright, Billy?"

"Yes thanks, Mam, I'm hungry though," and he eyed the scallops covetously as they were discharged from their wrapping and onto a plate.

"Can I sit to table?"

"Aye go on, I shan't be a minute but you can start; save 'em getting cold and listen, I'm going to spread two slices of bread but if you want any more you'll have to eat it dry."

"That's okay, Mam, I don't mind." Billy went about constructing his famous scallop sandwich. A thick slice of bread upon which he carefully laid a layer of scallops, then a liberal sprinkling of crunchy batter bits, followed by even more scallops. When the sandwich was finished it was a good two inches thick.

"Don't thee go and drop that on thi foot, Billy," Tim was loading the tray as he eyed Billy's handiwork. "Big enough to gag a donkey is that," and he gave a running commentary to Vera as he climbed the stairs.

"Vera, tha wants to see what Billy's got; without a word of a lie he's got a sandwich there that must be six inches thick, I'm not kidding." He laughed at his own exaggeration as he carried the tray into the bedroom.

"Well he's a growing lad; he'll enjoy it, bless him," enthused Vera. While in a louder voice, "Don't you skimp on the margarine, Annie; me and Tim will be alright for rations so let Billy have what he wants."

A muffled "Aye, alright," drifted back upstairs but in the kitchen Billy knew that if he wanted to make any more sandwiches it would be with dry bread. For the moment however, he was content as he bit into his gastronomic delight.

"By gum, this is grand; I'm glad I came now." The words were barely audible as his jaws grappled with their prodigious task, and at the end of the meal his face had a look of contentment.

"Thanks, Mam, I'm full up, alright if I go back to the Garden of Remembrance, till it's time to catch bus?"

"Don't forget we'll be catching the same bus that our Susan will be on, so come when I call you. What are you doing over there anyway?"

"Just looking at birds in the aviary and there's some goldfish in the pond, so can I take a piece of bread? There's an old man from across the road sits in there nearly all day – he always has some bread with him." Annie put half a slice of bread in some newspaper.

"Here you are and don't forget, come when I call you and try and keep clean."

As Billy left, Tim came downstairs. "Don't mind if I slip out for a bit, do you, Annie? Only I want to see how the arrangements are going for this fete we're having next weekend. The committee decided that this year would probably be the last until the war is over, which reminds me, will Jack still be on leave next Saturday?"

Annie confirmed that he would.

"Right, well listen, if you want a nice piece of meat for dinner, tell Jack to turn up for the boxing tournament next Saturday afternoon. It should start about three o'clock and it will be in that field leading into Anston Stones, same as it always is. There's nobody round here much better than your Jack when it comes to fisticuffs, and a nice joint of pork would be nice, wouldn't it?"

Annie sighed; she didn't like boxing but she promised to pass the message on.

"Right, Annie, I'll be off, so what time will you be wanting me to get back here? So I can mek sure I'm back before you go."

Annie explained about the bus times so Tim promised to return before 5.30. He slipped a jacket on then changed his mind and hung it back in the hall.

"A bit warm for a jacket and this waistcoat; I'll see you

before half past." He then called upstairs, "I'm off Vera, be back before your Annie goes."

"Right you are."

Tim left by the back door to cut across the yard towards another terrace of houses running at right angles to his own. Half a dozen starlings took flight as his boots crunched along a stone path. Annie meanwhile, busied herself in the kitchen, washing a few baby clothes then spent the rest of the afternoon chatting to her sister with hardly a murmur from the baby, except when he decided he was hungry again. Just before five o'clock Annie said she would go down and set the table and a tray.

"It'll be ready for when Tim returns then you two can have your meal when you please. Me and Billy will have ours when we get home but I don't know what, not until I have a look in the pantry – something quick and easy probably."

A little while later, Tim returned as promised, bringing word that everything was set for the planned fete the following Saturday including the featured boxing competition. The prize for the winners would indeed be a piece of pork donated by a local butcher.

"Don't forget to tell your Jack, because as I said before, there's nobody round here that I know of can touch him."

"Yes, yes, I won't forget!" she promised, then went outside to give Billy a call. She could hear laughter on the other side of the high wall so her son was obviously not alone, but he answered promptly enough when he heard his name.

"Right you are, Mam, won't be a minute, just got to finish this game."

"You've got two minutes because I don't want to miss that bus and you'll need a wash, do you hear?"

More laughter accompanied the sound of scuffling before Billy's head bobbed over the top of the wall, minus his cap. "I'm coming," he shouted, then with someone's help he was hoisted upwards until he could straddle the stone coping, and with a rolling action he was over, to drop in a heap at his mother's feet.

"Just look at you, can't you keep clean for five minutes, and where's your cap for goodness sake?"

There were giggles on the far side of the wall and a voice chortled.

"Here you are, Mrs Foster," followed by the cap sailing over to clear the top of the wall by a good six feet.

"Thanks," shouted Billy, slapping the green and yellow cap on his buttocks to get rid of the dust. This was followed with an innocent, "Right, Mam, I'm ready."

But Annie was having none of it.

"Oh no you're not, just look at you! How can you get so mucky in such a short time? Off you go inside and have a wash; you're not catching the bus looking like that, and don't take all day. When you've finished, go up and say 'cheerio' to your Aunt Vera and Uncle Tim."

"See yer, Billy," chorused voices from the other side of the wall, which Billy acknowledged as he made his way indoors. "Yeah, see yer, maybe next week at the gala, bye."

A few minutes later he was offering up his face for inspection.

"Well it looks clean enough but I bet you haven't washed the back of your neck, but it'll have to do till we get home. Now go and say 'cheerio'."

Billy called from the bottom of the stairs, "Cheerio, Aunt Vera," but his mother wasn't satisfied.

"Go and say 'cheerio' proper." Her voice was vexed and she followed a reluctant Billy up to the bedroom where Vera held out her arms as he walked through the door.

"Come on, come and give your Aunt Vera a kiss," and with a chuckle she planted a big kiss on Billy's cheek.

Annie meanwhile, walked round to the cot to stand looking down at the sleeping infant. "You've got a little treasure here, our Vera, so tek care of yourself luv and the little 'un." She too embraced her sister warmly.

"I'll see you next Saturday with Tim being at the fete, because my lot will be there if Jack is boxing. All being well you'll be out of bed, but remember what I've said and don't go trying to do too much. I'll say bye for now and see you next week." Another embrace was exchanged then she and Billy made to go downstairs.

"Thanks for coming, Annie, and thanks for the baby clothes. Bye."

Annie gave a little wave as they went through the door followed by a call to Tim as she was halfway down the stairs.

"Bye, Tim, I'll be over next week. Do you reckon I should get some pork stuffing and apple sauce ready?"

Tim came to the doorway and laughed. "I'm telling thee, Annie, that leg of pork or whatever it is, is as good as in your oven, you'll see. Anyway, thanks for coming over, and thee Billy, did tha enjoy it in t' garden? I could hear thi laughing.

"Yes thanks, Uncle Tim, see you in t' Stones next Saturday, all being well." Billy opened the front door and stepped onto the little path, and Annie called upstairs as she was halfway through the doorway.

"Off now then, Vera, is there anything you want me to bring next week? Owt you need for the baby?"

"No ta, Annie, remember me to everybody. Bye luv."

Annie closed the door behind her and hurried to catch up with Billy who was already heading towards the church, its steeple visible above the roofs of the houses.

"Right you are, Billy, best foot forward."

When the bus arrived, it turned out to be a single-decker private coach run by a local firm who only operated on the Bennington to Worksop route. Annie was pleased for she preferred it to the big lumbering double-deckers; she said the coach was quicker and had better seating.

Susan waved through a window as the bus came to a halt and Billy, being Billy, pulled a funny face so Susan retaliated by sticking her tongue out, much to the amusement of the other passengers. Only one seat was available so Billy went to stand behind the driver; he liked to watch the gear changes as the bus negotiated the hills and the bends en route to Bennington.

'Pity I can't see his feet' thought Billy, but the partition obstructed his view of how the driver manipulated the clutch, throttle and brake pedals. Despite this drawback he 'drove' the bus all the way back to their destination and in no time at all the bus was drawing to a halt near the avenues. Music greeted them as they entered home and Les could be heard warbling an accompaniment to Billy Scott-Coomber singing with Jack Payne and his orchestra on the wireless. Les was eyeing himself in the mirror over the sideboard as he too sang "It's a lovely day today" but his voice trailed away, leaving Billy Scott-Coomber to carry on alone as three pairs of eyes took in the scene.

A slow handclap from Susan resulted in an unabashed "Thank you" from her brother, followed by a low bow.

"I was just checking on my presentation: it's important for us vocalists when we perform in public."

"If you ask me you were just fancying yourself." The dry comment came from Annie as she took off her coat. "What with all this crooning, have you had anything to eat, and where's your Dad and our Jack?" The two questions came one after the other so Les answered them in the same order.

"No, we decided to wait till you came home, and Jack is down at pigeons wi' father; they said to send Billy down as soon as you came in."

Annie nodded to Billy and he shot off to give Jack and his father a call from the end of the avenue. Meanwhile, Annie was donning her apron and giving instructions to Susan and Les.

"Right, Susan, I'm going to mek a salad for quickness; if

you set the table our Les can fill the kettle and get teapot ready, it won't take but ten minutes."

During the meal Les enquired of his sister. "Let's see, Clarke Gable at the pictures tonight, in't it, Susan? Going with anybody I know?"

"Shouldn't think so but that reminds me, Betty came into the store today asking about you. Apparently she's finished with that Canadian. "Not as nice as your Les", she said and I thought, 'Blimey, he must be a right lummox then,' but anyway she wants remembering to you, seemed pretty keen too."

Les chewed on a piece of luncheon meat, with a self-satisfied look on his face. "It's a big responsibility you know, having this power over women."

Billy laughed out loud. "We caught him singing into mirror, didn't we, Susan?"

Les raised a finger. "Ah well, you see when you perform in public ..." but he wasn't able to continue because Susan interrupted.

"Yes, Leslie, you told us, stage presence and all that."

"Yes that's right, I got asked to do an encore at Red Lion last night, didn't I, Jack?"

Jack nodded, "He did an' all, mind you the request came from the landlord. He'd already shouted time and wanted to clear the place so he asked Les to sing ... it worked like magic."

There was laughter from everyone round the table, including Les.

"Just you wait till I get on the wireless singing wi' Ambrose or Joe Loss. I can hear the announcer: 'Ladies and gentlemen, Britain's answer to Bing Crosby ... the one and only Lee Forest!' ... That's what my stage name'll be."

John gestured with his fork. "Sounds reet enough, but I wouldn't give mi job up at pit just yet if I were thee." He winked across at Annie but she raised her eyebrows before answering. "Oh you never know, miracles do happen. Now then, more bread anyone?"

Billy had two more slices.

"Where does tha put it all, Billy?" Jack asked in amazement. "You scoff like a horse yet you're like a yard of pump watter; where's it all go to?"

Billy flexed his arm to display a small lump in the region of his biceps. "It's all muscle Jack, look. By the way, has Mam told you about the boxing at Anston?"

Jack shook his head. "What's all this, Ma?"

Annie hadn't forgotten about the fete and she would have mentioned it eventually, even though she wasn't all that enthusiastic.

"Oh it's their gala next Saturday, apparently there'd been some doubt as to whether it was going to be held this year with the war being on, but a committee decided to hold one more. It's in The Stones like it usually is."

Anston Stones was a local beauty spot with a stream, rocky crags and caves, hence its name, and to get to the area one had to cross over a field. This was where the gala would be held as it was ideal for accommodating the tents, the stalls and the many competitions, like tug-o'-war, greasy pole climbing, etcetera, etcetera.

"Our Vera's Tim reckons you couldn't help but win the boxing and the prize is a piece of pork, so he said to be sure to put your name down. I shall be going to our Vera's but if I wasn't I shouldn't be watching you box – you know how I feel about that."

Billy momentarily stopped feeding his face to look excitedly at his brother across the table. "Are you going to put your name down, Jack? If you do, can I be a second?"

Jack gave a slow smile, "A nice bit of pork, eh? That wouldn't come amiss for Sunday dinner, before I go back off leave."

Billy gave a cheer. "Yeah, good old Jack, how about you being t' other second, Les?"

Les frowned questioningly. "Do they bother with seconds at these village dos? I shouldn't have thought so."

Jack shrugged his shoulders. "You can have seconds if you want but as likely as not there will just be a couple of first aid men in attendance, plus the ref. He can stop a fight if it's looking too one-sided but there's usually more puffing and blowing than owt else. Yes … for a nice bit of pork I reckon I ought to put on a pair of gloves again." He looked at Billy, a serious expression on his face. "Okay, you can be my second but you'll have to do it proper mind, you'll need a bucket, sponge, water, towel, smelling salts, styptic, grease, stretcher." He ceased when he saw the concern on the lads' face. "Only kidding, Billy, but you can be at my corner if you like, also that mate of thine, Jimmy what's-his-name."

Billy's delight revealed large white teeth, "Great, I'll tell Jimmy tonight." Annie was less enthusiastic. "Just can't fathom out what you see in knocking one another about, can you, John?"

"Village boxing is nowt serious, lass, beside I bet tha'll have a smile on thi face when tha's cooking meat in t' oven."

"Oh you reckon I will be cooking it then?"

John winked at his two elder sons. "You can count on it lass so you might as well get big roasting tin ready."

Jack and Les looked at each other but didn't comment. After that the talk turned to the evening's entertainment. Susan would be going to the Regal with a friend; Annie and John would as usual, be spending a couple of hours at The Working Man's Club. Billy would stay with his pal, while Jack and Les would go to Worksop, but on a later bus than Susan.

"Okay then, first stop will be the Golden Ball, a jar or two in the Kings Head and finish off in the Central. That way we are only a cock's stride and a jump from the Palais when they shout time; that sound good to you, brother?"

Jack was about to reply when Susan butted in: "That reminds me, Betty also asked if you still went to the Palais Saturday nights. I told her you still fancied yourself on the dance floor, among other things, but that I didn't know about tonight with our Jack being home on leave."

"Who's this Betty, anybody I know?" Jack's eyes

widened. "First of all she wants remembering to you because she's finished with some Canadian, then she wants to know if you'll be at the Palais tonight. Who is it, Betty who?"

"It's Betty Cooper, from off New Street."

Jack thought for a moment. "Wait a minute, Cooper you say? Lives on New Street? I know her sister, Connie. I'll tell thi what, if Betty is owt like her sister then she's a warm lass; there's also a brother, Tom Cooper. He nearly got sent down for pinching timber from wagon repair yard two or three years back, remember?"

Les shook his head, "No I don't, and anyway, Betty's not like that ..."

Annie had been listening intently to the conversation. "You be careful my lad, you hear?" She knew Les had a lot of bravado but he was not as worldly-wise as he tried to make out. Jack could look after number one and would size people up carefully, but Les was different. He tended to take people on trust and in some respects was still very naive, so a frown momentarily furrowed her brow. It was a good job she didn't know the full story regarding the girl under discussion otherwise the frown would have been less fleeting. The Betty in question was, as Jack had succinctly put it, 'as warm as her sister Connie.' She had broken off with Les some months back in favour of a Canadian soldier, but had recently found out he was married, with a family, and she now thought she might be pregnant, hence her sudden interest in Les again. She knew Les had been pretty keen on her, so at the back of her mind was the notion they might get back together again and present her with a chance to solve her problem.

Les shrugged his shoulders in a nonchalant fashion. "If Betty is at Palais I might favour her with a dance or two." He tried to make his remark sound casual but deep down he hoped she would be there, for it was she who had aroused his initial serious interest in the fair sex. As he pensively rubbed his chin the memories returned, so for the remainder of the meal he tried to think of what he might say to Betty if she did happen to be at the dance – perhaps a casual approach.

'Now then sweetheart, I hear you've been asking after me and I bet any money you have only just realized what a fantastic bloke I am. Tell you what, play your cards right and I might let you take me to the pictures one night next week, back row of the one and nines and we'll get one of them double seats, how about that?'

Les pondered on his opening gambits but had to accept the fact that she might not be at the dance hall; 'When she'd spoken to Susan she may have had a row with her Canadian chap and been feeling somewhat miffed, so best wait and see instead of thinking too far ahead.'

When everyone had finished their tea, it was John to have first turn at the kitchen sink; after that it would be free for the two brothers to use.

When they both stripped to the waist the contrast in physique was quickly apparent. Jack was tanned, well-muscled with strong broad shoulders and one could well visualise him being quite at home in a boxing ring. Les, on the other hand was lean and wiry but nonetheless, he was no weakling and he squared up to Jack in an exaggerated pugnacious stance. His fists however, were unconcernedly brushed aside and he ended up in a bear hug with his feet dangling clear of the ground.

"Put me down, you bugger," he gasped as the breath was squeezed from his body and Jack had no sooner complied before Les was attempting a half nelson but this too ended in abject failure.

Jack laughed as Les squirmed, trying to escape. "What's it to be, little brother, a ducking in t' bowl or pay for me to get into Palais?" Les groaned; "You wait, you sod, I'm going to tek a bodybuilding course then you can watch out. Ouch! Alright, I'll get tickets for the dance." He rubbed the back of his neck but also added a quiet 'maybe' under his breath.

Jack washed first before starting to lather his chin for a shave. "Here, I hope you're not dipping into Ma's packet of lard again – you're not, are you?"

Les splashed water over his face before answering. "No, I bought some Brilliantine today, smells just like a Turkish brothel – want some?"

Jack paused with razor in hand to give his brother a look that left no doubt as to his opinion on the use of Brilliantine.

"I just thought you might want to improve your image, that's all."

Les was confident in the knowledge that he could get

out of reach if he had to, but Jack carried on shaving and merely flicked a blob of lather in Les's direction before replying.

"I don't need owt out of a bottle, just rely on good old sex appeal, works every time."

Les didn't intend to let it end there, ribbing his brother had been one of his great pastimes and ten days leave wasn't very long so he had to make the most of it.

"Aye you could be right, but I just thought that going to Worksop with me, well perhaps you could do with all the help you can get. I mean with me being so good-looking and attractive to women it just don't seem fair, still ..."

He got no further; Jack had finished shaving and was drying his face but suddenly he pounced. "Right you bugger, you bin asking for it," and with a sweep of his foot he wrestled Les to the kitchen floor and in no time had the upper hand and was sitting astride Les's chest, pinning his hands beneath his knees. From past experience Les knew that escape was well-nigh impossible so he resorted to the only tactic that had ever been of use in the past, stamping his feet and yelling for his mother.

"Ma! ... Jack's got me again, help me, Ma."

Jack threw back his head, guffawing loudly: "Shouting for yer Mam as usual, eh? Well, we'll have to put a stop to that, won't we?" With a free hand he reached for his well lathered shaving brush. "Now then, what was it you were saying about me needing all the help I could get, eh?"

Les clamped his mouth tightly closed while Jack

carefully worked the soap laden brush up his nostrils and into his ears. The only sound from Les was a muffled moan as he endeavoured to avoid the obvious. After a minute or two, Jack could envisage a stalemate so he decided to exploit a well known weak spot. He knew his brother could not bear to be gripped or squeezed just above his knees so Jack's fingers and thumb searched for the vital points of torture. As he did so his grin grew even wider and more demonic while poor Les, eyes widening in dismay, writhed in silent apprehension. When he spoke, Jack's voice was menacing and low, it sounded almost sinister.

"Yes, I think a thumb here and ... fingers there, then squeeeeeze."

The 'squeeze' was delivered through clenched teeth with sadistic pleasure.

Les let out a yell, only to have it immediately stifled as the shaving brush found its target. A dreadful muffled wail rent the air, interspersed with retching sounds, not unlike a cow regurgitating; rich lather had disappeared into the reluctantly formed orifice only to be swiftly ejected in a frothy stream. After a few seconds, Les lay with his head to one side still spitting and coughing, but nevertheless smiling weakly at his own undoing. Jack meanwhile, calmly sat astride his brother's chest laughing his head off.

They were both still chuckling when Annie and Billy finally popped their heads through the door. Billy, as always, took in the scene with a huge grin while Annie shook her head in mock disbelief.

"Won't you two ever grow up? You're just as bad now as you were when you both went to school."

The two looked up from the kitchen floor as Les slowly recovered.

"It's alright, Ma, I was just teaching Jack a lesson; he was getting a bit too big for his boots so I thought I'd better show him who was boss."

There were hoots of derision from everyone at this remark and Annie answered in a somewhat scoffing tone, "Oh I can see that, Leslie, it's obvious you've got the upper hand as usual."

Jack jumped to his feet and extended a helping hand to his brother. "Come on, youth, up you get. I'll tell you what I'll do, I'll treat thi to a whisky wi' first pint, help get rid of the taste – I can't say fairer than that can I?"

Les was hoisted to his feet and he immediately put his head under the tap, filled his mouth with cold water and gargled noisily. After a final spit he put an arm around Jack's shoulder to ask cheekily, "Could tha mek that a double?"

Jack matched his grin as they set about diligently applying themselves to the task of getting ready for a Saturday night out. There would be plenty of beer to be drunk and hopefully there would be a lot of unattached ladies at the Palais. It was a serious business this Saturday night gallivanting and not to be undertaken lightly.

When Susan appeared, looking lovely in a blue summer dress, she received a round of applause from her brothers and the customary caution from her mother.

"Now you be careful, our Susan, and don't miss that coach back; it'll be better than the double-decker cos you can get off at the top and you won't have so far to walk in the dark. Are you listening?"

"Yes, Mother, I have done it plenty of times, you know."

"Aye, I know that; have a nice time, luv."

Susan wiggled her fingers in a farewell gesture, stepped outside, shouting "Bye" as she did so. Annie watched through the window and smiled proudly as the young figure passed through the yard entrance to turn left towards the top of the avenue. It didn't seem like any time at all since she had been doing the same thing on a Saturday evening. 'How time flies,' she mused, then concentrated on getting rid of Jack and Leslie so that they could catch their bus, leaving her to could get ready in peace.

"How much longer are you boys going to be?"

A voice from upstairs answered her in a rather wry tone – it was Jack.

"I'm ready, I'm waiting for Percival here. He's combed and parted his hair at least ten times."

Annie could hear Les whistling and she could visualise him in front of a mirror. "If he's trying to get his parting right he'll be at least another ten minutes; worse than any woman, he is."

Jack sat on the edge of his bed checking the contents of his wallet while he waited. Two one pound notes, a ten shilling note, then some change in his trouser pocket. 'That's more than enough,' he reasoned, 'might even last me into next week as well.' He glanced across to his brother who was still trying to get a quiff in his hair that was to his liking. A cigarette dangled from his lips curling smoke and he closed an eye as he peered into the mirror to inspect his latest attempt.

"Don't know why you're going to all that bother; come ten o'clock and it will be all over the place unless you want me to borrow a net off Ma for you."

Les ignored the attempted sarcasm and stepped back from the mirror to blow a smoke ring as he removed the cigarette from his lips.

"It's like I've always said, Jack, you've got to have style. When I step on that dance floor all the heads will swivel – you'll see."

Jack sounded unconcerned, "Look, pal, the only time you'll mek any heads swivel is if you fall on your backside."

Les gave his brother a beatific smile before taking a last glance in the mirror. "Right, what are we waiting for then?" He made it sound as if it was he who had been hanging about and not Jack.

Jack rose and followed downstairs. "We're off now, Ma; can't say what time we'll be in." He kissed his mother on the cheek and Les followed suit but also allowed her the benefit of a big wink.

"Don't get drunk, Ma."

"And don't you be cheeky, my lad, have a nice time both of you and be careful."

"Always are, you know us, see you later."

John was sat in a chair, listening to and looking at the wireless as if he could see the owner of the voice emanating from its speaker. He swung round as the two called his name to say cheerio.

"You two off then? I'll leave the door unlocked," before returning his gaze to the wireless.

CHAPTER FIVE

A Night on the Town

Jack and Les went outside and stood in the yard for a few minutes as Annie came to the door.

"Aren't you putting a coat on, Jack?" Her tone sounding slightly concerned. "What if it turns cool?"

"No, I shall be fine, Ma; where's Billy?"

Annie pointed down the avenue and Billy could be seen playing football; he shouted as his two brothers emerged through the yard entrance.

"See you Jack, see you Les."

They both waved farewell as their strides took them in the opposite direction.

"Let's cut through here," suggested Jack and he changed direction so that their path now proceeded between the houses instead of following the avenue to its end then turning right. He had made the change to avoid passing Valerie's home but he didn't say so and Les followed this change of direction without questioning why. "One road is as good as another so it don't mek any odds." They reached the main road and Jack looked at his watch.

"We've time to stroll up to the square to catch the bus – okay by you?"

"Yes, why not, may as well be walking as hanging about here, but just remember, you promised me a whisky."

Jack grinned. "So I did but tha did ask for it and anyway you knew what would happen if tha tackled me."

Les knew well enough and gave his brother a friendly dig in the ribs.

"I'm chuffed to have thi back home, Jack, after yon bloody Dunkirk job; it set me thinking did that, I were worried."

"Me too, Les, I don't mind admitting it."

When they at last reached the square, Jack again looked at his watch. "We've about ten minutes to wait; fancy a swift half in t' Red Lion or do you want to wait till we get to Worksop?"

Les glanced across the square. "If we have one in there the beer in Worksop won't taste all that clever; you can't beat Fred's bitter, let's wait."

As it happened, the South Yorkshire Corporation bus was a bit early so they didn't have to wait the full ten minutes. It was nearly full but they both managed to get seats and Jack occupied one near the front. More passengers boarded but they had to stand, and as they edged down the bus, Jack became aware of a very trim waist moving into vision. It halted opposite his right eye and belonged to a young woman in her early twenties. Jack looked up, allowing his eyes to follow the contours of a well-filled blouse then to a very pretty face staring out of the window. He checked the third finger of the young woman's left hand, noticed the absence of any gold band, gave a cough, put on his boyish grin and gazed upwards. However, a second louder cough was required before her eyes were lowered to meet his.

"I've got a good pair of knees if you'd like to try them, mi duck, it's a long way to Worksop," offered Jack.

She looked down with smiling grey eyes but paused before shaking her head.

"No thanks," another short pause. "Maybe if this was the last bus home I might, but not just now thank you."

Jack feigned a look of sadness before rubbing his chin as if in deep thought. "Well in that case I'm going to be a gentleman," and rose to allow the young lady to occupy his seat. A few seconds later, the bus roared into life and its lurching progress almost resulted in Jack ending up in the woman's lap, much to her amusement.

"Nice try, but you're a bit too heavy for me." She gave a little chuckle before returning Jack's attentive gaze. "Thanks for the seat."

"You're welcome, lass," then it was Jack's turn to study the scene through the window as the bus trundled on its journey. A few stops later, some of the passengers alighted and Jack was able to sit down just behind Les who turned round with raised eyebrows. Jack interpreted this to mean 'Who's the girl?' So he leaned forward to speak in a low voice. "Don't know who she is but she's a tidy looking lass and I wouldn't kick her out of bed, that's for sure."

Les pursed his lips and nodded in agreement as Jack

leaned forward to speak again. "Mind you, with a bit of luck I might be able to find out on t' bus home."

Worksop was about a half hour journey so it wasn't long before the outskirts came into view. First a large sawmill, followed by shops and houses.

Jack stood up and nodded to the conductress to ring the bell and the bus came to a halt. The Golden Ball was over on the opposite side of the road so they decided to let the bus pull away before attempting to cross, and Jack took this opportunity to walk alongside the bus to a point that was level with a window giving a view of the young lady he had surrendered up his seat to. Jack was a handsome devil and when she saw him she smiled, so he went through the motion of doffing an imaginary hat and that brought an even wider display of radiance. She gave a little wave as the bus finally set off to wind its way through several streets until it reached its destination at the main depot; here it would discharge her and the remaining passengers. As soon as the bus was clear, Jack and Les crossed over the road to enter the Golden Ball through revolving doors giving access to a carpeted foyer. This led to a large lounge with a bar that served it and several more small rooms, but Les made straight for the bar. He put his hand in his pocket but Jack restrained him.

"Nay it's my shout, Les, and as I promised thee a whisky I reckon I might as well join thi."

He waited until an elderly barman approached before laying a ten shilling note on the bar. "Two pints of bitter and two malt whiskies please, barman."

The elderly gentleman nodded. "Straight glasses or pint pots, sir?"

Jack had been asked this question many times so he was ready with his stock answer. "Oh glasses please. Do you know I once saw the handle come off a full pint pot and it upset me for days – I think I'd rather have seen blood spilt."

The barman laughed; he recognized a rough diamond when he saw one and it made a pleasant change from the usual clientele that frequented the lounge of the Golden Ball.

"I know what you mean sir; water or soda with the whisky?"

Jack raised a hand. "Just as it is – my brother here needs it neat, in order to clean his tonsils."

When the drinks were poured, they each raised a whisky glass in salute, downing the golden liquid in one gulp. Les screwed up his eyes and quickly reached for his pint to take a generous mouthful, shaking his head slowly from side to side as the beer eased the stinging in his throat. "Oh I shall be glad when I've had enough," and although the joke had whiskers on it, Jack joined in with his contribution.

"Aye, and women always think we come out to enjoy ourselves."

Now they both laughed out loud before draining the contents of the glasses and replacing them on the bar.

Les rubbed his hands together. "I think we had best have the same again, barman, the contents seem to have evaporated."

The barman picked up the empty pint glasses. "And the whiskies, sir?" he enquired, nodding towards the empty tumblers.

"Aye, go on then, I've only got this scoundrel for another week then he's back in the army."

The barman started to fill Jack's glass. "I thought you might be a military man, sir – I was in the last show. That one was supposed to be the war to end all wars but we don't seem to have learned much do we?"

Jack shook his head before answering. "I don't think we ever will but it's not up to the ordinary man, is it? It's the politicians and big wigs, and if I had my way, I'd line both sides up, give 'em a balloon each, then tell 'em to go ahead and knock the stuffin' out of each other. But you know what they say: 'Ours is not to reason why, ours is but to do or die,' isn't that how it goes?"

Both pints were now ready and the barman nodded in agreement as he placed the whisky glasses under the optic while Les dug into his trouser pocket to bring out a handful of coins.

"What's the damage, barman?" He was busy sorting silver coins from the copper.

"That'll be three and tuppence altogether, sir."

Les pretended to be shocked, "No, no! I only want to buy the drinks, not the fixtures and fittings as well."

The barman smiled but nodded in acknowledgment. "Yes I know what you mean but I'm afraid these are hotel prices."

Les wagged a finger to indicate that no asperity was intended. "Nay don't fret thissen, I know the score. Look, give me twenty woodbines and have a drink yourself; the cigs aren't dearer are they?"

"Cigarettes are normal price, sir, and thank you, I'll have a half if you don't mind, and I'll just have to get your cigarettes from the main bar."

Les counted the correct coins from his loose change and slid them forward. "There you are, I suppose you can remember when beer was only tuppence a pint, eh?"

The barman pulled himself a half of bitter. "Your very good health, sir," after which he took a sip before replying. "Tuppence a pint? No, not quite as cheap as that but very nearly so. When you both get to my age you will probably think back and remember how cheap the beer was tonight even though you don't think so at the moment." Another sip was taken before having to move down the bar to serve another customer.

The brothers now held the tumblers aloft with Les grinning as he saluted Jack with the glass. "Over the tonsils, round the gums, look out stomach here it comes – cheers!" He downed the drink but gave a cough as the spirit hit the back of his throat. Jack held his glass, tilted his head back and slowly drained the contents until the last drop had disappeared. They stood looking at each other quizzically for a second or two before Jack spoke. "I've a funny feeling we shall both have a bit of a list to starboard come eleven o'clock; how about making the Unicorn the next stop? We can always end up at the Central before going into the Palais – they'll have music on in the big room."

Les nodded agreement. "Aye alright, but they get a lot of officers in t' Unicorn nowadays so there won't be many spare women floating about for the likes of us.

Jack looked a bit nonplussed. "In t' Unicorn?"

Les drank a third of his pint before answering. "Oh aye, Polish, Canadian, French, all sorts. The place has changed."

"Is it still a good pint?" Jack was curious.

"Beer's still the same, just the trade that's different."

"Ah well, a few shoulder pips and rings on sleeves don't worry me, you know what t' owd man says: 'When we all strip down to our birthday suit there's no difference between any of us, except where it matters', and he's right."

Les smiled at the thought of his father divesting himself of his clothing in the Unicorn. "Aye, he'd stand out alright; probably rank as a Colonel-in-chief or Air Marshall – what do you reckon?"

Jack didn't answer because he was busy quaffing beer but he signalled acquiescence by raising his eyebrows. When the glass was nearly empty he wiped his lips with the back of his hand and nodded vigorously.

"Do you remember when I left pigeon coop undone and a cat got in? He walloped me from one end of our avenue to the other, then back again." Les threw back his head, laughing. "I wasn't very old but I remember it alright, you were rubbing your arse for days, but you didn't leave coop undone again did you?"

Jack shook his head in recollection. "No, I have to say the old man has a knack of impressing people so that they don't forget things, but he's not a bad owd stick really."

Les opened the packet of cigarettes he had purchased and shook one out, but pondered on Jack's remark before lighting it. "He's well respected down pit, though he frightens some of the men, but it's only them silly buggers who do owt daft or get his back up, even the deputies tread a bit wary. We know he doesn't swear in t' house, I mean really swear, but you want to hear him down pit. I don't work on the same coal face but I've been told what a bugger he is; on the other hand he's usually finished his stint first then he helps his mates until the end of the shift. I wouldn't like to try and keep up wi' him, he's like a bloody machine."

Les took another long draw on his cigarette before downing the remains of his pint. "But what am I prattling on about pit for? Sup up, youth, then we'll go and show our faces in the Unicorn." Turning towards the bar he raised his hand. "Cheerio, barman, hope to see you again if the good Lord spares us."

A returning gesture came from behind the bar as Jack also finished his drink and the brothers made their way into the foyer, through the revolving doors and out on to the forecourt. Once outside, Jack took a deep breath, clapping his hands together as he contemplated the night ahead. "Well that's a nice steady start to the evening, so let's see what we can find in the Unicorn – and you reckon it's still a good pint there?" Les nodded, "I've told thi, there's nowt wrong wi' beer."

Jack clapped his hands together once more. "Right then, what are we hanging about for?"

The night was still warm and the street busy as Jack and Les turned out of the forecourt to make their way past shops to cross over a once busy canal. This was fed by the Ryton river, spanned by the same road they now traversed to go past Susan's place of work and finally to a crossroads. As the traffic lights changed in their favour, Jack and Les hurried across the junction to stand outside the stone facade of the Unicorn.

A central entrance gave access to doors leading left and right so Jack followed the sound of music and turned left which, when opened, revealed a smoke-fogged room crowded with groups of men and women. Smart costumes and chic summer dresses seemed to be the order of the day for the females, while nearly all the men were in uniform, predominantly khaki, but the blues of the Royal Air Force and the Senior Service were also represented. A jukebox was belting out music, consequently all conversation was louder than normal until the record ended then the chatter reverted to a quieter level. Jack beamed and made a beeline for the bar. "This is more like it," he called over his shoulder as he threaded his way through the various groups. Some men were there with their wives but most were there with someone else's, or a girlfriend, or a friend of a friend, or a total stranger, but what the heck? With a weekend pass in your pocket the idea was to enjoy it, and as Jack often said, "You're a long time dead my friend, so make the most of it while you can." He did manage to get an elbow on the bar but empty glasses were being waved all over the place to try and attract the staff, so he decided a well-timed wink was called for, plus a bit of chat. "A pretty lass like you shouldn't be working on a Saturday night, but as you are, pull me a couple of pints when you get a minute please, sweetheart."

He very nearly received a 'hold your horses' look but his boyish grin did the trick.

"Tek your time, luv, everything comes to them that wait you know and some things are worth waiting for," she countered.

"They are if they're as bonny as you." Jack waved his hand at the throng. "A good job there's not many in tonight."

The barmaid laughed; she had a sense of humour so decided to join in. "Don't worry," she said, "it'll get busier as the night goes on but I'll see to you in a minute – you can hang on that long, can't you?"

Jack gave her another wink. "For somebody like you I'd hang on till doomsday."

A few minutes later, two pints were placed on the bar much to the chagrin of a young officer who had been standing there waiting to be served. Jack ignored the mutterings as he paid and when he received his change he picked up the two pints before turning to look for Les who had taken up a position near one of several pillars located throughout the room. Before moving away from the bar however, he leaned forward to speak to the young officer and purposely gazed at the pip on his shoulder. "Shall I give thi a bit of advice, sport? It don't allus pay to be a gentleman, tha wants to shout up, you might get served a bit quicker." The impish look on Jack's face must have been apparent as he made his way towards Les who held out a hand for his drink as Jack approached. "What did yer say to that young lieutenant, he gave thi a funny look as tha walked over here?"

"Aw it were nowt important, I were just having a dig at him and anyway he'll have worse than me to deal wi' before that new uniform of his gets to see some service. Jack took a drink before continuing.

"But never mind him, tek a dekko at them two t' other side of this pillar? Not married neither or at least they're not showing owt on their fingers."

Les took a glance. "I've already noticed them, Jack, but they're not in here for the likes of you and me."

The 'two' were a couple of women in their early thirties and looking as if they had just stepped out of a beauty salon. Both wore plenty of make-up, smart two piece costumes and high-heeled court shoes that made their long legs look even longer. Les wagged a finger under Jack's nose. "They won't be on their own for very long and it's no use you getting any ideas, because you've more chance of being struck by lightning than getting it away wi' one of them. It'll be uniforms only, preferably foreign and nowt less than captain, you'll see."

Jack gave a nonchalant shrug and grinned. "Didn't fancy 'em anyway – their eyes are too close together."

Les laughed at the second old joke of the night then pointed eagerly towards another bar. This one served another room on the far side and from their present position they could see several of the waiting customers.

"Bugger me, look who's there; it's Tommy, Tommy Riley, he must be on leave an' all."

A fresh-faced lad was just about to pay for his drink when he spotted Les. The dark blue uniform of a serving matelot suited him to a tee and he gave a thumbs-up sign before beckoning the two to join him. Jack and Les looked at each other to nod in unison.

"Might as well," suggested Les. "The beer is a penny cheaper in that room and it is a bit throng in here, come on."

They threaded their way towards the connecting doors then on into the next room, where Tom had managed to confiscate three chairs at one of the long tables. The three exchanged handshakes before sitting down.

"How long you home for Tommy, still down at Plymouth?" Jack asked the questions between quaffs of beer which nearly finished off his pint.

"I got home last night on a weekend pass; we've been busy picking some of them poor sods up off Dunkirk. I'm not joking it were a real bastard; I don't know how many lads managed to get away but there were still a lot still left on the beach when we had to return – part of our rudder got shot away. You weren't among 'em, were you?"

Jack finished off his pint and pushed the empty glass towards Les.

"I bloody well was; eventually I was able to wade out to a lifeboat then picked up by HMS Windrush, but what a sodding cock-up. I'll tell thi what, Tommy lad ..." The beer and the whiskies were beginning to have an effect and he tapped the table before continuing. "I shall never," tap, tap, "ever again," tap, tap, "allow missen to get into a position where I have to stand like a silly bugger and be shot at, shelled, bombed and not be able to do owt about it. In future I shall look after number one and the powers that be can get stuffed." Beaming like a Cheshire cat he slapped the table with the flat of his hand. "Meanwhile, how about us three," pointing first to Les then to Tom, "how about us three making a night of it? I mean sloshed, pickled, stoned, blotto, call it what you like but well and truly ..." His grin stretched from ear to ear as a conclusion to the question.

Tom and Leslie exchanged knowing looks, so Tom answered.

"Well it looks as if I've got a bit of catching up to do but I'm game. Where have you two been anyway? You weren't in the other room a short while back."

Jack pointed to his empty glass but Les ignored him because he wanted to answer Tom. "Oh it's not all spit and sawdust for us lads, we partook of a beverage or two in the Golden Ball, but it got too rowdy so we left."

The attempt at a joke went unnoticed by Jack who again stabbed a finger at his empty glass. "Are you getting the beers in, or not? And I notice it's your round when we get to the cheap bar." He looked at Tom. "Do you want Les to bring you a fresh glass?"

Tom's pint was still at three quarter level. "Nay," he grinned, "it's a convenient depth." The beer was swiftly consumed then he too slid his glass across the table.

"Right, three pints – anything else?" queried Les.

There was no immediate answer so he collected all three glasses for replenishment, but as he neared the bar Tom called out in a loud voice.

"Yeah, while you're there see if you can get hold of three beautiful sex maniacs wi' plenty of money." Heads swivelled in his direction so he beamed to all and sundry.

Les returned, expertly holding the three pints, while a cigarette in the corner of his mouth had him screwing up his eyes to avoid the curling smoke.

"How's that for service? I didn't manage to get any nymphomaniacs but I reckon you're on wi' a promise, Jack. That barmaid from t' other side came over especially to serve me and she was asking who you were. I told her you were on the lookout for a good woman and at that she said, 'Is that so,' in a real deep voice, lecherous like. Which reminds me, you haven't told me yet where you got to last night."

Jack half closed his eyes. "I wasn't far away, little brother, just minding my own business as it happens, like you should be doing." Les could pry all he wanted but that was all he was going to get.

Les grunted. "Fair enough, if you don't want to tell me, but I might ask you again later, when you've had a few more."

Tom meanwhile had been at work on his fresh pint. "Going down like wine is this, are you two ready for a refill?"

Both men raised their hands in protest before Les answered, "You get yourself a pint, my back teeth are floating."

"Fair enough," said Tom and stood up, trying to finish off his remaining half but unfortunately dribbling beer over the man sat next to him. He was a surly looking character with a brick red complexion acquired by hours employed as a farm labourer, and he didn't take kindly to Tom's carelessness.

"Hey, pal, if I wanted a bloody shower I'd go and stand under a hosepipe or out in rain, watch what tha doing."

Tom winced in mock alarm, quickly brushing the man's damp shoulder.

"Sorry, mate, I haven't been ashore for six months and I'm a bit excited, you know how it is." He directed a half grin, half grimace towards Jack and Les before hurrying to the bar.

"Your bloody mate drunk or what?" spluttered Beetroot Features.

Les answered, trying to keep a straight face. "Er no, not yet, but I've an idea he will be before the night's out – he's just glad to be home for a bit."

There was a grunt from Florid Face who said something to his companion before turning his gaze towards Tom at the bar. Jack remained quiet, determined not to get involved so he started humming and tapping his foot in tune with the music coming from the next room.

"Hey tha knows this one, Les, it's your mate, Bing," and he gave Les a nudge as he accompanied the voice on the record: "'... south of the border down Mexico way,' – come on, sing up."

Les took a sip to wet his whistle then accompanied his brother: "'... That's where I fell in love when stars above came out to play.'" They were in full voice by the time Tom returned so he too contributed.

Cherry Chops glowered as they went into the second verse but as more people had joined in the singing, he didn't remonstrate further. As the record ended, Tom leaned forward to speak to both Jack and Les in a low voice. "Do you know why he's so niggly? Well apart from having a face like a farmer's arse, which would make anybody miserable, he's got a great big boil on the back of his neck."

Les tilted his chair to get a better look and as he scrutinized the angry looking furuncle showing above the man's collar, he gave a low whistle. "Poor sod, I hope it hurts like hell." He was still grinning when the juke box started up again but this time the record was a slow sentimental dance tune and the three all pulled faces. "Can't sing to that," said Les, "but then we don't have to, do we?" He started singing a number he had heard earlier, so Jack and Tom joined him in full vocal support.

Gargoyle Features spun round in his chair to face Tom who had the misfortune to be sat nearest so he received the full blast. "Why don't you put a bloody sock in it?" he growled. "I don't care if you've been at sea six bloody years, don't keep singing in my ear hole cos I hate it, do you hear?"

Tom ceased his warbling but answered with a beam on his face, "Why don't you join in? You never know you might enjoy yourself."

A fat finger was jabbed into Tom's chest and the farmer's voice took on a rasping tone. "Look, I've warned yer, just shut yer cake 'ole or I'll shut if for yer, and that goes for yer mates an' all."

Tom sighed before taking a copious draught of beer while Jack also lifted his glass, but he drained the contents. "Right lads, I'm off ... otherwise ..." His voice trailed away and he shook his head before continuing. "I'm going across the road to the Central, there'll be a piano going in there. I'll get the beer in and you come across when you've supped up here." Jack slid his empty glass forward; he knew very well that if he stayed he would end up in a brawl and he wasn't looking for that, not again.

Tom and Les agreed, so when Jack had left the room they put their heads together to confer in a low voice before emptying their own glasses. A crafty nod to each other signalled the time to rise from the table with Tom taking up a position just behind his chair while Les gathered all three empty glasses to stand opposite Cherry Chops. After a slight pause there was an almighty clatter as the glasses were virtually dumped on to the table, causing the choleric farm hand to focus his attention on the rebounding glasses and give Tom just the opportunity he needed. Like a mischievous schoolboy he took up a position behind Florid Features before lunging forward with outstretched arms. His eyes gleamed as two eager thumbs found their mark on either side of the inflamed swelling and squeezed. Vesuvius itself could not have erupted more fiercely as the liberated constituents soared aloft to embellish the ceiling of the Unicorn Hotel.

The victim froze as if in suspended animation but by the time a howl had escaped from his anguished lips both Les and Tom were well on their way towards the exit. They heard a clatter as Claret Chops overturned his chair in his haste to follow in pursuit, but they were through the door and instead of turning left to go out on to the main street they re-entered the room Jack and Les had gone into initially. It was even more throng than before and as they weaved their way through the crowd they heard the door from the taproom being flung open followed by a voice bellowing obscenities as its possessor ran along the short passage towards the roadway.

Tom and Les pushed their way forward until they were behind one of the pillars and this enabled them to keep an eye on the door they had just entered, and also a sight of their table in the other room. The chair that Red Face had overturned was being righted by some thoughtful gentleman, while the chair next to it was also vacant. Tom pointed towards the door, grinning. "They're both out looking for us, so keep an eye on that door. Hey! Did tha see it burst?"

Les stifled a laugh. "No, I was watching his face; Christ you should have seen it, I thought his eyeballs were going to pop out. Thar's a cruel bugger, Tom."

Tom bit his lip, "Well he got my bloody goat. You come on leave for a good night out then you light on a miserable sod like him, so he's only got himself to blame. Anyway, he'll feel the benefit tomorrow so really I've done him a favour."

Just at that moment the door opened and the man who had been sitting next to Red Face popped his head through and looked round the room. Tom and Les quickly lined themselves behind the pillar so as not to be spotted so Les spoke in a low voice. "You might think you've done matey a favour but I bet he's not looking for thi to give you a kiss. Just stand still, I don't think his mate is coming in."

The man gave a few more glances around the room then withdrew.

"Let's see if they go back in there;" said Les, "they've still got some beer on the table."

A few minutes later, both men were back in the other room. Red Face was holding a red spotted handkerchief to the back of his neck and the man who had righted the overturned chair spoke to him and laughed; this prompted Les and Tom to nod towards the exit. After waiting a few seconds, they were safely out of the building where thumbs-up signs were exchanged before hurrying towards a structure bearing a hand painted declaration that it was the Central Inn. Double doors opened into a passage with two further doors at the end held ajar to reveal a large room possessing a bare wooden floor and a bar running the length of the whole of one side. A tinkling piano and singing greeted the two young men as their eyes probed the swirling cigarette smoke searching for Jack. He was leaning against the bar talking to one of several barmen, a half empty glass in his hand. As they approached, he put his own glass on the bar, picking up the two full ones to hand to the two rascals.

"I don't like to ask what you've been up to."

They looked at each other, trying not to laugh and Les eventually answered. "Well it's like this: Tom here reckoned Red Face needed cheering up so I gave him a hand, that's why we were so long in coming over."

Jack waited expectantly. "And?" he asked.

Les looked at Tom and this time he did burst out laughing. "I think we can safely say it was mission accomplished – you reckon so, Tom?"

Tom agreed and Jack thought of enquiring further but after scrutinising the two faces before him he thought better of it, so he waved his hand to the centre of the room instead.

"Look, we can get three stools round the end of that table there."

After ten minutes or so, some of the regular clients started chanting, "Come on, Billy, let's have you up, it's show time. Where are you, Billy?"

A little man in his thirties was sitting at a table near the back wall and he cocked his head to one side and smiled as his name was called out. Those seated at the same table leaned forward, urging him on. "Come on, Billy lad, do yer stuff." Eventually the man rose to his feet and was guided through the maze of tables and chairs to the small stage where he was helped up to stand in front of the piano. From his jacket pocket he produced four flat bones about eight inches long and four large spoons; these he placed on a stool just in front of him. Lifting his face to the ceiling, he cocked his head to one side listening to the music. He was blind but once he started playing the knick-knacks he was in perfect rhythm with the music. First with one hand, then the other, finally with both hands, changing from bones to spoons without any pause or break. All the while looking up toward the ceiling with a smile lighting his face as his head shook from side to side. The performance ended, as it always did, with all four spoons being played at a frantic rate, followed by a dramatic leap from the low stage with the man sinking to his knees, arms outstretched above his head. The leap from the stage showed great faith in his fellow man because he had to rely on them to ensure he had a clear space in which to land. A fresh pint was waiting on the table by the time he had been guided back to his seat and he raised the glass to acknowledge the clapping and plaudits from the crowd, his moment of fame over for another week.

Jack turned to Tom and Les, jerking his thumb in the man's direction.

"You've got to hand it to him, he's good with them knick-knacks and he's got some pluck."

Les smiled. "He's been playing the bones for years but that bit at the end is new, I don't think I'd like to do it with mi eyes merely closed, would you?"

Both lads agreed it needed guts.

The piano playing and singing now resumed with Les discarding his jacket and loosening his tie, while Tom was beginning to look very much like the proverbial drunken sailor. Jack tapped the top of the table in time with the music and was thoroughly enjoying himself, so when the pianist launched into a Spanish-type tune he was tipsy enough to climb on to the table and attempt a heel-stomping flamenco. There were whistles and shouts of encouragement from the Saturday night revellers while Tom and Les clapped their hands to provide the right tempo for Jack's impromptu display of acting the role of a Spanish toreador. After a few seconds, there were even louder cries of incitement from the room as he was joined on the table by a middle-aged lady who was, to put it kindly, exceedingly well proportioned. Les threw Jack his coat to be used as a toreador's cape, while the pair improvised a paso doble dance. After a while the woman raised both hands above her head and positioned herself in front of Jack, looking up into his face and vibrating her buttocks. Not from side to side as would a Hawaiian dancer performing the hula-hula, but in a cheeky suggestive back and forth movement that brought gales of laughter and whistles from the crowd. Jack tried to carry on but the display of the pulsating female form was too much to compete with and he sportingly conceded by stepping down to join in the acclamation. As the pianist quickened his playing, so the woman increased the speed of her pelvic movements until that region was just a blur and eventually outpaced the fingers on the piano. In the end it was the pianist who stopped first, prompting the woman to clap her hands in triumph before carefully climbing down to rejoin her friends amid noisy appreciation from the onlookers.

"What's it like to get upstaged by a middle-aged woman?" The query came from Les and Jack laughed.

"Nay ... I've allus said I appreciate talent when I see it and that woman's got plenty; I bet her owd man thinks so too, providing she hasn't worn the poor sod to a frazzle."

They all rocked with mirth as their imaginations went to work. Les was still chortling when he screwed up his eyes to look blearily at his watch. "Here, have a guess what time it is."

Jack placed his fingertips to his forehead as if calling on some inner power. "Nearly ten o'clock?"

"And the rest, it's gone half past. Too late to get into the Palais so we might as well get 'em in again. I haven't heard 'time' shouted – who's round is it?"

Tom decided it was his, so after weaving an unsteady path to the bar, he returned a few minutes later with three pints and three whiskies. "Hell, Tom, it's not thi birthday is it?" asked Les, blinking owlishly at the laden tray.

Tom swayed ever so slowly before sliding the drinks carefully on to the table. "No, not yet it isn't, but it will be in about three months' time and besides, you know what Jack said in the Unicorn?"

Jack selected one of the whiskies, picked up a pint also, before holding both glasses before him. "I remember what I said Tommy, so here's to your very good health and stuff the army."

Tom did the same, scrutinising the drinks carefully before he too spoke. "Well, in that case I say stuff the navy an' all."

They both looked towards Les who collected up the remaining whisky and pint but having done so, stood with a quizzical look on his face. "What can I stuff?" he asked plaintively.

Tom and Jack swayed to and fro with furrowed brows until Tom's eyes lit up. "Owt you can get your leg over," and Les grinned at the advice.

"Great, I'll drink to that, cheers!" All three downed their whiskies, with differing reactions. Tom shook his head from side to side, blowing noisily, while Jack curled his lips to display strong white teeth as the spirit cursed a fiery path to his stomach. Les, on the other hand, merely rolled his eyes before sinking quietly into his seat, giving a little cough as he did so. After paying homage to their pints the boys decided it was singing time again but by now the pianist had finished for the night and several customers were beginning to leave. One of these included

Jack's dancing partner who made her way towards the three as they started on the second verse of 'Roll out the Barrel' but they stopped as she reached their table. She smiled down at Jack.

"Thanks for being a sport, luv, I couldn't resist getting up on t' table with you; I wish I were ten years younger." She tried to ruffle Jack's short hair before kissing him on the cheek.

Jack laughed. "Hey! From what I saw tonight, if you waggled that backside of yours any faster ten years ago you must have set your bloke alight! I tek it you're married?"

"Aye, poor luv's in the army but I didn't mean it like that, cheeky sod. I meant that ten years ago I was a lot slimmer and I wasn't married. I don't know, you lads are all the same – a one track mind, the lot of you." There was a little giggle before she added, "Thank goodness." Returning to her friends she paused to wiggle her bum in a farewell gesture. "Goodnight, boys. If you can't be good, be careful."

This prompted Les to start singing, "You must have been a beautiful baby." And as she passed through the door all three voices were raised in rhapsodic discord as the drink took its toll on their harmony. The singing ended when the lights flashed on and off and a voice called out. "Sup up, lads, so we can have yer glasses please."

Tom looked towards the bar. "It's alright, landlord, you can put lights off – I can sing just as good in the dark. How about three more pints?" The owner of the voice approached the three revellers and they blinked through fuddled eyes as he placed both hands on the table to address them in a cordial tone.

"Hey, lads, towels have bin on pumps a good quarter of an hour or more; you wouldn't want me to get in trouble wi' bobbies, would yer? Tell you what, somebody left a nearly full pint on the bar, you can split it between yer while I collect glasses. No singing mucky songs mind. Had a good night, have yer? You looked to be enjoying yourselves."

Tom raised a beaming face. "Aye, have that, I was lucky to bump into my mates here and we've had a reet good night together; mind you it's not over yet. There'll be all them lasses on t' bus going home and owt could happen; they might want to mother mi with me being in mi sailor suit."

Les let out a hoot of laughter. "More like want to smother thi."

At that the landlord smiled. "Okay then, I'll get that pint if it's still there. I like to see lads enjoy themselves without mecking trouble, so tek care when you leave here." He looked at Jack; "Haven't I seen you in uniform?"

"Aye, I'm just on a spot of leave; it's good to be home for a bit." The landlord agreed and expounded on the folly of the war then went to the bar to fetch the drink he had promised but came back with an extra half as well. "Here you are, lads, split the pint between the two of yer then somebody can have this half – all the best." He then went to help his staff, busy clearing tables. While Jack tipped the fresh half into what was left of his pint, Les shared the nearly full one between Tom and himself. As they all raised their replenished glasses, Jack turned to Tom. "I suppose you'll have to travel back tomorrow, eh, Tom? Well all the best and here's to the next time." They clinked glasses, knowing full well that 'next time' could mean next month, next year, or quite possibly never? But the pensiveness was brushed aside and they broke into a ditty that had the staff singing along with them as they tidied the place up. "'We'll meet again, don't know where, don't know when, but I know we'll meet again some sunny day.'" As the words drifted through the now nearly empty room, Jack, Les and Tom had their arms on each other's shoulders, swaying from side to side in time with the melody.

The night's drinking came to an end as the singing hushed and the glasses were drained of their contents. Jack took a deep breath. "Right lads, I reckon we can call it a night; we've had a good session so let's tek our glasses back to the bar, and don't drop any." He pushed back his chair, collecting the glasses before him while Tom and Les did the same to make a meandering course for the bar. The landlord was drying glasses and he chuckled as they approached. "You seem to have a bit of a list to starboard, young man."

Tom gingerly placed his glasses on the surface of the bar.

"Naw, not really; it's being on dry land what does it. Be alright once I get back on board ship." Tom swayed back on his heels trying to look sober but the lopsided grin was a bit of a giveaway.

The landlord shook his head and smiled. "Glad to see

you enjoyed yourselves and thanks for bringing glasses over."

Jack also made sure their glasses were safe and extended his hand. "Thanks, landlord, tonight was just what I needed; hope to see you again soon."

His hand was firmly clasped. "I hope so too lad, now mind how you go, all of yer – tek care."

The three headed for the door but paused to shout cheerio to the staff, still hard at work, although one of them couldn't resist calling after Jack. "Hey, toreador, what do you reckon to our Daisy and her short strokes? You reckon you could stand the pace?"

Jack laughed. "Owd on, I'm too young to die just yet. Tell you what, slow her down to half speed and I might consider it, but in her present kilter she's too much of a woman for me." With that they departed.

Outside, on the pavement, it was Jack who spoke up again. "By 'eck, I could enjoy some fish and chips – how about you two?"

Tom nodded. "I fancy some; they'll still be open on Ryton Street, with it being Saturday night – what about you, Les?" Les fumbled in his pocket to examine his small change, rocking back on his heels as he did so.

"Don't worry about coining up," remarked Jack, "I'll treat yer, I'll treat both of yer, come on."

He wrapped an arm round Les's shoulder, did the same with Tom, then set an erratic course down the main street until they reached the crossroads. These were negotiated with total disregard for both the traffic lights and vehicles but luckily, of the latter there were very few so they were in no real danger. A right turn after passing two banks brought them into Ryton Street where the queues for the late buses had formed. Half way along the street, another group of Saturday night revellers were gathered to indicate that the fish and chip shop was doing its usual trade and an appetising aroma wafted towards the three as they approached its blacked out window and doorway.

"Well I'm having fish and chips," announced Jack, "how about you lads?"

Tom and Les looked at each other before nodding approval.

"Right, that's sorted then, fish and chips three times, a few batter bits and plenty of salt and vinegar." Jack rubbed his hands together as they came to a halt outside the entrance which was opened for him as a group of giggling girls emerged, each clutching her own individual package of gastronomic delight wrapped in white paper with newspaper reinforcement. As they spilled out onto the pavement, the girls wafted the packets under the noses of the three and Les was quick to respond. "Hey up lads, these lovely damsels have been and fetched us our supper, they must have known we were coming."

The first girl avoided Les's outstretched hand and was just as quick with a verbal response. "Go get your own, cheeky sod."

Les pretended to be crestfallen. "How can such a

gorgeous girl be so mean?" But he quickly switched his attention to the next girl and gave her the benefit of a wide grin. "You'll give me a chip, won't you mi duck? Tell you what, you give me a chip and I'll give you a kiss, how about that?"

The girl, about seventeen years old, was a demure little thing and she meekly offered Les her portion of chips. Les selected one but before popping the hot morsel into his mouth, he closed his eyes, puckered his lips and swayed forward. The young girl kissed him hastily then drew back, laughing. "You've been drinking," she declared, before offering her chips to Jack and Tom. They each took one and Tom asked if the offer still stood: "A chip for a kiss?"

"Not likely, I've heard all about you sailors."

"Listen, whatever you've been told is just a big fib to blacken us poor matelots. The only woman I've ever been out with is mi Mam and besides, I don't know how to kiss, you'd have to show me what to do." There were hoots of laughter as the remaining girls joined their friends but made sure their chips were out of reach. "You're not pinching our supper – go and stand in the queue like we had to."

"Not even for a kiss?" entreated Les.

"You must be barmy," they chorused then all four scampered away laughing as Les pretended to pounce.

Jack had been quiet while the bit of teasing had been going on but he spoke up now. "Well if you two Romeos have finished, can we go in and get served?"

"Aye, go on in," said Les, "we'll come in with you."

Once through the outer door, they had to draw back a black curtain to enter the warm interior where half a dozen customers were still waiting to be served. A man and a woman were behind the counter and both were flushed with the heat from the hot fat sizzling away in the stainless steel pans. Golden chips were piled into a holding section above the pans but the unit reserved for fish was empty. Pieces of cod were being dipped into white batter then slowly lowered into the hot fat to splutter away where they too turned crispy brown. Jack joined the queue and wrinkled his nose in appreciation.

"By they smell good, I haven't bin able to get hold of owt like that for months."

The man dipping the fish paused and looked over his shoulder. "Been somewhere where you couldn't get food like this, have you lad? Well you'll enjoy these when they're ready, if you're wanting fish, are you?"

Jack nodded, "Aye, fish and chips three times and a few batter bits if you've got any to spare."

The man inclined his head towards the lady behind the counter. "Missus will serve you when it's your turn, these won't tek long." He slid the last piece of fish into the pan before turning round. "On a spot of leave?"

Jack gave an expressive nod; "Light Infantry, but I can count mi blessings, some of my mates can't."

"That's right lad, thee count thi blessings while tha can and mek most of what you can get. By the looks of yer, you three seem to have had a good night."

Jack smiled; "When I get them fish and chips down, it will just finish night off a treat. We've had a good booze-up, a good sing-song and now for a good feast – what more can a man ask for?"

Behind him, Tom and Les had their arms round each other's shoulder sharing a joke while they waited, but from time to time Les broke into song as he took advantage of his captive audience.

"Don't clap him for goodness sake," implored Jack, "otherwise he won't stop and Tom there is capable of passing his hat round, so be warned."

The waiting customers took it all in good part until the fish were ready and they were served one by one and it was Jack's turn to stand before the perspiring proprietress.

"Now then, young man, one of each three times did I hear you say?"

"Aye please, Missus, and could you drop a few of them batter bits in an' all, with plenty of salt and vinegar?" Jack licked his lips. "Don't bother to wrap them up, we're going to eat 'em straight away when we get outside."

The woman smiled at Jack's obvious contemplation of enjoying fish and chips for the first time in months and she scooped three separate portions of crispy brown chips into three squares of white paper. A fish was added to each one, along with some batter bits, particles of batter that had broken away in the hot fat and came free to those who asked for them. Jack eyed the three steaming repasts as each one received a liberal sprinkling of salt and vinegar, enhancing the mouth-watering aroma, and he licked eager lips. "Now then mi duck, they look good enough to eat so how much do I owe you if I pay cash?"

The woman decided to go along with Jack's badinage. "Well seeing as how it's you I'm only going to charge you ninepence. Anybody else mind and they'd only get thrupence change from a bob; can't say fairer than that, can I?"

Jack laughed at the canny reply. "True enough and if they taste as good as they look, then they're worth every penny, thanks, Missus."

He handed over the correct change and beckoned to Tom and Les to step forward to collect their portions, while he carefully arranged his to fit snugly into one hand. "I'll tell yer summat, shall I? You can keep yer frogs legs, yer snails, yer caviar, I'll mek do wi' these any day; thanks again, Missus, and a good night to you both."

There was an answering "Good night, lad" from a back room and a "Cheerio" from the perspiring lady as she busied herself serving the next customers.

Jack followed Les and Tom outside to lean against a wall as he tucked into his supper.

"Thanks for these, Jack," remarked Tom, "a bit of alright, aren't they?" Jack grunted an affirmative but he was too preoccupied to say much.

Les too was enjoying himself but kept casting apprehensive glances in the direction of their bus stop. "I'm sure our bus is in and there are people standing on the pavement; it could be full up you know."

Tom gazed through bleary eyes at the coach but he fed a generous portion of fish into his mouth before speaking. "Aye I think you might be right, Les. Unless they've got a duplicate coming on behind, we'd better get down there. Come on, Jack, otherwise we could be walking back home."

Tom and Les set off in the direction of the stationary vehicle but Jack remained leaning against the wall and he didn't move until every morsel of his meal was devoured, at which point he gave a sigh of contentment. 'By heck they were good,' he pronounced to himself before screwing his wrapping paper into a ball, tossing it into the air then deftly heading it into a waste bin. In the meagre light coming from the interior of the bus he could just discern a group of people gathered on the pavement and as he hurried towards them he could hear Les trying to converse with one of the passengers on the vehicle. He was rocking back and forth, both hands deep in his pockets, gazing up at a window and speaking in a conciliatory tone. "Never mind, Betty luv, I'll tell you what; how about if I tek you for a walk tomorrow afternoon, eh, say about three o'clock? You be at the end of your street at three and I'll tek you for a nice walk like I used to do."

Jack had now drawn level and Les turned as he heard his brother's step. "Look, Jack, it's Betty, isn't she a smasher eh? Right put out she is because I didn't manage to get to Palais."

He turned back to the window. "Don't forget, three

o'clock tomorrow afternoon." Three fingers were held in the air as if to endorse his intentions and to aid Betty's memory.

Jack looked up at the window and he saw a girl nod her head then giggle to her friend sitting next to her as Les swayed back and forth. There wasn't much light but Jack recognized the likeness to an older girl he knew as Connie so this was her younger sister. Dyed blond hair framed a pretty face to which far too much make-up had been applied but Jack could see the reason for his brother's interest. He hoped for Les's sake she wasn't a carbon copy of Connie because the word 'fast' was synonymous with the older sister.

While Les stood like a dummy grinning up at the coach window, Jack looked for Tom and he heard him remonstrating with someone who was sounding a bit agitated.

"Look, I'm only allowed to carry so many passengers and if I were to count how many were on now, even without you lot, I'll bet you any money I'm over the limit so I just can't take any more. I'm sorry, that's all there is to it, I can't let any more on."

Tom was waving his arms in the air. "What if we sat on somebody's knees? Or they sat on ours?"

The conductor shook his head and stepped back, but now the driver butted in. "Wouldn't make any difference because they're already sitting on each other's knees as it is. I'm afraid it looks like you'll be walking home, sorry mate." He held a pocket watch up to his face. "Time we were off, no point in hanging about."

Tom dropped his arms as the driver went round to climb into his cab and the conductor stood on the steps to ring the bell. A second later the engine roared into life and the last bus to Bennington was on its way. Tom threw his hat on the ground but Jack didn't seem unduly perturbed at the prospect of walking six miles and he shrugged his shoulders. "Tell you what, young Thomas, if we come across a wheelbarrow I'll borrow it and give thi a lift to the top of your street, or better still, how about a ride in a pram like Ebb and Flo?"

Tom laughed at the prospect because Ebb and Flo were a couple of local characters who lived rough and took it in turns to push each other about in an old perambulator that probably contained all their worldly possessions; they were a familiar sight on the roads between Worksop and Lindrick.

"Fair enough, but by the looks of your Les perhaps the pram ought to be big enough for two." Tom then called out to Les who was still gazing after the bus as it turned a corner leading into the main street.

"Hey, Don Juan, how do you fancy a six mile hike? Are you up to it?" Les still had his hands thrust deep into his trouser pockets.

"I suppose I'll have to be but we'll have to get going while I'm still able, and I don't know how long that will be for."

They set off and were soon on the outskirts of town.

Retford was to the east and Sheffield lay in the opposite direction, so they headed westwards.

Three quarters of an hour later they were making weary steps through the village of Woodsetts with its stone cottages and farms set on either side of the winding road, and as the last of the dwellings receded behind them they gazed at the daunting sight ahead.

Stretching before them was a very long, very steep hill that would take them past Dead Man's Wood, so called because years earlier some unfortunate had decided to end his days by hanging himself from one of its large oaks. However, it wasn't the wood that distressed them it was the steepness of the hill, just distinguishable in the starlight, as they gazed forwards and upwards. They were also aware that after the summit was reached their journey was far from over; through their bleary eyes it looked a heck of a climb to the top of that hill.

Les slowed to a halt before moving to lean against an open five-barred gate giving access to a field of freshly mown meadow grass, for here and there sweet-smelling hay was heaped ready for carting away to make silage.

"I don't know about you two but I'm ready for a bit of a rest." Les let out a sigh as he invited comment from his two weary companions. Tom stood with head bowed and hands on his hips while Jack nodded his head several times before answering.

"Aye, wouldn't do any harm to have a bit of a breather, that hay looks inviting so we might as well have a bit of comfort."

They headed for the nearest pile of hay to flop backwards, with arms outstretched. The grass felt warm and its fragrance hung in the still June air, but what had been intended as a breather turned into something rather longer lasting. The drink, the singing, then the miles already covered, took their toll and the three weary young men were soon asleep. Not a peep escaped any of them for the remaining hours of darkness and the sun was well into its ascendancy before the Sunday morning activity on the nearest farm roused them from their slumber. The clanging and clanking of buckets and milk churns, intermingled with the mooing of a dairy herd, welcomed them back to wakefulness.

Tom gave a little cough. "Hell's bells, my mouth's like the bottom of a bird cage and mi throat ... it's like sandpaper; must be all that warbling I did."

Les too stroked his Adam's apple, sticking his tongue out as he sat up to observe his brother. "You alright, Jack? You look like death warmed up."

Jack covered his eyes and slowly rocked forward into a sitting position. His mother had once told him that merry nights made sad mornings and that everything had its price ... Well, the thumping behind his eyes was the price he was now paying for last night's little spree in Worksop. He groaned, looked skywards and decided things could only improve. The sun was shining, the birds were singing and his head would get better; he rose slowly to his feet.

"Hey, I'm soaking, my clothes are wet through."

Tom and Les too rose slowly to their feet, feeling the dampness of their clothes as they did so.

"It's from the grass – I bet it was only cut yesterday. What's the back of my jacket like?" Les pivoted in order to get an assessment from his companions.

Tom inspected the jacket through a pair of bloodshot eyes. "It's okay, pretty wet mind, but it's not stained so it'll be alright."

Jack stretched himself and yawned. "We've still got that hill to climb and no chance of a lift, so it's Shanks's pony, gentlemen."

Tom looked wistful; "No chance of that barrow or pram you were on about last night?"

"Ah that was last night, this is a brand new day and I'm now sober. Look, if we get a move on we could get home before Ma's up; how about you, Tom? Are they early risers at your house?"

"Not on Sundays, and it depends how long it teks us to get home; how long do you think?"

Jack shrugged his broad shoulders, "Three quarters of an hour or so, at a steady pace."

He led the way out of the field to face the long incline.

"Right then, you lucky lads, there's only one way we can get to the top of that bugger and that's by putting one foot in front of the other – are you ready?"

They set off with the sun on their backs, while overhead a skylark tried to sing its heart out while the sweet smell of hay gradually faded, left behind in the meadow. Away in the distance a church bell rang out an early summons to its Sunday service but, even without such an indicator one instinctively knew it was a Sunday morning, a bit different, a bit special.

"I could murder a cup of tea," declared Tom, "how about you two?"

Jack licked dry lips. "Aye, wouldn't say no, not even if it were a cup of NAAFI tea wi' bromide in it. Run on ahead, Les and put kettle on."

"You must be joking," protested Les. "It's alright for you infantry bods, but if I ever join up I'm going for tank corps."

"Tom's not complaining," retorted Jack, "and he's in t' navy. Anyway we shall soon be at top then it will be easy going."

Sure enough, ten minutes later they had reached the brow of the hill with Bennington in the distance bathed in morning sunlight. A lone cyclist, on his way to work at one of the farms they had left behind, pedalled towards them whistling merrily at the prospect of freewheeling down the steep hill ahead. As he approached he shielded his eyes as if to scrutinize the three wayfarers but as he drew level his whistling slowly ceased and there was a squeal of brakes as he halted to gaze back in amazement. On hearing the brakes, Tom, Jack and Les also stopped to look back.

"Summat the matter, lad?" enquired Jack, but before the young man had time to answer the reason became obvious. While walking abreast of each other they hadn't noticed anything unusual, but the scene to the young cyclist as he approached must have been quite a sight as they were now able to appreciate. Apart from their tousled hair, rumpled attire and unshaven chins, the trio also looked like phantom wraiths as steam rose into the morning air from their wet clothing to give them a ghost-like appearance.

"Had a bath and forgot to take yer clothes off?" asked the wide-eyed lad. "Wait till I tell 'em at farm – wish I had a camera wi' me!"

Then he was off, pedalling towards the hill as his laughter startled wood pigeons roosting in the nearby wood.

"No wonder he stopped for a closer scan," declared Jack, "we look a right spectacle – look at this." He flapped his arms, sending more wisps of steam spiralling upwards and it was a good five minutes before they stopped falling about with laughter and were able to resume their journey.

Eventually they did so until a junction was reached where Tom needed to go one direction, and Jack and Les in another to head towards the tall pit chimney clearly visible against the blue of the sky. For a few minutes they stood facing each other, remembering the night now past. The humour, the beer, the songs and the sheer pleasure of a night shared with good companions were all reflected in their laughter and handshakes, but there was also a serious note too.

"Enjoy the rest of your leave, Jack; it's a pity I have to travel back this afternoon but I must catch train from

Sheffield." Tom looked Jack squarely in the eyes before gripping his hand once more. "Just you tek care, eh?"

"You too, Tom. We'll do the same again next time we get some leave together. Remember me to your folks – cheerio."

Les also bid him farewell and they stood while Tom walked to a turning that would take him out of view, but before it did so he paused to wave his hat and do a hornpipe, then he was gone. For a few seconds Jack and Les stood in silence; each knew what the other was thinking but they didn't openly voice their apprehension. Instead, Jack slapped his brother on the back and spun him round to face the tall chimney.

"Right, let's go and get that pot of tea; haven't you got a date this afternoon? What time was it, three o'clock? Mind you, you look shattered so if yer don't feel up to it let me tek her for a walk over Skinner's fields. We can do a spot of sunbathing behind that stone wall at far end and I'll tell her you send your love, how about it?"

"You must be joking, but I'll fix you up wi' her sister if you like; you know Connie, you reckon?"

Jack gave a drawn out whistle. "Yes I do but no thanks, I'd rather go and keep t' owd man and his pigeons company, I'd be safer there."

They turned down between Collier Avenue and Jubilee Avenue but apart from the sound of a wireless here and there, all was quiet. Their clothes had more or less dried so they no longer created the spectral appearance of earlier. Jack turned into the yard first so it was he who raised the latch on the back door; it was not locked, it hardly ever was and inside, all was still.

A pot of tea was soon mashed and after the first appreciative swallow, Les collected a third cup from the kitchen. "I'll go and give Ma a surprise, I bet she hasn't had a cup of tea in bed for ages; don't think Father would welcome one though, do you?"

Jack pulled a wry face, "Depends on how much beer he had last night, he might send you back down wi' a flea in yer ear hole. I should play safe if I were you and just tek the one."

Les mounted the stairs and Jack heard the surprise in his mother's voice as

Les woke her.

"What are you doing up at this hour? You never get up early on a Sunday morning. You've just got in, haven't you? Is our Jack in?"

The questions stopped, to be replaced by the sound of the tea being savoured.

"Ah that's grand, have you only just got in, Jack as well?"

There was the sound of Les chuckling as he explained the reason for the early morning tea, which evoked a "tut-tut."

"I don't know, you were bad enough as kids but you're supposed to learn a bit of sense as you get older. Look at your trousers, is your jacket as bad?" There was the sound of a big sigh before she continued. "Go on, I'll be down in a minute, thanks for the tea."

Les rejoined Jack downstairs to drink his own cup of tea before going over to the sideboard to gaze in the mirror.

"Good grief, where's that debonair young man that was here last night? I'd better get my head down for an hour or so – how about you, Jack?"

"No, I'm alright, I haven't got a date at three o'clock. You reckon madam will turn up then?"

"She'll be there, brother – you mark my words, a good looking chap like me?" Les took a closer look in the mirror. "Well, when I've had a kip, a wash and a shave, that is."

Jack rested his head back on the chair. "Just watch yourself, that's all, they're a rum family."

Les was about to reply but Annie started down the stairs and they both fell silent.

"I'll just have a wash," said Annie as she negotiated the last step, "then we can have breakfast. One of you put the kettle on again, I shan't be a minute."

She disappeared into the kitchen to return with a pan to collect hot water from the boiler. "Give the fire a bit of a stir, Jack, it needs a bit of coal – can't do without hot water." She looked at her son. "Looking forward to Sunday dinner then?"

Jack smiled and nodded. "Yorkshire pud? Roast tatters?"

"Of course, then I thought I'd do a jam roll for afters; what do you fancy – steamed or baked?"

"Whatever you put on the table, Ma, will be fine."

Ten minutes later they were enjoying scrambled egg on toast and a fresh pot of tea. The aroma must have drifted upstairs because it wasn't long before there was more activity as the rest of the household stirred into wakefulness and prepared to greet the new day.

Sunday dinner was always the meal of the week, but this one would be extra special as every chair around the table would be occupied for the first time in months. Annie excelled at making Yorkshire pudding so when it accompanied a bit of beef, roast potatoes, green vegetables and lots of thick brown gravy, it was a repast fit for a king. Billy was despatched to fetch a bottle of dandelion and burdock so that he and Susan had something to drink with the meal. Later, he would go to the off-licence to get a jug of ale for the men while Annie would also share it by making herself a shandygaff.

The morning passed quickly as each of the Fosters occupied themselves with their individual pursuits, then it was time to be seated round the table, raising their tumblers and mugs to toast each other's good health. Les was soon regaling everyone by recounting the episode of Tom and Red Face, which brought an "Oh, how could he?" from Susan, but Billy thought it was great. Then the incident when the farm labourer had to stop cycling in order to stare back at the spectacle of the three steaming early morning hikers also had everyone chortling. Annie had heard the tale earlier but she nevertheless joined in the laughter as Les revelled in his role as storyteller, albeit with assistance from Jack. As they sat there, enjoying the food and the bonhomie, it was hard to envisage the same table just a few days earlier when anxiety and apprehension had hung like a dark cloud over its occupants. Annie had to remind herself that it was only three days ago they had listened to the news on the wireless with foreboding, as information was slowly released concerning the plight of thousands of troops trapped on a Dunkirk beach. Jack had been one of those troops and she bit her lip as she contemplated how it might have been this Sunday. She closed her eyes. "Oh thank you, thank you," she whispered.

CHAPTER SIX

Les Takes Betty for a Walk

"Hey Romeo, it's a quarter to three. I hope you're not going to keep the lass waiting, you were eager enough last night!"

Jack raised his voice in order to be heard upstairs where Les was changing into a cream, short-sleeved shirt.

"She'll wait, Jack, and anyway it'll only tek me five minutes to get to the end of New Street, from there I can see right down to where she lives." A thump of feet heralded Les's descent into the living room. "Just comb my curly locks then I'm off." He took a comb from his back pocket and made his way over to the sideboard, where a couple of passes with the device and a pat with his right palm settled a kink just over his forehead. "You lucky girl, you," he announced to his reflection as he bared white teeth for inspection and blowing himself a kiss.

A snort came from Jack who looked up from reading the Sunday paper. "I'm not joking, it's a wonder that bloody mirror don't crack, whatever the lasses see in you I just do not know. Are they all short-sighted or what?"

Les turned to wink at his brother. "It's obvious in't it, eh? Poise, charm, good looks, wit, a fantastic animal magnetism, and before you say owt, Ma reckons I tek after you, when you was my age."

"What a load of rubbish, you'll never be as good looking, as witty, or as sexy as me as long as you've got a hole in yer backside." They both burst out laughing, prompting Les to take one last look in the mirror before making his way through the passage and out into the sunshine.

"See yer, Dad," he called, walking briskly to the yard's entrance, pausing only momentarily to glance upwards as a cloud passed over the sun, but it was only a fleeting obscuration and the fluffy stratus drifted on its way.

"Aye, alright lad, will thar be back for tea?"

Les hesitated. "Er ... should be, but tell Ma not to hold things up on my account, just in case."

He gave a final wave and was soon turning between the houses to take him on to the main road and towards New Street.

As he hurried along, his thoughts went back to when he and Betty had gone out together on a regular basis. After starting work down the pit his leisure hours had been spent playing snooker or billiards, or going to see the latest film at the picture house. That is until the Saturday night dance became included in his social activities then life became very interesting. It was there he had met Betty and after she had allowed him to discover the pleasures to be enjoyed between girls and boys he had decided that that particular activity had snooker or billiards beaten hollow. He gave a little smile as he crossed the main road in order to pass an area of enclosed public garden, but now it was having its iron railings removed in similar fashion to the park. He recalled having spent quite a few pleasant hours in there with Betty so as he hurried along he found himself looking forward to being with her again. He checked his reflection in a shop window as she came into view for he could see she had taken care in getting ready, and her make-up was not as heavy as usual. She was wearing a blue skirt and white blouse with a light blue silk scarf tied loosely round her long delicate neck. Her hair, a shining glossy honey hue in the warm sunlight, was held back with a matching silk band, while white-flowered earrings complemented the outfit nicely.

"Hey, you look great," expressed Les warmly. He approached to stand before her and took hold of her hand. He was a good few inches taller than Betty so she had to tilt her head back to look up into his face.

"Ta, I didn't know whether or not you'd turn up; you'd had one or two last night and what with having to walk home, what time did you get in?"

"It was late, well early really, early this morning," and he gave a little chuckle as he mentally reminisced on the previous night's happenings.

"Do yer fancy a walk?" Betty looked down at her feet; "My heels are a bit high but as long as it's not too far."

Les rubbed his chin; "Just a walk over Skinner's, like we used to, eh?"

Betty nodded but gave a wary look. "Okay, just as long

as we don't end up walking right the way across – I know you when you get going."

Les shook his head, "Not today, I had enough tramping last night, we'll just go as far as that first stile then have a sit down. Besides, I want to get back for tea, with our Jack being on leave."

Holding hands, they set off with Les making sure he was nearest the pavement's edge; he had read that it was correct for the man to be positioned so.

"What happened to this Canadian chap then?" The question was broached as they matched stride for stride down the main street. "I bet you couldn't get me out of your mind, am I right?"

Betty turned her head and she gave Les's hand a squeeze; "Yeah something like that." She was pretty sure Les still fancied her and he would make a good father if she really was pregnant but she needed him to think the baby was his.

"Yeah, I kept remembering how it used to be between you and me – it was a bit special Les, don't you think? Anyway I couldn't forget you and I guess I just lost interest in him."

She had no problem concocting the lie and she gave the hand holding hers another squeeze for good measure. Les welcomed this adept massaging of his ego so he made a slight adjustment as they walked side by side, allowing him to slip his left arm round her waist. There was no denying that Betty could make heads turn but it was obvious her brassy attractiveness was superficial, though not so to Leslie for where Betty was concerned he suffered from impaired vision. The stroll down the main street with his arm around her waist was doing him a power of good. He chattered on happily as their steps took them past Collier Avenue and Jubilee Avenue before heading towards an imposing red brick structure boasting a high clock tower. It was the technical college and their route ran alongside its grounds in the form of a narrow path between high railings, so it was only suitable for single file. Les however was reluctant to relinquish his embrace for it had moved higher and Betty's left breast was now virtually resting on the back of his hand. So while she walked on the path he struggled along beside her but quite content to accept the inconvenience as the ample orb bounced in compliant tempo with every step they took. Some two hundred yards were covered in this fashion until the path terminated at a wrought iron swing gate set within a half circle of railings and allowing only one person through at a time. From that point the vista changed to open grassland where a right of way was clearly defined across the meadow leading to the first of several stiles set in stone walls dividing the area into individual pastures. Les gave Betty a peck on the cheek as he manipulated their passage through the confined space; he had done the same thing lots of times before and was delighted to be resuming the practice. He displayed this by encircling her waist with both arms as she emerged through the opening so that her whole body was pressed tightly against his.

"Hey, it's broad daylight, you never know who might be looking," protested Betty, but at the same time making sure it didn't sound too much like a protest.

Les looked over his shoulder; "I can't see anybody, – the only audience we have are these heifers." He nodded towards the herd of Friesian cows quietly grazing away at the clover-rich browse, their tails swishing away any irritating flies that settled on their rumps. "I don't reckon they'll get upset by my bit of canoodling, because when owd man Skinner turns his bull loose among 'em, they get a bit more than just canoodling, whether they like it or not."

"Leslie Foster, ... you don't improve one bit."

Betty gently prised herself free but not before brushing Les's lips with her own. "When was the last time you brought me a walk over here? I bet you can't remember."

"Er, let's see, last time we came for a walk over here was last summer. We finished up in Skinner's barn because Ma wanted to know where I'd bin to get corn and chaff in mi trouser turn-ups. I told her I'd given one of the farm hands a bit of help to get some stray heifers back into their yard but she wasn't convinced; Ma can see straight through me."

Betty gave a cheeky smile; "No, you're not very good at hiding things, are you? When you held me back there at the gate I had the feeling you were pleased to be here with me."

"You cheeky sod," replied Les and gave her bosom a gentle squeeze. "Anyway it's your fault; you always did have that effect on me – you used to call me 'Ever-Ready', so I don't suppose?"

Betty uttered several tuts. "You're really romantic, Leslie Foster. We haven't been out together for months and the first time we are you want to have your wicked way, is that why you suggested bringing me over here?" She poked him in the ribs; this wasn't the time or the place – she had other plans. "I can't, pet, it's the wrong time."

Les shook his head and grinned; "Didn't want to, not really. It's just that I didn't want to disappointment you."

There followed another poke in the ribs. "Liar," she said softly.

By now they had nearly reached one of the many stiles set in the stone walls but Les steered away from it to a part that was in need of repair where several of the stones had been dislodged and one or two were large enough to sit on.

"Here, you can sit on my hankie," offered Les.

"Ta, you're a real luv, no wonder I missed you."

"Aye, there aren't many of us about, like gold dust we are," and he held Betty's hand while she lowered down.

"I've really missed us going out together, Bett." The acknowledgment was spoken softly as he too tried to make himself comfortable.

Betty raised her eyebrows. "You've bin out with other girls though; I know you have cos I've seen you two or three times and you had your arm round one of 'em."

"Oh aye, pictures and that but nowt like when we were going out together."

Betty reached across to place her hand on his knee. "We can go out sometime next week if you like, just like we used to." She allowed her eyes to widen fully as she gazed intently into Les's own. "I still get home from work about half four so I could be ready for half past five, if you want to, that is." Les covered the hand on his knee with his own and pressed hard.

"Tha knows very well I want to, how about tomorrow? I'm on days regular so I could get my head down for a couple of hours when I've had dinner, then we could go to first showing at pictures and I could still be in bed at a decent time."

Betty thought quickly – going to the cinema had not been quite what she had in mind, but still …

"Yeah, okay, that's fine, not a cowboy film is it?"

Les grinned, he liked the westerns but he shook his head.

"No! No, it's an Abbott and Costello comedy so it should be a good laugh, and the supporting feature is 'Crime Does Not Pay.' Les pronounced the title in an affected American drawl, pretended to draw a pistol, fire it, blow smoke from its barrel and return it to its holster.

"Us G-men always get our man," he drawled again.

Betty giggled. "You're as soft as a brush, do you know that? And besides, it's the Mounties who always get their man … But let's see, tomorrow night? Yeah and we'll be able to get in after six because on Mondays, it's a continuous performance. How about half seven? I could meet you at the top of our street at twenty past."

Les readily agreed and reckoned his shift at the pit

would be a bit more bearable if he had a date with Betty to look forward to. He looked at her as she sat with her hands clasped around her knees and wished they were over in the corner behind the wall, having a bit of naughty. 'It was true he had been out with other girls but they hadn't been like Betty; she liked sex and she didn't mind showing it, so next week with a bit of luck'. The hint of a smile flickered across his features but he forced himself to think of other things.

"Hey, how about coming for a drink with us tonight? There's nowt fixed up definite as yet but me and our Jack were thinking of taking Ma and the owd man for a bevvy at the Comrades. We don't go in there very often but Father likes it – what do you say?"

Betty pursed her lips; "I don't think so, Les, if you're taking your mam and dad they'll enjoy having just the two of you with Jack being on leave, so some other time, eh?"

Les nodded, "Aye okay, it was just a thought, like."

He glanced at his watch then across to the clock on the college.

"Time's flying, have to be mecking a move shortly." He stretched out his hand. "Come and give us a kiss."

Betty rose to her feet and covered the short distance with easy strides before sliding on to his lap and encircling his neck with her slim, warm arms. She tilted her face until her full red lips were merely brushing his before allowing them to slowly fuse together. This was Betty's forte and she enjoyed sensing the precise moment to tantalise his eager mouth with her pink tongue. Les gave a soft groan when she finally prepared to ease herself away.

"Well, sir? Was that alright, sir?" A provocative cheeky wriggle accompanied the mocking overtones.

Les rolled his eyes; "I reckon you'd better get up before I have a mishap! Jump up, please."

Betty obliged but not before delivering another big kiss.

"You've got lipstick on you – want me to wipe it off?"

Les rubbed the back of his hand across his mouth before offering it up for inspection but Betty shook her head.

"No, you need that hankie I was sat on and you might want a bit of spit as well." Les retrieved his handkerchief and tried to get rid of the telltale sign, meanwhile Betty had brought out a small mirror and was viewing her reflection.

"I'm not joking, I always end up looking like this when I've been out with you; why don't you learn to control yourself. Just look at my make-up."

The rebuke was accompanied by a simulated kiss to ensure the reproach was recognized in its true light.

Les rose to brush and straighten his trousers, giving Betty a wicked grin as he did so.

"Don't mention control, what do you suggest I do with this, cut it off?"

Betty's kissing had had its effect and she chortled as she glanced down to view the consequences. "Race you to the gate", she called, before setting off with Les in hot pursuit.

A few minutes later, they were back between the high railings, arm in arm and heading toward the road.

"No need to walk all the way home with me, Les, I'll leave you at the top of your avenue."

When they had to go their separate ways, Betty looked up into Les's face.

"Give me a peck and I'll see you tomorrow, twenty past seven."

She felt sure things would eventually work out as planned.

Five minutes later and Les was walking into the yard of number 16 Jubilee Avenue.

"You're too late, pal, they've all sat down to tea at your house, but there might be a few scraps left." The voice came from Stan, ensconced in his outside toilet but with plenty of opportunity to view comings and goings through the cracks in the door.

Les chuckled, "Thanks Stan, don't suppose you know what they had for tea?"

"Yeah, bread and dip," came the muffled reply.

Les paused in his stride, "for a bloke who's busy on the thunder box you seem to know more than tha should. Just be careful you don't fall down the pan; easy done when you try to do too many things at the same time. Wouldn't like me to push a book under the door so you can have a read an' all?"

"No need, I've got Sunday paper."

The clatter of crockery greeted Les as he entered the house.

"Sorry I'm a bit late," but it turned out he wasn't. The table was laid and his father, Jack and Billy already seated but his mother and Susan were not yet settled. "I'll just wash mi hands, not be a minute."

"Might as well wash that lipstick off too while you're about it."

The advice came from Susan so Les gave a sigh as he realized he hadn't made a very good job of removing Betty's trademark. He ran his hands under the tap then rubbed the area where he suspected the telltale smear to be, and a red stain on the towel proved he had picked the right spot. As he seated himself he detected Jack's quizzical gaze but decided to ignore the scrutiny.

"Oh pork pie, pickles an' all, go down a treat, eh Dad?" Les looked across at his Father and John nodded.

"Aye, can't beat a bit of pork pie wi' a good crust, and them pickles are what your Mam made, last back end." He looked approvingly at his wife. "Am I right, Annie?"

Annie confirmed that he was and waved her hand to another plate on the table.

"I've opened a tin of luncheon meat as well, so everybody help themselves to what they want," she paused momentarily, "except you, our Billy, I'll see to your plate cos your eyes are bigger than yer belly sometimes and I expect you'll be mecking a doorstop as usual."

Billy looked a bit crestfallen but at least he could still make his specials. "Anything for afters, Mam, wi' our Jack being on leave?"

Annie laughed, "Anybody would think we didn't eat proper when Jack wasn't here, but yes there is. Connie's

Wilf from across let me have some rhubarb out of his allotment so we're having stewed rhubarb and custard, is that to everyone's liking?"

They were all busy helping themselves to bread and whatever they fancied in the way of pie and luncheon meat but there were sounds of approval from all and Billy licked his lips.

"Oo-er, that's great, Mam," he said, beaming as his mother handed him back his plate.

Les sorted his own refreshment out before turning to Jack and nodding to his mum and dad. "Have you asked Ma and Father, about tonight?"

Jack looked up from his plate; "No, I thought I'd wait until you got back but I can do it now." He looked at his mother, then to John. "How do you fancy a night out with your two big sons? Anywhere you like."

John approved straightaway. "Aye, grand, as long as it's Working Man's Club mind, cos I allus goes in there on a Sunday – that alright with you, Annie?"

Annie nodded; "My word, out twice, two days running – so yes, that would be lovely."

Les grinned with satisfaction. "At least I'll get to bed at a decent hour; how about you, Susan, fancy a couple of hours or have you got a date tonight?"

Susan glanced at her father, "Does it have to be Working Man's Club, Dad?" The look on her face told its own story.

"Nowt wrong wi' Working Man's Club; it's a good pint

and it's a penny cheaper than yer pub prices. Besides, I allus goes there of a Sunday night."

Billy had been listening intently, and now he chirped up. "What about me, can I come?"

Jack displayed an exaggerated expression of doubt and slowly shook his head.

"I don't know what you think, Les; I reckon the school cap might be a bit of a giveaway – what do you reckon?"

Les pretended to be deep in thought as if weighing up the situation.

"Well, he is a tall lad and I suppose we could paint a moustache on him, summat like Ronald Colman's; could work if he didn't blow his nose."

Jack impaled a pickled onion, studied it carefully before switching his gaze to Billy then ruefully shook his head. "No, it can't be done, there's all them freckles to contend wi,' I say it's too risky."

There was a cry from Billy as laughter broke out round the table.

"Aw, it's not fair, I should be able to come with yer."

Annie looked at her youngest. "It'll come quick enough, our Billy, it don't seem five minutes since them two were your age and look at the great lumps now."

Billy felt better as his mother redressed the balance of humour away from him although he knew his brothers were only pulling his leg. Jack too decided to make amends and he gave Billy a serious look.

"Hey, I'll tell you what, I wouldn't mind being your

age, and knowing what I know now, suit me fine would that."

He swung his gaze back towards John. "Working Man's Club it is then, about eight o'clock, Father?"

"Aye, about eight o'clock will be fine because four steady pints does me nowadays, but I suppose you two can sup more."

Jack and Les pretended to be shocked. "We don't, do we, Les?"

Les grimaced. "We may do, because I think we might have done last night, but that was Tom's doing – he was a bad influence."

Annie gave both of them a scornful look. "If there was any influence I know who was responsible, so don't go blaming poor Tommy. I bet you were all as bad as one another and you deserved to miss last bus."

Jack and Les pretended to be chastened but they didn't fool anyone and talk turned to the village fete now less than a week away.

"Will you be going to Anston next Saturday, Father?"

John cleared his plate before leaning back in his chair to brush crumbs from his waistcoat and to answer.

"Oh aye. I'll be there right enough; you going to win that piece of pork then?"

Jack shrugged his shoulders. "Might as well, I reckon I stand as good a chance as anyone round here; besides, I've already signed up a couple of seconds for my corner."

Billy received a wink and he proudly stuck his chest

out. "I've told Jimmy, he thinks it's great. Can I borrow a towel, Mam?"

Annie snorted; "I don't know about a towel, stretcher more like. I've no patience with the lot of you – what do you think to it all, John?"

John looked passively at his empty plate then towards the stove. "Did you mention rhubarb and custard, lass?"

Another snort was delivered before Annie waved to all and sundry.

"Pass your plates because I might as well talk to a brick wall, so give me a hand Susan, love."

Susan smiled as she rose to help clear the plates. "Nobody gets hurt at these village dos and our Jack can look after himself, you know that."

"That's as maybe but I still don't like it." Annie too rose from the table and the rhubarb and custard was duly served and passed round.

"Hope it's sweet enough; have to be careful with the sugar," she remarked.

Jack picked up his spoon but before sampling his dessert he tapped the side of his plate. "Ma, if it's really going to bother you I'll withdraw mi name, do you want me to?"

With a sigh Annie looked down at her plate. "Oh I don't know what I want ... I never bothered when you boxed for the army; perhaps it's with just getting home from Dunkirk ... I don't know."

She lifted her head and jabbed her spoon aggressively

in Jack's direction. "But you'd better win or I'll give you what for, do you hear?"

Jack threw back his head and laughed out loud as did the rest of the family. "I'll see what I can do, Ma." He affirmed.

John however gave his son a discreet glance as he enjoyed his rhubarb and custard.

CHAPTER SEVEN

The First Shift of the Week

Five thirty on a Monday morning and three pairs of boots trod a well-defined path through thick gorse towards the distant pit baths. Fair weather was still dominant but the dawning sky was grey with a light mist obscuring the morning sunrise.

Stan Norbury was the last of the three figures striding along in single file and he raised his voice to call to John who was leading the trio.

"For a minute last night, John, I thought you were going to get up and do a turn; you and Annie sounded in good voice."

John glanced over his shoulder before tucking his snap tin a little more firmly under his arm.

"Nay, not me, I reckon one nightingale in t' family is enough; I enjoyed it reet enough mind and our Annie did."

Les smiled: he knew his father would have preferred his usual game of dominoes but everyone had had a good night out together. Jack had ended up with a widow virtually sitting on his lap at throwing-out time, so he reasoned his brother's failure to return home until the early hours could make for interesting conversation.

However, he also knew the likelihood of that was very doubtful, as Jack never gave much away with regards to his love life.

"What did yer reckon to Widow Twanky then, Father?" Les gave Stan a wink as he asked the question.

"She were alreet I guess, and anyway she's a free agent same as our Jack, so nowt to do wi' me or anybody else. Did tha fancy her then?" Les smiled; "No! No, I just wondered what you thought to her, that's all, Father."

John glanced up at the smoke belching from the pit chimney before he elected to respond any further. "None of my business, lad ... nor thine."

At this point, Les would normally have deemed that particular topic to be concluded but he had his date with Betty to look forward to so he was feeling a bit chuffed. As a consequence he again half turned to Stan and made a rude gesture allied to Jack and the widow, then continued. "Aye, I know that, but I thought she was a bit of alright, just what our Jack needed. I bet he gave her what for. Don't you reckon so, Stan?"

Stan pointed a finger back at Les, but grinning broadly as he did so.

"Don't thee involve me in this, I'm keeping my nose out of it."

"Best thing, Stan, instead of rattling on like yon silly sod." John nodded towards Les; "Is he like it down pit?"

Stan was quick to support Les. "No, no, I'll give him his due, when he's on t' face he gets on wi' job, only I do reckon he talks to himself quite a bit – I can sometimes hear him chuntering on."

"I'm not chuntering, you balm pot, I'm singing to myself."

John gave another backward glance. "Tha wouldn't have any breath for warbling if tha worked wi' me."

Les scoffed; he didn't feel like letting his father get the upper hand this morning so he thought fast.

"Hey, let me tell thee summat for nowt now, shall I? Your mates have begged me to go and work on your seam but I've always refused; I reckon they were looking for a younger bloke." Les made a face behind his father's back as he concocted the story; he wanted him to bite back and John duly obliged.

"I'm going to tell thee summat now, sunshine, are yer listening?" Les made another face as John continued.

"If tha can get same yardage of coal out as me and as fast as me, I'll pack the job in, but I'll tell thi what, it won't be just yet awhile."

Les stuck his thumb in the air for Stan's benefit for he had managed to get the old man going, which didn't happen very often, so he felt a perverse sense of satisfaction.

After that they fell silent as the tarmac road, leading towards the pithead baths, came into view and they climbed a fence to reach it. Les looked skywards; he was always relieved if the sun wasn't shining when they made their way to work; it made the thought of eight hours underground a little more acceptable.

Inside the baths, men who had just finished their shift

mingled with those getting ready to go down and it didn't require a great deal of sagacity to ascertain which were which, with or without the coal dust. Those who had completed their shift made more noise than those who still had to, and one group shouted to Les as they passed on their way out.

"Got the Monday morning blues, Leslie? You want to try nights for a change – we're all going fishing this afternoon."

They didn't receive a verbal reply but Les gave them an appropriate gesture, which earned a "Same to you wi' knobs on" before they passed through the exit doors.

After changing into their pit clothes, the two younger men lit the last cigarettes they would enjoy until their return to the surface eight hours later.

"Taking Betty to pictures tonight and ... I reckon I'm on to a promise later on in the week." Les couldn't contain a grin as he confided his expectations to Stan, who pursed his lips and noisily inhaled pretending great distaste.

"You randy little sod you. I bet thy arse is like a fiddlers elbow when tha's performing." He pointed a censoring finger in Les's direction. "Just don't expect me to help thi if tha comes to work knackered because I didn't get any sympathy when I came back off honeymoon, remember?"

Les blew a smoke ring and nonchalantly tried to pierce it with his cigarette as it drifted slowly upwards.

"No fear of that, Stanley my son, I'm what you might call a sexual athlete – just born to mek women happy."

He wasn't allowed to continue any further because Stan

rose to his feet to tilt the bench they had been sharing so that Les landed in a heap on the floor.

John, seated a few yards away, shook his head. "I bet you're not as lively when you've finished yer shift."

After picking himself up, Les pretended to throw a punch at his mate. "It's Stan here, Father, I think he's a bit jealous if truth's known."

"Oh aye, I can't for the life of me think what of." John rose slowly to his feet and prepared to make his way outside.

Both younger men took one last draw on their cigarettes before dropping the butts on to the concrete to crush them underfoot.

"May as well get a move on," Stan suggested, so both men slung dudleys over their shoulders, tucked snap tins under their arms and followed the tall figure through the doors. Once outside, they headed towards the pithead with its two giant wheels that were part of the hoisting gear.

Les glanced at the sky. 'Don't shine just yet, sun, not till I've gone down.'

However, eight hours later it was doing just that; the grey sky had cleared to be replaced by an expanse of blue that was almost cloudless. Stan blinked as he, Les and a group of other miners stepped on to the gantry then out into the sunshine.

"Well that's first 'un over, roll on Friday." Stan spat out a piece of chewing gum while Les did likewise. Most of the older miners chewed twist tobacco but the boys found the taste too strong; they preferred to chew gum to alleviate the taste of breathing in coal dust while working underground.

"Aye, that's first one under our belts, just four more to go, Stanley."

They were both as black as the ace of spades except for a band of white on their foreheads where helmets had covered that area.

Stan gave his mate a dig in the ribs. "Hey, why do you allus give me black looks when we've been down pit? Is it summat I've said?"

The joke had been repeated time and time again over the months they had worked together, but it always made Les smile.

After the usual banter, Les looked back to the pithead then towards the baths.

"I wouldn't be surprised if the owd man isn't already showered and changed; I hope I'm like it at his age. But hey, I had him going this morning though, did you notice?"

Stan chuckled; "I don't think I'd push mi luck too much if I were thee; one of these days you might just catch him in a bad mood."

"Get away, Father's alreet, him and me are just like that." Les crossed two fingers on his free hand to indicate a close unity between his father and himself, but he grimaced as he did so and to elucidate he displayed the crossed fingers again and pointed to the bottom one. "I think that's me."

Stan nodded vigorously in agreement.

On entering the baths, they made straight for their

lockers and had just started to discard their work clothes when John returned from the showers. He was holding a towel around his waist and made a point of flicking water at the pair as he passed.

"Come on, you two, I've been up top at least ten minutes."

Muscles rippled as John reached for the key round his neck in order to open his locker. Both Stan and Les were not exactly puny, but compared to John they, shall we say, appeared small in stature.

"Shan't be two minutes, Father, see you outside if you like."

Les was divested of all clothing, with Stan nearly so and when he too was completely naked they set of at a sprint for the showers, their white bottoms contrasting starkly with the remainder of their grimed torsos.

John gazed after the pair, turned to a couple of work mates and shook his head.

"Bloody young 'uns these days, meks you wonder," he grumbled. But one of his mates paused from getting dressed to wag a finger in John's direction.

"Now then, John, tha was just as bad at that age, in fact I dare say tha was a damn sight worse. Who was it got stripped starkers as we were walking home in that thunderstorm, before we had pithead baths, eh? It were dark, I know, but I bet your Annie got a shock when you walked through door wi' just thi clogs on."

John fingered the whiskers on his chin. "Ah, that was a

long time ago, before kids came along, in fact I reckon our Jack were upshot of that night. Me and Annie ended up in tin bath together because most of the muck had washed off in t' rain so we said it were a shame to waste watter."

The two workmates laughed as John gave a wry smile, finished getting dressed, picked up his snap tin then went outside to wait for his son and Stan.

He didn't have to wait long and soon they were retracing their steps of just nine hours earlier, only now the sun was shining and the course was for home.

CHAPTER EIGHT

To the Pictures with Betty

"Been waiting long, pet?" Betty's eyes were bright as she took hold of Les's hand.

"About five minutes, but you look worth waiting for." Les straightened up from leaning against the stone facade of a chemist's shop and squeezed the hand now in his.

"Oh flattery," purred Betty, "I like it, more please."

Les gave a half smile. "Play yer cards right, and you never know."

"Don't I get a kiss first?" Betty closed her eyes, face upturned.

"No! I read in t' paper today that kissing can shorten your life and I want to live till I'm ninety."

Betty poked him in the ribs. "Yes, but think of what you'd miss and besides, you didn't say that yesterday, remember?"

Les assumed an air of innocence; "Can't remember but it might come back to me when we get on the back row, come on."

They crossed over the main road and in less than ten minutes they were standing at the bottom of half a dozen marble-effect steps leading up to two adjacent ticket booths.

"Just a mo, Les, I want to see what's on later in the week."

Betty led the way to one of three glass-fronted cabinets displaying photographs of forthcoming films.

"Hey look, it's a horror, I like them. 'The Mummy's Hand': Thursday, Friday and Saturday – fancy seeing it?"

Les shrugged, undecided. "What's on next week?"

They walked to one of the other display cases and studied the stills. One photograph showed Bette Davis looking up into the face of Paul Hendri and in another, Paul was lighting two cigarettes with Bette reaching to take one of them.

"Oh that should be good, I like Bette Davis. I wish I was like her." Betty gazed longingly at the photographs so Les stepped behind her and slipped an arm around her waist.

"She's got nowt you haven't got," he whispered.

"I know, but just look at that face, isn't she beautiful?"

Les nibbled the lobe of Betty's ear, "Aye, not bad, but as for that cigarette trick I can do that, light two at the same time. I'll do it when we get inside if you like."

Betty smiled, "you daft ha'p'orth, I don't smoke."

Les led the way up the steps and made for a ticket booth depicting ticket prices of one and ninepence or two and thrupence.

The other booth had sixpence, ninepence and one shilling signs over the grille but those seats were for the days when he was a bit short. He peered through the aperture. "I bet all the double seats on the back row are full up, eh?"

There was a chuckle from the other side and a middle-aged woman looked at Les over her glasses.

"I should think so, we opened at six and you young

chaps always make a beeline for them double seats when you bring your girlfriends."

Les winked, "Well you've got to be comfy when you come to pictures with a young lady, but if you reckon all the doubles will be taken I might as well have two in the one and nines please."

Les placed two half crowns on the stainless steel top and received his tickets, together with a shilling and a sixpenny piece change.

"Can I have my money back if it's no good?" he called over his shoulder, before joining Betty in the foyer.

"You can try if you want, but it won't make any difference; we don't give refunds, only when the projector breaks down."

The reply prompted Betty to take Les's arm and they passed through thick curtains and into a make-believe world of a darkened cinema. A disembodied hand checked their tickets by the light of a torch, before pointing the way to vacant seats.

On the screen the bad guys were exchanging gunshots with the good guys as the G-men attempted to prove that 'crime did not pay'. Gunfire was echoing round the auditorium as they lowered their seats and Betty gasped as one of the figures on the white screen crumpled to the floor in a pool of blood.

"It's alright," whispered Les, "he won't die cos he's one of the stars; I don't fancy the other bloke's chances though."

They settled themselves in their seats so Les lost no time in slipping an arm around Betty's shoulder.

"There you are look, he's gritted his teeth and stemmed the flow of blood, now he's firing his gun with the other hand – what did I tell you?"

Betty giggled, held the hand that was round her shoulder then nestled down to enjoy the film.

It was still light when they emerged from the cinema but thunder was rumbling in the distance and rain threatened. Les looked at the sky as they descended the steps.

"I suppose the main picture was a good laugh – did you enjoy it, Bett?"

Betty nodded; "It was alright, yeah, I enjoyed it. I prefer a nice love story but yes, it was okay thanks, Les." She slipped her arm around his waist.

"Hey come on or we're going to get caught."

Their hurried steps soon brought them to the corner of New Street and as a few heavy drops of rain began to fall, they made their way to a shop doorway for shelter.

"I hope the good weather isn't going to break up," remarked Betty, "because I've been thinking, perhaps we could go for a picnic. You know, later in the week when I get home from work say on Wednesday; I could make some sandwiches and maybe get some biscuits – what do you think?"

They were standing with their arms around each other and Les had dropped his hands until they were resting lightly on Betty's bottom. He was tempted to grasp her cheeks but he resisted.

"Yes, if you get home at about half four I could meet you after dinner, sounds fine does that."

Betty pressed her body a bit closer.

"We could go to the Grips; I could meet you at the end of your avenue, say half past five then it would be just you and me, like old times?"

Les swallowed and gave a little cough.

"Half past five? Yeah, half past five would be great, end of our street at half past."

Betty closed her eyes; "Give me a kiss, Les."

He brushed her lips but pulled back to look up and down the street; what few people were about were hurrying to try and avoid the impending storm.

Betty raised herself to her full height. "I mean a proper one, I'm not bothered about people seeing us."

Les raised one hand until it rested in the small of her back; his other remained on her bottom, as he gave her a long ardent kiss.

"That's better," whispered Betty, "that'll have to last till Wednesday, can you wait that long?"

Les pulled her even closer. "I suppose so if I have to, but what if it's raining?"

Betty raised her shoulders. "Let's wait and see, eh?"

Another look at the advancing black clouds brought the embrace to an end. "Come on, better get going; do you want me to walk you home?"

Betty shook her head. "No pet, if we both hurry we might make it without getting too wet; see you Wednesday."

Les released her and stood while she ran across the road to pause momentarily, wave, before running on again. Returning the gesture he too set off at a brisk pace for home, just managing to get indoors before the heavens opened.

"Jack not in?" he asked, as he stepped into the living room.

Susan was struggling to put her hair in curlers so it was Annie who answered.

"No, I reckon he's seeing that widow what's-her-name but your dad says it's none of our business."

"Aye, he told me that. Where's Billy then, in bed?"

"Not yet, he's doing his homework. He will stop out playing and then he has to do it at last minute. If you go upstairs, just make sure he is, because I don't want him getting into bed without having a wash. Do you want something to eat?"

Les smiled; "I'll have a look at him in a bit but I'm not hungry. A cup of tea though ..."

Annie looked pleased; "Oh grand, mash a full pot, your dad will be in any minute and me and Susan can enjoy one, can't we luv?"

Susan paused from her task to nod then give a sigh. "Why weren't I born with naturally curly hair, Mam? You and Dad slipped up."

Annie sniffed; "If you had curly hair you'd want it to be straight – I suppose the colour's wrong an' all, is it?"

There was another sigh from Susan. "Colour's alright, it's all this rolling up I get tired of."

Les was in the kitchen filling the kettle so he called out as he ran the tap. "It could be worse, Sue, you could be bald – ever thought of that?"

Susan sniffed; "No Les, I hadn't thought of that but thanks for telling me." There was a hint of sarcasm to heighten her retort but Les disregarded it and returned to the living room to position the kettle on the fire.

"Tell you what, Susan, just let me get teapot ready then I'll finish rolling your hair for you – how's that for brotherly love?"

Susan laughed; "Can you hear him, Mam? What do you think?"

"I'm saying nowt, it's your hair."

Les spooned tea into the teapot before going to stand behind Susan, flexing his fingers. "How does madam prefer her rolls? Soft? Tight? Medium? Would madam care for a little moistness? I can spit on my fingers if you like."

Susan tilted her head in order to look at her brother.

"You've been out with Betty, haven't you? I can tell." She gave a soft laugh before continuing. "Er, not too tight, do 'em like the ones I've already rolled up please."

Les confirmed he had been to the pictures with Betty, as he set about his task as a hairdresser. After a few attempts, he achieved a reasonable result so Annie offered to mash the tea, and when her son's endeavours as a coiffeur were completed she had to nod approval.

Susan noted this so she inspected the achievement in the mirror.

"Hey, thanks, Les, you've made a right good job."

Les held up his hands to again flex his fingers. "I know I just can't help it. Singer, dancer, snooker player, now hair stylist, I'm just a walking phenomenon."

The two women laughed loudly enough to provoke a call from upstairs.

"What you all laughing at?" Billy, not wanting to miss out on anything interesting was being inquisitive.

Annie opened the stairs door slightly before calling back.

"It's alright, it's just your big soft brother, Lord help us if you get like him. You finished your homework yet?"

"Nearly done."

"Well be quick, it's time you were in bed and don't forget to come down for a wash. Your school socks are here, I've had to darn 'em again."

"Okay, shan't be long."

Annie poured the tea then looked at the clock. "I bet your dad is waiting for the rain to ease – he's not usually late."

Les walked to the window and grimaced. "It was starting to come down like stair rods when I came in and it's still throwing it down."

He sank into an armchair, letting his mind wander as he took a sip from his mug. 'Let's see, Tuesday tomorrow, if Jack isn't busy with the merry widow we could have the afternoon at Langold Lakes, weather permitting.'

Jack was a good swimmer and he liked to show off his diving skills. His speciality was to perform a handstand on the edge of the diving board then launch himself into the water like a dart. Les, on the other hand, was quite happy to dive in at ground level, which, at Langold Lakes was off the wooden jetty that protruded out over the lake's deep point.

'So if the good weather does return, a day at the lakes would be very nice and that would mean the following day would be Wednesday.' Les sucked in his breath as he contemplated the forthcoming picnic with Betty. 'Don't rain on Wednesday, even if you rain tomorrow, please don't rain on Wednesday.' All further reverie was interrupted as Billy came clattering down the stairs.

"Can I have a slice of bread and jam please, Mam? I'm starving."

Annie gave him her usual wary look for she was used to his regular ploy.

"I want you in bed in ten minutes so one slice. Get me the things out of the pantry and I'll cut the bread, otherwise it will be an inch thick. After that it's a wash then upstairs – you're late as it is."

"Ta Mam, hey up, Les, been on the back row wi' Betty then?"

He disappeared through the passage to collect bread and jam from the pantry.

"There's just enough left of this loaf to mek a sandwich, will that be alright, Mam?"

Annie knew Billy was testing so she employed her special tone.

"Bring the things out here and put them on the table; I said one slice – I meant one slice."

There was a low whistle from Billy as he reappeared with a pot of jam, some margarine and the remains of a loaf of bread.

"You crafty monkey, there's enough bread there to cut into four slices, never mind just a sandwich."

Billy winked at his brother but Les pretended not to notice, otherwise Annie's special tone could be launched in his direction if it was thought he was condoning Billy's artfulness, so he made a point of studying his mug of tea.

Annie cut a slice off the loaf, before spreading the margarine and finally the jam.

"Now then, you were on about a sandwich, do you still want one?"

Billy's eyes lit up at the thought of getting two slices after all.

"Yes please."

Annie picked up the bread knife, deftly cut the one slice in half and folded the two portions together.

"There you are, one sandwich."

Billy smiled weakly as Susan stifled a titter and Les chortled at the disconsolate look on his face.

"Thanks a lot, Mam." There was just a hint of sarcasm in his voice.

Annie savoured her tea and gave him the benefit of a sagacious look.

"I want you to get that down, go into the kitchen for a wash and I don't mean a cat lick, then straight upstairs."

"Yes, Mam."

CHAPTER NINE

Let's Go to the Lakes

After Monday's thunderstorm the Tuesday turned out to be quite a bright day, albeit with more cloud than of late. So when Les and Stan stepped out of the pit cage and into the afternoon sunshine, Les was eagerly contemplating the forthcoming trip to Langold.

"Hey does tha fancy a few hours at Langold Lakes this afternoon, Stan? Me and our Jack are going."

Stan lengthened his stride to fall into step as they made their way to the baths before carefully considering the proposal.

"It's alreet for you two buggers, you're fancy free but I've got t' owd lass to contend with. Mind you, as it happens I wouldn't mind, cos it's a while since I've been and I must admit I did enjoy going.

There was a pause as he gave the matter some more thought.

"Aye, why not, though I expect I shall be in t' dog house for a couple of days if I do, but what the hell; what time are you thinking of going?"

"Straight after dinner; it'll mean catching a bus to get there, but with a bit of luck we could get a lift back. Some of

Lerigow's men are doing some building work t' other side of Langold and their van comes back about six. If we stand at the end of that lane that runs down to lakes we might get a ride back; you game then?"

"Aye, but if our lass starts playing up I shall send her next door, then it will be up to you to pacify her."

Les gave a wicked grin. "Hey if I pacify her, she'll never be content wi' thee again."

Stan swung his dudley in Les's direction but with no real intention of making contact.

"Here, when is it you're seeing this Betty what's-her-name?"

White teeth contrasted starkly against a black face as Les grinned and positioned his helmet at a jaunty angle.

"It's tomorrow, all being well in just over twenty-four hours I shall be having mi wicked way." A dirty laugh accompanied this optimistic prediction, followed by a few nifty dance steps so Stan immediately affected huge disapproval.

"You horny little sod, there should be a law against single blokes like you getting their end away, it'd serve you right if yer winkle dropped off."

Les gave Stan a convivial nudge with his elbow.

"Now then, Stanley, you know you don't mean that, and besides it all depends on the weather." With head tilted back to gaze at the heavens he placed his hands together as if in prayer.

"I don't mind a bit of damp grass but please don't rain, not tomorrow afternoon."

The supplication was just audible enough for Stan to repent so he gave Les a friendly slap on the back.

"I've got a groundsheet you can borrow." He then pointed to the baths. "What's the betting your father is already showered and getting dressed?"

"Oh I'm not going to give odds on him not being, we don't often get to be in the baths first, and hey up there he is – look."

Sure enough, as they made their way between the rows of lockers they could see John drying his feet prior to putting on long woollen socks.

"Alreet, Father?"

John replied without looking up, "Aye, don't tek all day."

The pair exchanged humorous glances as the predictable interchange was conducted, for it hardly ever varied.

"I'll say one thing for yer father, you know where you are wi' him."

"Aye, he don't alter provided you keep right side of him, but if you don't, well you can watch out. When me and our Jack were kids he took his belt off to us once or twice and he made our arses red hot. I dare say we deserved it but I'm sure that belt should belong on a cart horse, what do you reckon?"

"Oh it's a good 'un alright – made you whistle did it?"

"Whistle? It made me bloody yodel, never mind whistle."

Les pulled a face at the recollection of those few occasions and he gave his buttocks a sympathetic rub.

Just over an hour later, Stan, Les and Jack were outside their respective back doors preparing to set off for Langold. Jack had his towel and trunks under his arm patiently waiting, while Les listed the items he wanted to take with him.

"Let's see, cigarettes, matches, bathing trunks, a towel, half a crown and a clean hanky. Right, I'm ready."

Stan was smoking a cigarette so he placed it in the corner of his mouth as he unrolled his towel.

"Just a mo, chaps, what do you think to these?"

He held up a pair of bright red bathing trunks.

"Ma knitted these for me years ago and I've never worn 'em, but a bit of alright, eh? Got a white belt with 'em, look."

Jack looked a bit dubious. "You've never worn 'em in the water then?"

"No, why, what's wrong wi' 'em?"

"Nowt, they look very smart; that white belt should set 'em off a treat."

"Cheerio, we're off, should be back about seven, all being well."

There was a muffled reply from Annie when they had shouted their adieus.

Langold wasn't a great distance away but they had to go by bus via Worksop.

"Let's hope we can cadge a lift back, eh, lads?"

Stan's comment was repeated when they finally alighted at their destination and headed for the popular picnic area. "Lerigow's van will be a lot quicker than any bus, providing we are lucky enough to see it when it's on its way home."

Access to the lakes was eventually reached via a turnstile, and in the distance they could be seen shimmering in the sunlight. Progress was through a small wood and it wasn't long before the sound of laughter and splashing water became audible, so any tranquillity created by the trees was suddenly transformed as boisterous activity in two pools came into earshot and sight. Both pools were almost full of yelling children revelling in the twin delights of warm sunshine and water. One of the pools had toddlers splashing and pretending to swim in it, while a larger and deeper pool resounded to the gleeful din of bigger, older youngsters, diving and jumping into the water sending spouts of blue-green spray high into the air. Jack indicated in the direction of the larger pool.

"Fancy turning the clock back and jumping in wi' them, Les? The little buggers are having the time of their lives."

"I wouldn't mind but some of them young sods look a bit too rough for my liking; I reckon I'll be safer in t' lake."

On hearing Les's remark, Stan pointed to the larger of the two lakes and gave a low whistle.

"I don't know about being safer but it could be a lot more interesting – just look at them two."

Jack and Les followed the direction of Stan's outstretched arm pointing to a couple of young women poised on the edge of a jetty, about to dive into the water. Both girls were wearing white costumes, emphasizing their tans to perfection and they had the kind of figures such costumes were designed for.

Jack's 'tut-tut' was uttered to remonstrate with his next-door neighbour.

"Now then, Stanley, tha's not supposed to notice things like that, being a married bloke an' all. No wonder your Vera weren't very keen on thi coming – I can see why."

"Sod our Vera, she's not here to see what I get up to; just you wait till I get mi trunks on."

The three made their way to an expanse of grass that served as a picnic area but also somewhere to change into bathing suits. Shoes and socks were discarded, belts and buttons undone, then with a towel round their waists they dropped their trousers, stepped out of them, pulled on bathing trunks and hey presto, the job was done.

Jack and Les had black trunks, but Stan, of course, had his bright red ones with the contrasting white belt, and he was convinced he looked the cat's whiskers. Dropping his towel, he paraded for a few minutes to savour his colleagues' approval. Whistles were interspersed with remarks like: "Spitting image of Tarzan" and "I'm not joking it could be Mr Universe, in person".

Stan puffed out his chest even though he knew the comments were mordant. "Watch this," he called, then ran along the pier to where the two girls, now in the water, were about seven or eight feet away from its edge. As he drew level he launched himself into the air, grasped his knees and entered the lake with an enormous splash to engulf the two girls. Stan surfaced to a tirade of abuse from both females before they made their way back to the pier and climbed out.

"If you do that again, we'll jump on you," they protested, which was just the reaction Stan was hoping for so he too swam to the pier and climbed out. Squeezing water from his hair he straightened up to grin like a Cheshire cat but he froze as the girls shrieked and two hands pointed in his direction. He looked down to ascertain the cause for the commotion and the reason was plain enough. In their dry state his bathing trunks were all they were meant to be – practical, functional, smart even – but after their immersion in the lake their function to cover naughty bits was virtually non-existent. Stan quickly swung both hands in front of his body to conceal his conspicuous appendage and leapt back into the lake with peals of laughter ringing in his ears until his head disappeared below the surface.

By this time, Les and Jack were halfway along the jetty just as the two girls ran past, still giggling, and one called out as they reached the bank. "You want to be careful if you go into the lake because I think your mate's caught an eel in his swim trunks … or else it's a big worm."

There was more laughter as the two nymphs ran across the grass.

The brothers exchanged amused glances before their steps brought them alongside Stan's bobbing head whereupon Les addressed his workmate.

"Now then, Stanley, what have you bin up to wi' them

two young lasses? Don't tell me you've lost yer trunks and you pretended to be a nudist? Whatever it was it made 'em scarper pretty quick."

Stan swam to the pier, a sheepish look on his upturned face.

"No!" he protested, "I didn't lose mi trunks, it's just that when I climbed out of the water you could see my what's-it and everything. You'll have to fetch me a towel before we go to get changed."

Les gave Jack a wink then shook his head as if in doubt.

"Oh I don't know about that, Stan, a few minutes ago you were bragging about them new trunks of yours; I shall have to think about it."

With that he stood beaming, determined to make full use of the opportunity to pull Stan's leg as his mate gave him a plaintive look. "Come on Les, I can't walk back wi' all them folk about – I'd do it for you."

Les remained silent, arms folded.

Stan gritted his teeth as he realized he was getting a real ribbing, so he did the only thing he could. He made a grab for Les's ankle and jerked hard, with the result that Les joined him in the lake amid an almighty splash.

Jack shook himself as water cascaded everywhere so he ran to the end of the pier and performed a racing dive and this propelled him almost halfway towards a three stage diving platform. It was located in the deepest part of the lake and when he surfaced he struck out in an effortless crawl towards a ladder fixed to the rear of the platform.

Climbing up to gain access to the first board he walked to its end to ensure there were no swimmers below and after this precaution he retraced his steps. A few deep breaths followed before running forward to bounce once before launching into an arc, high enough to allow him to straighten his body and enter the water with hardly a ripple. After surfacing, he swam back to the platform, only this time he climbed up to the second stage from where he executed a jackknife that had spectators sitting up and taking notice. There were a few handclaps as Jack surfaced so he raised an arm in acknowledgement before floating on his back to gaze up at the topmost board. He had to shield his eyes in order to see the protrusion silhouetted against the blue sky but for Jack this was not just any springboard. This one represented a challenge, an intimidating hazard that had all the enticement of an artful siren. Many times in the past he had contemplated diving from that height but had never plucked up enough courage, yet now for some reason it was important that he did so. Why? Why so suddenly irresistible? He shook his head as the aspiration became almost compelling and thought back over the last few days: 'It'd begun with that soldier in the Red Lion. I could've ignored the silly sod but no, I had to retaliate and punch the poor bastard, even enjoy putting him on his back. Then outside the pub, I just had to go and jump those bloody upping stocks because they were standing there daring me to try, even though I knew failure could cost broken bones, but what the hell did that matter? Then to top it all came the icing on the cake, the lovely Valerie. Well done, Jack, round off the night by having it off with another man's wife – it's just what you need. But it shouldn't've happened; I'd already walked away, lifted the catch on the back door, all I needed to do was open it and step outside, but oh no, I had to go and prove something. Now that bloody thing up there is challenging me, looking down and scoffing, "Still scared are you? Still a little boy then?"' Jack gritted his teeth in exasperation for he had dived off the top board in the swimming baths, so what was so special about this particular one? He again gazed skywards and felt his stomach tighten – it was over twice as high, that's what.

In the distance the sound of children enjoying themselves drifted over the lake and Jack envied the carefree simplicity of their lives, but he knew those days for him were over, and he swam towards the ladder.

For the third time that afternoon he climbed onto the staging and again shook water from his body before ascending to the next platform. He climbed slowly, trying to clear the thoughts in his head. 'If I wanted I could dive off the second stage again, nobody would be any the wiser, nobody but myself that is.'

Like a sleepwalker he grasped the handrails and climbed. Ten, eleven, twelve, just two more steps, thirteen, fourteen and there it was, over twenty feet of springboard, stretching out over the shimmering lake. Jack could feel the sun on his shoulders but there was no pleasure in its warmth. For five minutes he stood against the rails, breathing hard before looking down. 'Christ, it is high, why am I doing this? I must have a screw loose. I don't have to be up here, I can turn round, go back down the ladders and just swim over to the pier.' He looked towards the grassy area where people were shading their eyes and pointing to the lone figure on the top platform. Down below, swimmers were treading water as they too gazed upwards and two of these were Stan and Les.

"To my knowledge he's never gone off that top board but I'll bet you any money he will today; he hasn't climbed up there for nowt."

Stan's reply was apprehensive; "Rather him than me. I don't think I could tackle that first level, never mind that top bugger up yonder."

"Our Jack will, thee watch him."

High above the lake Jack turned to face the springboard, his jaw tightening as he took the first of eight paces that would place him a foot from the end. Once there he felt better, he had reached a point where he needed to concentrate his mind and he knew exactly what he had to do. One more step and he was standing on the end of the board with his toes curled over its edge. His movements had caused it to oscillate but he counteracted this by flexing his leg muscles until the vibrations ceased and the board remained quite still. 'Surely they can hear the beating of my heart all around the lake.' A deep breath filled his lungs as he stood, poised, perfectly still, arms outstretched until a slight bending of the knees gave him the impetus needed to tilt forward and the dive was in progress. There was no fear now, just complete concentration as the water rushed ever nearer while he brought his hands together to ensure a clean entry into the lake.

During the descent everything became enhanced, his senses heightened, his awareness intensified. The blue of the water and the cloudless sky were vivid colours, while the sun's shimmer on the surface of the lake made it appear as if sparkling diamonds had been scattered over its surface. Even the exclamation of 'Ooh' from the onlookers was carried with crystal clarity to his ears, but in a split second it was all over. As Jack's hands incised an entry into the water he experienced an overwhelming feeling of satisfaction and achievement. Blue turned to indigo as he plunged deep enough to start encountering weeds growing on the bottom before arching his body to take him heading for the sunlight above. Strong kicks gave him the necessary impetus to break the surface with enough force so that the top half of his torso rose clear of the water to be greeted by hand claps, whistles and shouts from the onlookers as they acknowledged his skill and daring.

Jack clasped his hands above his head and grinned like a happy schoolboy – he felt good. After a final look upwards, he struck out to where Les and Stan were now sitting on the pier, clapping. When he drew near, Les jumped back into the water to slap his brother on the back.

"Nice one, Jack, I told Stan tha would dive off top 'un today."

Jack trod water, laughing as he lied through his teeth.

"Aye, it were a piece of cake; I only wish it had been twice as high!"

With another chortle he disappeared underwater to put his head between Les's legs then kick upwards so that they both rose clear, only to fall back with a splash.

Stan sat enjoying the spectacle but Jack swam towards him and held out his hand.

"Give us a pull up, Stan," he requested, but as Stan tried to oblige he too ended up in the lake.

When they had recovered, Les pointed towards the diving stage.

"Hey, let's swim out to the platform and do a spot of sunbathing; there are one or two lasses on there now."

"I can't," protested Stan, "what about mi trunks?"

"Oh aye, I forgot, you frighten women away you do, displaying that bobby's helmet of thine. Tell you what, when you get there, climb out of the water backwards then go and lie on your stomach, me and our Jack can chat up the girls while you'll have to pretend to be asleep."

Stan sighed, "You wouldn't like to go and fetch me a towel would you?"

"Not likely, we're going over to the platform, so come on, Mr Allcock, I'll race you there."

The remainder of the afternoon was total enjoyment and to cap it all, they managed to obtain a lift back to Bennington in time for a late tea.

CHAPTER TEN

Betty's Plan Works

"Hey, today's the day in't it? Lusty little Leslie going to get his end away and I reckon you already had a bit of a semi on when you were in t' shower, you horny sod."

Les was having the nape of his neck clasped while Stan made the indiscreet enquiry.

"Ger off, tha knows very well I've got a date wi' Betty so don't go on about it. I've been thinking about nowt else all morning."

He signalled in his father's direction to indicate caution while they made ready for the short walk home. Their third shift of the week now over, they were showered and changed so he called to John.

"Right you are, Father, we're ready when you are."

There was a non-committal grunt and a "Let's go and get some dinner then."

As usual the two younger men brought up the rear so were able to chat.

"By the way, was your Vera in a good mood when you got back from Langold?"

"Oh aye, she was alright, we had a good laugh when I told her about mi trunks. They're in t' dustbin now but I reckon your Jack had an idea what would happen to 'em when they got wet. It was still a good afternoon though and hey, that were some dive off top board weren't it? If somebody offered me a hundred quid I could never do it."

"No, me neither, no wonder our Jack were chuffed, but he didn't go on about it, did he?"

John had heard the conversation from his customary three paces ahead.

"Our Jack dived in off top board then? It's a fair height is that and he never said a thing about it last night."

Les raised his voice to answer. "Aye, it were a cracking dive, but funny thing was, it didn't seem to be important to him after he'd gone and done it. It was as if he'd tested himself and passed, you know, as if to prove something."

John nodded knowingly as he strode forward; "Aye, that's Jack alreet."

The remainder of the walk home was in comparative silence and it wasn't long before the thumping of their boots was heard on the concrete of their shared yard. John and Les turned right to go indoors while Stan wheeled left, but couldn't resist giving Les the benefit of a rude gesture.

"Hey, if tha can't be good, be careful," he added.

Les hung his coat in the passage before popping his head into the living room.

"Don't mind if I have a quick wash and a shave before dinner, do you, Ma, just to save a bit of time?"

Annie had just poured boiling water into the teapot,

for with Billy at school it meant she had no early warning of when John and Les were on their way across the Grips.

"Oh a rush job is it, that there Betty Fletcher, then?" Annie knew it was but she asked just the same. "I hope she's worth getting indigestion for; what time you seeing her?"

Les turned his shirt collar down in preparation for having a shave as he waited for the tea to mash.

"Oh I don't have to rush, it's just that I thought I could save a bit of time if I have a shave now, have mi dinner, then get my head down for a couple of hours. When I get up I can get ready more or less straight away."

"Going anywhere nice?"

"Er, haven't decided yet."

Just why he lied he didn't know but he felt a bit irritated at the disapproval towards his friendship with Betty: he wasn't a kid any longer.

"We might go for a picnic; does it matter?"

His tone was sharp and he cut short any further comment when he caught his father's eye.

"Alright, no need for that," said John.

Les took a mug of tea from his mother.

"Thanks, Ma, I didn't mean owt."

Annie gave Les a steady look as she took a sip from her own cup.

"I weren't being nosey, just concerned, like I would be if it were our Susan or Jack." She nodded towards the kitchen. "Go on, go and have a shave; it won't tek you long will it?"

The question was added to indicate that the former topic was over and done with, for the time being at least.

"Shan't be more than five minutes, just need a drop of hot water then you can start putting the dinner out. I shall be done and dusted by the time you want to sit down."

After the meal, Les took himself upstairs to have forty winks.

If the weather held then the picnic should be on, so he called to his mother as he made his way along the landing.

"Give me a call in a couple of hours, if I'm not already up, please."

An affirmative reached his ears so he settled down on his bed, content in the knowledge that he would get a call after the agreed length of time.

His first reaction after being awakened was to look out of the window to check the weather again. 'Good, a bit of cloud but still fine – thanks, pal.' He gave a thumbs-up sign to the heavens or to whoever was in charge of meteorological conditions for that Wednesday afternoon then began to marshal his thoughts on his date.

'Now let's see, I've had a shave, so a quick wash then I can get ready.' He rubbed his chin reflectively while chewing over what to wear. 'Not a lot of choice really, so it will have to be the fawn trousers and sports jacket, my cream shirt, mi brown shoes and a packet of you-know-what in mi wallet.' As he descended the stairs he could hear Jack's voice so he wasn't surprised to be greeted by a wisecrack or two.

"Look out, here it comes, the Casanova of Jubilee

Avenue. I bet Betty's only just got home from work and you've bin snoring yer head off you crafty varmint. By the way, when I came in it was definitely looking like rain, big black clouds over Sheffield and it's a sure sign is that."

Les gave his brother an angelic smile.

"I've already checked the weather kiddo and there's no sign of rain ... at ... all." The last two words were dragged out to add extra emphasis, just as Annie's voice floated through from the kitchen.

"If you want to put a spot of hot water in the teapot you can get yourself a drink; it hasn't been mashed too long."

Les checked and found he was in luck; there was still a good measure in the teapot so he helped himself before calling back to his mother.

"I'll just have this drink, ma, then can I get to the sink to have a wash, just a quick one?"

There was a muffled reply, which he took to be a "yes", so he sat down to enjoy his tea and glance across to the sideboard: the wireless would give him the correct time soon.

Jack followed his gaze. "What time have you arranged to meet her today?"

Les inspected his mug of tea. "In about half an hour." There was a pause before he continued. "What don't you like about Betty?"

Jack shrugged his shoulders. "Nowt, I don't know the lass but I do know the rest of her family and I think I know her type. Can I ask you something, I bet she were the first 'un you had it off with, am I right? If so, that can sometimes kind of prevent a bloke from seeing things as they really are, or from seeing people as they really are, know what I mean? I'm not saying there's owt wrong with the lass but ..." At this point, Jack raised his hand as if signalling halt, "Just don't have a one track mind; open yer eyes a bit, that's all I'm saying."

Les nodded, "I know you mean well, Jack, but I reckon she's right enough, I allus have done."

"Fair enough, so just bear in mind what I've said and don't do owt daft."

Les stripped to the waist to have his wash and twenty minutes later he was greeting Betty as she walked towards him swinging a paper carrier bag. She was wearing a light blue summer dress, white sandals and no stockings, which she knew helped to compliment the light tan of her long legs. Les waited until she drew level then took hold of her hand.

"I timed it just right, I got to the top of our road and I could see you just turning to come down Main Street; brought owt nice?"

Betty gave him a peck on the cheek before replying in a provocative tone.

"What, besides myself you mean?"

"Oh I know you're nice, I mean owt nice in the bag?"

"You'll just have to wait and see but we could do with a drink of some kind, any ideas?"

"Er yes, I can call in baker's across from the school and get a bottle of pop, two if you like."

"One will be fine, I've brought a couple of cups and an old cut-down blanket so we should have all we need."

When she mentioned the blanket, Betty made quite sure she was gazing deep into Les's eyes and he pursed his lips to give a low whistle as the intimation got through loud and clear.

"Right, no point in hanging about, let's be on our way," and the whistle was replaced by a broad smile as he entwined his fingers around the hand that Betty was using to carry the bag.

They followed the same route as on the previous Sunday, only this time when they reached the junction near the school, their path led them towards the pit instead of turning right to go past the technical college. First however, Les had to call into a small corner shop to make his purchase.

"Can I have a bottle of Tizer please, Missus?"

"Large or small, luv?"

"Oh mek it a big 'un, it's for two of us."

Les handed over the required coins and received his bottle of fizzy drink: 'Tizer, The Appetizer' as stated on the label.

"Penny back on bottle, Missus?"

"Yes, when you return the empty."

"Right oh, thanks, good day to you."

"Cheerio, luv."

Outside the shop, Betty made room for the bottle in the carrier before they continued towards the pit in the distance. On their left was the short cut the miners used to reach the baths, while on the opposite side of the road lay another area of gorse but this was hardly ever visited. It was to this spot that Les now veered in order to search for an easy access through the barbed wire.

"Hold on, Bett, we can get through there, look."

Les pointed to a section of fence that was in need of repair so they made their way over for a closer inspection. With a bit of manoeuvring it would be possible to gain entry and Les nodded in satisfaction.

"Okay, this will do, now listen. Let's put the bag down, then I'll hold the wire so you can get through. I'll then pass the bag over to you, okay? Then you hold the wire so I can get through and Bob's yer uncle."

Betty laughed and gave a mocking salute.

"Yes, sir, right you are, sir, three bags full, sir, anything else, sir?"

Les sighed. "Sarcasm, madam, is the lowest form of wit, you do know that?"

He nodded towards the barbed wire. "Just keep yer head down and yer backside down and be careful, because you'll blame me if you get snagged, I know you."

He placed his foot on the lower strands of wire and held the higher ones up in order to create a gap but as Betty wriggled through he pinched her bottom with his free hand.

"You sod, Les, you just wait."

"That's for being sarcastic," he grinned.

Betty grunted as she straightened up. "Don't forget you've got to get through as well."

"That's okay I shall be coming through head first."

Betty was busy straightening her dress but she blobbed her tongue out in retaliation and the action didn't go unnoticed. "Is that a promise or are you just being rude? Anyway, catch hold of this." Les handed over the bag, with instructions on which wires to hold up and which to hold down but only a nifty manoeuvre saved his backside from a retaliatory pinch.

"You wait, my lad, I'll get my own back." Her tone was one of feigned indignation but she didn't resist as Les slipped both arms around her waist to whisper in her ear. "I'll have a look later to see if there's a bruise."

Betty pouted. "What if there is?"

"I might let you have a drink of Tizer."

Betty gave him a thump before wheeling away to dart between the clumps of gorse, swinging the carrier bag. "But I'm the one who's got the Tizer, so what do you say now?"

Les gave her a few paces start before setting off in pursuit and it wasn't long before he was wrestling her to the ground. They gazed at each other, breathing heavily until Les kissed her on the mouth, his body pressed against hers. As their lips parted, Les eased himself up, extending a hand to assist Betty to her feet.

"Come on, let's go find a spot for just me and thee, eh?"

The tone of his voice convinced Betty her plan was going to work and she eagerly led the way as they threaded their way between shoulder high gorse until the road was lost to view. When at last they halted in a small clearing, only the pit chimney was visible to indicate there was any existence beyond the confines of their own little Arcadia.

Betty handed Les the carrier but removed the blanket to give it a good shake before spreading it neatly on the springy turf.

"There we are, Mr Foster, how about that?" she asked, somewhat proudly, sinking to her knees and beckoning for the bag to be placed beside her. Les obliged, removed his jacket and before joining Betty on the blanket, laid his coat on the grass beside them.

"What have we got then?" His eyes widened in anticipation.

Betty removed the bottle of Tizer and peered into the bag.

"Well I made some potted meat sandwiches and Mam also put something in a paper bag, so I think we might have a couple of buns and some biscuits as well and ... guess what, Uncle Sam let me pick a few strawberries out of his garden."

Les chuckled. "Bugger me, we've got a feast. Pass the cups and I'll open this pop while you see to things – I'm hungry."

Betty handed over the cups then a small white cloth appeared which she unfolded and placed on top of the blanket. On this she arranged several wrapped items and a jar with nine or ten strawberries inside.

"There we are, I've cut the sandwiches into triangles cos I think they look better, don't you?"

Les opened the largest of the bags and nodded; "Hey these look posh, are they all mine?"

"No they're not, we've got to share but I made some extra for you."

Les smiled; "I know they're not all mine, I was only kidding." He offered the bag to Betty; "Ladies first."

Betty took one and scrutinized it; they did look quite special so she was rather satisfied with her handiwork. Les also selected one but his bite nearly consumed the whole sandwich as he was more used to the full slices that fitted neatly into his snap tin, but he didn't complain.

"Hey, a bit of alright are these, make 'em bigger and you can get my snap packed up anytime."

When they had finished the sandwiches, Les took a peek in the other bag and confirmed that Betty had guessed right. It contained two buns and half a dozen arrowroot biscuits so these were shared, then it was time to sample the strawberries.

"Oh I love these," Betty exclaimed, so Les moved the jar to her side of the cloth.

"Then you enjoy 'em; I had most of the sandwiches so you tuck in, go on."

Betty shook her head vigorously. "No, they're for both of us – I want you to have some ... please."

Les was about to refuse but he couldn't bring himself to be so unyielding.

"Tell you what, I'll have a couple, then I want you to enjoy the remainder."

Betty selected the largest strawberry in the jar and held it between her thumb and finger. "Right, now close your eyes and don't open your mouth until I tell you to."

Les did as he was requested and he could feel a hand on the nape of his neck as Betty leant forward bearing the sweet scent of fruit. But it wasn't a strawberry that brushed his lips; it was the tip of Betty's tongue as she merged her mouth to his. The kiss was warm, lingering, full of promise, and when she drew back her voice was soft.

"Now open your mouth, nice and wide."

Like a child, Les obeyed the instructions and duly received one of the succulent fruits, his eyes remaining closed as he savoured its sweetness.

"You can open 'em now; I didn't mean for you to keep them closed, but was it nice?"

Les opened one eye. "Marvellous, and the strawberry wasn't bad either."

"In that case let me give you another one?"

"If you mean kiss, then yes, but you have the rest of the strawberries and tell your Uncle ... Tom is it? Tell him they were smashing."

Betty indulged herself until the last of the delicacies had disappeared at which point she gave a satisfied sigh.

"Oh they were lovely; can I have a drink of Tizer now please?"

Les filled a cup and passed it over. "Pretend it's

champagne!" He then filled his own, leaning forward to clink the cups together.

"Here's to me and thee, Betty."

Betty sank back, resting on one elbow. "You won't have to go in the forces will you, Les?"

"No, mining's a reserved occupation and we actually need more men down the pits, so I shan't have to go in – why?"

Betty cleared away the empty bags and folded the white cloth before answering.

"Oh, it's just that our Tom had his papers come the other day and I didn't like to think of you having to go in too." She smiled demurely. "Not now that we've got back together again."

Her voice had become almost husky as she decided it was time to put her plan into action. She was kneeling on the blanket in front of Les but turned away to reach towards a clump of buttercups.

"Let's see if you like butter."

Her action was slow and deliberate as she stretched forward, causing her dress to ride high. The more she stretched, the higher it rode and the more it revealed. Les stared mesmerized.

"Betty." He spoke her name almost in disbelief. "Betty! You're not wearing any knickers, you've got nowt on under that dress!"

Betty held a buttercup between her fingers. "Are you sure? I was in such a hurry to meet you I must've forgotten them."

Les was kneeling behind her now and he helped to elevate the dress another couple of inches.

"You can't forget something like that."

Betty spaced her knees a little wider apart then arched her back until it was almost a U shape. "What about this buttercup? Do you want me to pick it?"

Les was breathing heavily as nature took control. "No! Oh sod the buttercup, I've got a what's-it in mi jacket pocket."

"You won't need that Les, I should be alright."

"You sure?"

"Yes!"

Buttons were hastily undone and as he bared himself Betty reached behind her and Les gasped at her touch, before hastily placing both hands on her hips and pressing forward. Gritting his teeth he spoke between sharp intakes of breath.

"Betty, don't you move a muscle, are you sure it's safe?"

She didn't reply, merely rotated her buttocks against Les's loins in a deliberately sensual action until he threw his head back, closing his eyes as if in pain as the erotic stimulus quickly overcame what little self-control he had left and with a gasping cry his hold on her hips tightened with the intensity of the moment.

Betty curled her fingers over the edge of the blanket and she moistened dry lips while they both remained quite still, breathing heavily. Les eventually opened his eyes as his pounding heart slowly returned to a normal rhythm and he became alive to everything around them. The stillness and the silence within that small clearing, was broken only by busy crickets and a trilling linnet serenading only those who were within earshot and able to appreciate its song. Les listened and he looked around him. He looked at the sky, observing its vastness, then down at Betty, allowing his eyes to trace the arc of her body and the buttercups at her fingertips. Her eyes were closed but as he eased back she stirred and hurriedly placed a hand behind his thigh.

"Don't leave me, Les, not yet."

Les quickly obliged; his hands almost encircled her waist as he pressed forward to restore the closeness before allowing his fingers to glide over her hips in a caress. The movement continued down her thighs almost to her knees then back again but within her loins this time, and the arc of her back increased. Les was a young man at the height of his sexual prowess so it wasn't long before his ardour was again aroused and for the second time that afternoon his pulse quickened.

Later, they lay together on the blanket with Les resting his head on his jacket while Betty lay at right angles to him, her head on his chest. The afternoon had turned to evening with the promise of a fine sunset, now dappling their hideaway with its golden glow.

"Shall we stop here, Les, and forget everything else and everybody?"

"A nice thought, Betty, but in the morning I shall be going down yon pit and you'll be catching a bus to Maltby. We've got to live in the real world, luv, but they can't tek this afternoon away from us."

Betty murmured, "No they can't," and took Les's hand to place it lightly on her breast, wishing it was his baby she was pregnant with.

CHAPTER ELEVEN

Roll On Pay Day

"Well, how was the picnic then? I noticed the weather held up for you, so let's have all the details."

Jack broached the question as the family were getting ready to sit down for tea and Les gave a little cough before answering.

"Oh alright, yeah the weather was fine, it were a nice afternoon."

The answer was non-committal but he felt the need to change the subject so he looked to Billy.

"That reminds me, Billy, I've an empty bottle tha can take back to shop across from school – tha can keep penny back on it."

"Oh, ta, Les, I'll go straight after tea; have you any to go back, Mam?"

"Not at the moment," said Annie, "but I wish you were as eager to run to the shop for me when I ask you."

Billy displayed his toothy grin while rubbing a finger and thumb together.

"Ah, but this is called enterprise, Mam, you know – dosh, spondulicks."

"Oh aye, well you can wait till I need summat from that shop, then you can take the bottle back."

Billy looked a bit crestfallen so Jack winked at his young brother.

"I might have a bottle or two you can take back after the weekend, but it depends on how I do at Anston."

Billy perked up at the sound of that; "Oh yeah, it's the boxing on Saturday, don't forget you said me and Jimmy could be your seconds." His look was enquiring; "We still can, can't we?"

Jack gave him another wink before directing his attention to John.

"Did you say you were going, Father?"

They were all seated round the table now and John paused from spreading jam on a slice of bread studying it carefully before answering.

"Oh I reckon I shall show mi face for an hour or so; it could get interesting."

Susan addressed her mother: "That leaves just you and me then, Mam. I'll be working so will you be going to see Aunt Vera?"

With a wave, Annie indicated to the men.

"This lot can do what they like but I'm not watching any boxing bouts, so I shall go to our Vera's then catch that same bus back as last week, so try and save me a seat next to you if you can."

Billy interjected before his mother had stopped speaking so he received a sharp look …

"Er sorry, Mam, I just wanted to ask our Jack something." He looked towards his brother to start again.

"What time shall we need to go, Jack? Cos I have to let Jimmy know."

Before replying, Jack tapped on the table, deep in thought.

"Well let's see, have a late breakfast, shan't bother with any dinner. A wash, but no shave, then get ready and pack a bit of kit, so let's say about one, one to quarter past."

"Right, I'll tell Jimmy quarter to, because he's usually always late."

Billy chewed happily on his crust of bread as he contemplated his forthcoming role in Saturday's event, and when the meal was over he was beckoned by Les to join him outside. They went to lean against the wall, resting their arms on its top but with Les looking over his shoulder before speaking.

"Remember what I said to you about wanting a couple of lookouts when we had a tossing ring?"

Billy indicated that he did.

"Well I said it would be on a Saturday but ... we've bin talking at work and we've decided it would be best if we had it on pay day, in the afternoon or after tea. And we reckon tomorrow is as good a time as any, so do you still want to do it? You and Jimmy for a tanner each?"

Billy was eager and his eyes widened, but then suddenly he looked doubtful.

"Yeah, great, but hold on a minute, Les, we decided on a

bob each, remember? You agreed a shilling each because I said we could climb up them owd pylons in order to get a better view, me to Laughton and Jimmy towards Todwick. Come on you remember, I can tell by yer face."

Les grinned; "Oh aye, I forgot, but like I said, not a word to anybody and mek sure Jimmy knows that, an' all." Les jabbed his finger into Billy's chest; "I'm serious, so have you got that?"

"Yes! Yes! Yes! You must have told me a hundred times." Billy placed a hand over his mouth; "My lips are sealed," he mumbled impudently. Les clipped him round the ear and pointed a finger; "I mean it."

"Okay, okay, mum's the word," protested Billy.

By the time they returned indoors, the table was cleared and everyone had vacated the living room. Annie and Susan were in the kitchen washing pots, John had gone into the front room to try and fashion a pair of kneepads out of an old leather bag and Jack had disappeared upstairs. Les went to the half-open door to call to his brother.

"Doing owt special tonight, Jack?"

There was the sound of drawers being opened and closed then Jack's voice floated down.

"I'm taking somebody to the pictures."

"Oh anybody I know? Not the merry widow again is it?"

"Might be, then again it might not. What do you want to know for anyway?"

"Just wondered if you fancied a few games of snooker … for money?"

It was the day before pay day and Les was running short of cash. He knew Jack didn't play much snooker or billiards so he crossed two fingers for luck.

"Fancy yer chances, do yer?"

Les now crossed his fingers on both hands. "I just thought you might enjoy a game or two and a little side bet would make it a bit more interesting – I know you like a challenge."

There was a chuckle from upstairs. "Go on then, I'll have you a couple of frames with you before I go and meet madam; what's the size of this side bet, then?"

Les thought for a minute, 'I could make myself the price of a couple of pints here.'

"How about a tanner a game and the loser pays for the table?"

"You're on –make it a bob a game if you like."

Les was a bit suspicious. 'What if he's been practising?'

"No, sixpence is fine, I don't want to take too much off yer. I'll treat the games as a bit of a warm up session before I play Joe Davis next week."

Upstairs, Jack shook his head and smiled. "Aye, okay, Les, next week you're playing Joe Davis, next week I'm flying to the moon."

'Next week?' he asked himself, 'who knows where the hell I'll be next week.'

CHAPTER TWELVE

The Tossing Ring

Billy leapt from the bus and raced home; it was Friday, the day he had the chance to earn a whole shilling for himself and also one for Jimmy.

"Mam, can I have a quick sandwich? Me and Jimmy are going somewhere soon."

"Oh and where are you off to then? Les has gone out and he reckons he won't be back for tea; has he said owt about meeting Betty?"

"Les don't tell me where he's going to go. Can I have a sandwich please? I can mek it myself if you like."

Billy received his customary 'oh no you don't' look, plus a nod towards the pantry.

"There's a bit of dripping left in a basin; bring that then go and get changed out of your school clothes. No doubt you'll come in looking like a sweep as usual."

Billy did as he was told and when he came down from getting changed, his bread and dripping was on a plate on the table.

"Thanks, Mam, I'll put the two slices together and eat 'em on my way to Jimmy's."

"Don't you want a drink? You must be thirsty."

But Billy was halfway to the door and thinking only of the shilling he was going to earn.

"No thanks, Mam, I'll get a drink of water at Jimmy's." Then he was gone.

'Well,' thought Annie, 'it saves on the washing up.'

Jimmy was home from school before Billy so he was ready and waiting when he heard his name being called. He went outside and Billy pointed towards the tip.

"Come on, our Les has already gone; they might think we're not going and get somebody else."

Both boys raced to the end of the avenue then on towards the huge slag heaps forming the old tip which was a veritable mountain of coal, detritus and rubble. It had been created over countless years as valuable coal, but millions of tons of waste had been extracted from the mine then carried away and dumped to form huge slag heaps. Jets of water were being sprayed on any areas emitting noxious fumes and this process was continuous. Only the positioning of the hoses changed as resulting hot-spots determined their location and the length of time they would douse that particular area.

Billy glanced towards his father's pigeon loft but he couldn't see any sign of John and they were soon out of sight of the houses. With the tip on one side and allotments on the other, Jimmy pointed ahead, gasping for breath.

"I can see your Les – look, he's with those other men."

Sure enough, in a clearing ahead, a group of miners were gathered and eight pairs of eyes turned at the sound of their running feet. The two boys headed towards the men, panting for breath, Les stepped forward.

"I said they wouldn't let us down," he declared over his shoulder and the seven fellow workers nodded in agreement. They all knew, or at least recognized the boys so the men quickly returned to discussing tactics for the forthcoming gambling session.

"Get yer breath back then I want you to get up on top and keep a sharp look out for a sign of any coppers." Les waved a hand up to the summit of the piled waste.

"You down that end, Jimmy, watching that lane that comes from road to Todwick, and thee up there, Billy, where tha can keep an eye on Breck Lane. If any of the buggers come down from Laughton it'll be in a cop car down that road because I can't see 'em going all the way round past the pit towards Todwick. Tha'll be able to recognize it, won't tha?"

Billy nodded, "Yeah I saw it when there was that fight at football match last year. It's a black 'un with big headlights."

"Good, but as I say, any sign of a blue uniform anywhere and you let us know. Can you whistle Jimmy? Our Billy can."

Jimmy placed two fingers in his mouth and gave a demonstration that had Les nodding in approval.

"Good, that's fine, we should hear that down here. Now you didn't tell anybody about this, did yer?" A suspecting finger was raised but the boys shook their heads.

"Okay, off you go then and if you do climb those old pylons, be careful. You'll get yer shilling when we've finished. You never know, if somebody comes out winning a pile they might feel generous and give you a bit extra – now off you go."

The boys scanned the steep slopes to ascertain the easiest routes to their respective vantage points but before they set off, Les addressed them again to deliver final instructions.

"Hey, one more thing: if we do get a visit from the bluebottles, get down as quick as you can without being spotted. However, if you do get caught, you were just playing on tip – you saw nothing and nobody."

A thumbs up came from the boys to indicate they understood what was expected of them, then they made their way to the foot of the towering mounds. Billy pointed to the remains of a rusting pylon protruding out of the end spoil heap. It had been the turning point for the endless steel cable that had carried huge swing buckets from the mine. These had been upturned by means of a moveable trip mechanism positioned on the cable so that their contents would be discharged to form ever-growing heaps of black spoil. Over the years those heaps had merged to form a huge tip of such proportions that a fresh route for the buckets had been necessary and the new tip itself was now well established.

"If you go up there, Jimmy, I'll climb up to that third one, and we should be able to see as far as we want in both directions without being too far from the men down there, alright?"

Jimmy agreed and started to climb the black mass; most of it was firm, but in some spots the top layer was loose shale so then it was a case of two steps up and one back down again. Billy too, started up on a zigzag course so it wasn't long before both boys were standing on the apex and gingerly making their way to their specific lookout points. Billy reached his and stood looking up at the twelve or so feet of steel above his head, red with rust. 'Good job I've got mi old togs on,' he mused, then pulled himself up hand over hand until his feet were level with a horizontal bar that he could stand on and take a breather. This gave him the opportunity to look towards Jimmy's position and he saw that he too had climbed to a horizontal steel strut and was using it as a seat while checking the road that led to Todwick. Billy knew that if he also wanted a good view he would have to climb a bit higher and that would have to be to the next level section. From there he would get a clear view all the way up Breck Lane to Laughton so he gritted his teeth and tried to think only of the shilling he would collect later. As he edged his way up a diagonal bar his perspective of the surrounding area became clearly enhanced as more and more of Bennington came into view. 'Only a few more inches then I'll have a good look round,' he promised himself, and five minutes later he was in position. First he stood on the bar, and then he lowered himself into a sitting position. 'A look up Breck Lane first, just to make sure the coast is clear, then a sweep of the panorama in general.'

"Wow you can see for miles," he murmured. Over to the right was his old school and the technical college, and over there was the main street and all the shops. In front of him he could clearly see the big houses on Breck Lane where the 'nobs' lived, and then to his left was Pit Lane, with gorse on both sides leading all the way to the mine. From this vantage point, Billy could now appreciate what a large complex the mine really was; he hadn't realized there were so many buildings. He was familiar with the baths and the main entrance, but not all those sheds and workshops. These were dwarfed by the height of the cage-winding gear and alongside were the huge sheds used to house the screens. It was here that the waste was separated from valuable coal and where the endless steel cable started its perpetual task of carrying full buckets away and returning empty ones in a never-ending process. It was in operation now, forming a new tip alongside the old one that Billy was using as a vantage point, and he could clearly see and hear the operation of the trip mechanism as it deftly upturned the huge steel buckets. He twisted his head to look towards Jimmy's position and to give him a wave but Jimmy was still peering intently in the opposite direction. Down below, Les and his mates had formed a circle with one man in the middle, and on the ground someone had placed a cap. That cap would hold any stake money being bet on the outcome of how two coins would lay on the ground after being flicked into the air by the 'tosser', the man in the centre of the ring. He would need to cover all bets in the cap by an equal amount of his own money before the toss could begin. After all bets were laid, the tosser would then balance two pennies on two fingers of one hand, one coin showing heads, the other tails, then toss them high into the air. If the coins should touch while they were in the air, the toss would be deemed null and void, and the toss would be performed again. However, if executed correctly, the winner or winners would be determined by how the coins landed on the ground. All the action would have to be in full view of all the participants and the coins would have to lie flat on the ground when they landed. One coin displaying a head and the other a tail would constitute a void result and the toss retaken. Both coins displaying tails would denote a win for the backers and conversely two heads would mean a win for the tosser and therefore his right to the contents of the flat cap. It was gambling, pure and simple, and miners had been known to get drawn into a tossing game on pay day and lose the entire contents of their wage packets before going home to their wives. Consequently it was illegal, hence the enlistment of Billy and Jimmy to act as lookouts in the event of the police receiving a tip off.

Billy could see the tosser raise his hand in the air as he flicked the coins, and then hear the cries of the men as they craned forward to inspect the pennies as they landed.

Billy eased one cheek of his backside off the steel as he swung his gaze once again towards Breck Lane. 'I wish I had a cushion,' he reflected, 'they could be down there a long time.'

Jimmy too was having the same problem and when Billy glanced back he saw his pal standing on his perch, not sitting. From below he heard a cheer as the tosser lost and his cap was swiftly emptied, a few minutes later he was to be seen walking dejectedly in the direction of Jubilee Avenue; but as he did so three more miners were hurrying towards the clearing to join the circle. Les was still there and Billy wondered how his brother was faring; he could see plenty of arm waving as some of the men remonstrated with the current tosser. They probably didn't agree with his technique for launching the coins into the air because it was thought possible to manipulate the flight of the pennies to a certain degree and so gain a favourable advantage. If it was suspected that any cheating was going on and the culprit was considered guilty, then he would, without doubt, end up in one of the stagnant pools, sporting several cuts and bruises.

Billy shook his head at their show of fervour and hoped they were as enthusiastic when it came to paying out the shillings to himself and Jimmy who, he noticed, was shielding his eyes and scanning in the direction of Todwick, but due to the angle, Billy couldn't see what his interest was because that particular aspect was hidden from him by the end of the tip. He did see Jimmy straighten up and when he realized he was being observed, he pointed in the direction of the lane.

'I wonder what he's seen,' Billy asked himself.

In fact, what had caught Jimmy's attention was a lone

cyclist pedalling down the lane towards that end of the tip. That in itself was quite significant because the lane was hardly ever used unless someone was getting to the tip to scrounge a bit of coal, and the time for doing that was generally very early in the morning as the practice was well and truly discouraged by mine managers. Also, it was the bike and what the cyclist was wearing that was giving Jimmy cause for concern. The machine was a real sit-up-and-beg model, and surely that was no ordinary cap or hat on the man's head. Jimmy checked to see if Billy was still looking in his direction and when he saw he was, he again repeatedly jabbed a finger in the dramatic way one does when urgency is all important. Billy hoisted himself up to stand on his own crosspiece and quickly focused on Breck Lane and further beyond. A few people were walking, a bus was just about to pull away from the bus stop, the van parked outside that house was probably delivering meat or groceries, so nothing untoward so far except for a couple of cyclists. They were wearing shorts and were pedalling up towards Laughton so the only other detail of any interest was a car just starting to negotiate the junction that would enable it to proceed down Breck Lane. 'Just a minute,' Billy's eyes widened. 'A black car with wide running boards and it looks like an Austin, wi' big headlights? Bugger me it is ... it blooming well is ... it's that cop car from Laughton Police Station.' Billy placed two very brown-stained fingers in his mouth and his whistle almost coincided with Jimmy's own signal. He had decided that the cyclist pedalling down the lane was wearing a blue uniform and more importantly he was wearing a helmet, a bobby's helmet.

At the sound of the whistles, all activity at the tossing ring ceased momentarily, then there was a frantic dive for the cap with all the betters seeking to retrieve their stake money before vanishing from the crime scene. Most headed for home, but one or two made for the nearby allotments and the sanctuary of the conveniently located sheds.

Billy looked towards Jimmy's pylon and saw him sliding down a steel upright so he too swung his legs free and descended his lookout a bit quicker than he had climbed it. When he was about four feet from the surface of the tip, he released his hold and landed with a crunch. There was a cascade of waste as his boots loosened the slag and he quickly extended his arms to retain his balance. He was about to start down when he heard Jimmy calling his name so he waited until his pal reached him.

"I couldn't go down that end because there's a bobby cycling down the lane and I reckon he would have spotted me," gasped Jimmy.

Billy jerked his thumb in the direction of Breck Lane.

"There's some more coming from Laughton in that black car they use; I don't know how many will be in it, but if we look sharp we might get to mi dad's pigeon loft before they get here."

They looked down in time to see Les and some of the other men nearing the end houses on the avenue so they knew they would get clear. It was just themselves that were left to make a getaway and even though there was no longer any gambling in progress they didn't want to get caught on the tip. All policemen were a source of consternation to young lads like Billy and Jimmy; they had been told they locked people up.

"Come on, we'll have to get a move on; it won't tek that car long to get to the end of our avenue."

Billy led the way, stumbling and sliding as the shale and rubble was displaced beneath their boots. About half way down they were confronted by a large formation of slag several feet high; it had slowly built up behind several lumps of discarded rock during the development of the tip and over the years it had solidified into a sizeable mass. It was behind this that the boys came to grief, because years ago that part of the tip, like many others, had ignited and smouldered away for months on end until it had exhausted its immediate supply of combustible material and the fire had been extinguished. This had been hastened by constant dousing and due to the action of the spray the surface had remained intact to coagulate into a solid looking crust, but beneath this layer a huge void had formed and when the boys landed on its hardened surface their weight proved too much and they disappeared into the depths of a black crater.

Both boys yelled out as the tip fell away beneath their feet, then all was quiet except for the sound of the rubble as it followed them into the vaulted cavity. They fell several feet and the landing knocked the wind from their bodies.

Billy was concussed as a result of striking his head on a boulder, while Jimmy suffered a sprained shoulder but was too dazed to be fully aware of it as he and Billy lay motionless. The ash from the long dead fire rose, before settling again to cover their recumbent bodies as a grey-black mantle.

Down below, the cycling policeman had reached the end of the lane and had dismounted from his machine to climb a fence and gain access to the tip. He walked towards the clearing where the tossing had taken place, while a sergeant and another constable had driven as far as the terrain would allow, then they too were making their way forward, following the base of the old slag heap.

"See anything, Sanders?" inquired the sergeant who was now in earshot of the approaching constable.

"No, Sarge, no one this end, but I thought I spotted somebody up on top of the tip as I was coming down the lane, but there's no sign of anybody now."

All three custodians of law and order scanned the face of the tip and the surrounding area but the gambling miscreants had made good their escape. All except Billy and Jimmy that is, and of them the police were totally unaware.

"Right, either it was a false alarm or they got wind we were coming and legged it. There's nowhere else they would have set up a ring, because everywhere other than here, would've been too conspicuous. You might as well collect your bike, Sanders, then get back to the station; we'll have a wander through the avenues just in case anybody noticed owt, but I doubt it – off you go."

"Right you are, Sarge."

As the entry to the void confining the two boys was on the high side of the piled waste, it meant the hole was completely obscured from the ground so no amount of scanning from below would reveal its existence, consequently the police felt confident the area was deserted.

"Was the caller a man or a woman?" asked the sergeant as he and the other constable made their way back to the car.

"It was a woman, Sarge, from a phone box but no name of course. She just said there was some gambling going on, near the old tip. Well I reckoned it had to be this side because it was handy for the houses; if it had been on the far side that would've meant them going right round the end or over the top and they wouldn't've done that."

"Aye, thar's right enough, it had to be here. The last time we made a raid we caught 'em red-handed, before you joined the force that was. We had a bit of a scuffle an' all; hard buggers some of them miners but anyway they all ended up in the cells, them that we collared that is."

"Hardly a crime though, Sarge – they're not harming anybody."

"That is not the way to look at it, son; they're breaking the law and that's good enough for us. We just do our job, got it?"

"Right you are, Sarge."

They retraced their steps back to the black Austin and drove away, while up on the tip in the 'black hole of Calcutta' all was quiet. When the tossing ring had dispersed, Les had quickly reached the rows of houses, but instead of going home, which might have meant being spotted by the police car, he cut through one of the many alleyways to get to the main street, and had then made a beeline for the billiard hall.

He had envisaged a few games of snooker or billiards then a stroll up to the Red Lion, because a quick check on the cash in his pocket revealed him to be five bob to the good, so it hadn't all been for nothing. He would have liked to have had a go at tossing the coins with the chance of winning some real money, but 'best be thankful,' he reasoned.

It was gone ten o'clock when he left the Red Lion, so dusk had started to settle and as he walked home he reflected on his and his colleagues' quick departure from the scene at the tip. Billy and Jimmy would have made good their escape and would be looking forward to their well-earned shilling. He would have to see if he couldn't get them a bit extra – they had both done a good job. However, when he turned into the avenue and started to approach home he could see something was amiss. His father was talking to Walter Keats, Jimmy's dad. His mother was with another woman who Les later recognized as Mrs Keats. Les hurried forward, his heart sinking.

"What's up? What's happened?"

Annie turned on hearing his voice. "It's our Billy and Jimmy, they're still out playing, the little sods – our Billy knows what time to come in." Annie had her arms folded across her chest, as did Nora Keats who was standing beside her, nodding her head vigorously in agreement.

"Our Jimmy an' all, the little devil, he'll feel the back of my hand when he does turn up. I'm not joking, they get worse as they get older." She finished with a toss of her head.

Les stopped in his tracks. "Oh Christ!" he exclaimed.

John looked at him; "Does tha know summat – summat we don't?"

Les hesitated, his gaze lowered to the ground. "They were on the slag heap this afternoon."

John approached to stand before Les. "Well go on then, has it owt to do wi' coppers being down here nosing about?"

Les nodded an affirmative, his eyes still downcast. "Yeah, they were looking out for us, to give us a bit of warning like."

He couldn't continue further because John cuffed him as he would a small child, but such was the force of his leathery open hand that Les was sent reeling.

"You daft bugger, where were they? Up on top, I suppose?"

His voice vibrated with anger and everyone went quiet as he stood over his son. Les was down on one knee holding a hand to his ear, a thin trickle of blood running down behind the lobe.

"They should've got down safe, Father, they would've had plenty of time – perhaps they went hiding in one of the huts?"

"Oh aye, then why aren't they back home by now then?"

John stepped back to face Annie. "You stay here, and when our Jack gets in tell him to come down to owd tip. Go and see if Stan is still up and tell him we want him; get him out of bed if you have to and tell him where to come."

Les climbed to his feet as John stabbed a finger in his direction.

"Thee go and get a flash lamp, bike lamp, owt that'll shine a light and sod the blackout, then come to tip but knock on a few doors on thi way down, me and Walter is off. Nora thee stay here wi' Annie. Right, come on Walter, let's get a move on."

They set off, John leading and Walter almost running in order to keep pace. John was muttering as he hurried along.

"I can't see 'em being in any bloody shed all this time, they would know the coppers wouldn't still be here so summat's happened to 'em."

Walter, now a step behind John, panted, "Perhaps they did hide somewhere then fell asleep – our Jimmy can sleep on a clothes line."

John glanced over his shoulder; boots that had thudded on the concrete were now crunching the cinder path alongside the tip.

"Well maybe tha's reet, Walter, but I don't think so. I reckon they could've decided to slip down t' other side out of way of them coppers and got in a spot of bother somewhere. I'll tell thi what we'll do, Walter, we'll climb to top, then give a shout from there, eh?"

"Aye, right you are, John."

Fifteen minutes later, after scrambling in the gloom of approaching night, they stood on the summit of the tip gasping for breath.

"Right, Walter, get thi breath back then go to that end and give 'em a shout; I'll go this road and do the same."

John moved off, little thinking that he was passing above the spot where Billy and Jimmy had tumbled through the crusted surface of the tip.

John cupped two huge hands to his mouth and bellowed out their names; further along, near the end, Walter did the same while down below figures were hurrying to join them. Some veered away to check the sheds and huts on the allotments, but most of them began searching the tip itself. Flashlights were being used but the very size of the tip was making the operation a hit and miss affair until Jack arrived and realized some organisation was required. John and Walter were still up on top but without lights were unable to do much except call out the boys' names then listen for a second or two in the hope of hearing a response. It was during one of these listening periods that Jack decided it was time to get the search co-ordinated properly. He called for his father and Walter to descend then had the men pass the word for them all to gather where the tossing ring had been held. When they were all assembled, Jack spoke to his father.

"We've got to tackle this job right, Father, it's a bloody great tip and the lads could be anywhere, so let's think this out. Now, there are more than a dozen of us and we've got what, eight flashlights? Okay then, so I suggest we get in a line and start at that far end where our Les reckons Jimmy was on lookout. We'll work from the bottom up to the top and if we don't find owt we'll move the line of men over this way and work our way back down again. It's going to tek time so we'll have to keep calling their names then stop to listen for any reply, what do you reckon?"

John clenched his fists; "Aye, tha's mecking sense, Jack; we'll climb up twenty yards or so, looking and shouting, then stop and have a listen." He turned to Les. "Thee work next to me, son." A huge hand dropped on to Les's shoulder but it was not in anger and Les knew as much. He gritted his teeth and wished fervently that the boys would be found safe and well.

As soon as the plan of action was formulated, they all went to the end of the tip where Jimmy had climbed the pylon and where it was still just visible as it poked its remaining few yards of steel into the night sky. Men with flashlights were positioned at the ends of the line, while others, with lamps, were interspersed throughout it. Every now and then the clambering and calling was halted in order to listen for a response, but none came.

Everyone was aware that if the lads had fallen into an old fire void, then it was possible debris might also have fallen in and buried them.

They were also aware that the same thing could easily happen to them as they searched, but at least they had the assurance of knowing help was at hand. For nearly two hours the team of men searched, moving progressively along the tip so that every square yard was covered until finally their hard work was rewarded. It was after a period of calling the boys' names and the subsequent pause to listen, that a faint cry was heard and hopes were raised.

"Over there, Father, behind that pile of waste." Les's heart skipped a beat in hopeful anticipation. He quickly led the way to the mound and disappeared behind it, his flashlight probing the surface of the tip.

"Well? Can yer see owt?" called John.

Les moved forward, a spot of light preceding his steps and just as the beam of his lamp located the hole he too vanished, letting out a yell as he did so. Luckily Jimmy and Billy were not directly beneath his descent for Les landed a couple of feet away, accompanied by the inevitable cloud of dust and cohered waste. He landed with a crunch, coughing and spluttering as beams of light probed the blackness and he heard a shout of warning. Jack had noticed the speedy disappearance of Les and his light and was alerting the others not to do the same. But this warning was now unnecessary as the entire overhang had fallen into the crater and a lot of it was covering the three occupants. Les brushed dust and slag from his face as he raised himself to reach for his lamp that was still working. One of the heaps beside him stirred then it too heaved itself to a sitting position.

"Is that you, Billy? Are you alright?" The appeal was uttered between spitting and spluttering as he tried to clear his mouth.

"It's me ... Jimmy ... mi shoulder hurts; Billy's here, but he hasn't said owt for ages."

"Oh no," groaned Les, quickly directing the beam of his retrieved lamp on to a heap that he now knew to be the recumbent form of Billy. As he brushed debris away he uncovered the hands, the jacket, finally the face of his young brother.

"Billy! Awe come on, Billy lad, tha's got to be alreet."

The cry was anguished as tears streaked his dust-covered face and he cradled Billy's head on one arm then craned his neck to peer upwards. Circles of light ringed the opening above and he had to shout to be heard above the babble of voices seeking confirmation of the boys well being.

"Father ... our Billy's not moving, we need a rope or summat to get him out, and quick."

He heard Walter's voice enquiring after Jimmy so he continued.

"He's alright, Walter," then more urgently, "can yer get summat for our Billy, Dad?"

John's voice answered out of the blackness within the circle of lights.

"Jack and Stan have already gone to fetch summat; is our Billy breathing?"

The voice was husky with concern but under control and it pulled Les together.

"I'll have a see – thee hold lamp, Jimmy."

With anxious fingers, Les again brushed dirt from the young face in his arms as Jimmy held the light. He cleared the eyes and nose, then the mouth, finally blowing any remaining dust away with puffs from his trembling lips. He bent forward, straining his ears, first with his head tilted one way, then the other and back again.

'Was that a faint sigh, a little murmur? Don't thee be dead, our Billy, please don't be dead.'

Les bent down once more, his ear almost touching Billy's lips.

'There it is again, I can feel it on my ear. It is, it bloody well is, I can just hear it now.'

He craned his neck to speak to the ring of lights and his voice was hoarse.

"Father ... I think our Billy's alreet; I'm sure he's breathing but we've got to get him out of here – is Jack on his way back yet?"

There were gasps of relief from above before John answered.

"It's too dark to see, son, but he'll be as quick as he can – in fact I reckon I can hear somebody at bottom of tip now, but I can't see owt from here."

The pile of waste blocked any view of the ground below, otherwise he would have seen the beam of a flashlight as Jack and Stan were about to begin climbing up the tip carrying a ladder. It took another few minutes of slipping and sliding before the two exhausted men came into view, then several torches were swung round to light their path as they scrambled round the heap of slag. Jack and Stan sank to their knees lowering a heavy wooden ladder to the surface of the tip and Jack voiced some consternation.

"I hope the bugger's long enough: it's the only one we could lay our hands on."

John leapt to his feet and bodily picked the ladder up by himself, raising it over his head.

"This'll do, Jack," he declared. He then addressed the men around him. "Let's have as much light as we can down that hole."

He walked to the edge with the ladder and shouted down to Les.

"Thee watch thi back, Les, we've managed to get a ladder so thee shine thi light to a spot where I can lower it down to."

Men ducked as John swung the ladder until one end was over the edge of the crater, allowing him to start lowering it down. Les grasped Jimmy's arm to direct the light from their torch on to a suitable spot well clear of the three of them.

"Over there, Father, just there."

John lowered the ladder to the spot indicated by the ring of light and its bottom rung disappeared into the layer of dust. It sank even deeper into the detritus as someone's weight on the ladder caused another rung to vanish. Les could see someone grasp the stiles and start to descend and even before John spoke, Les knew it was he who was climbing down.

With six rungs still to climb down, John removed his feet from them and slid the remaining distance.

"You sure he's still breathing?"

Les raised Billy's head to enable John to get a close look.

"Aye, you can just hear him, only faint, mind."

John bent down, listening intently.

"The sooner we get him out of here the better. No time for stretchers or owt like that, he'll have to go over mi shoulder."

He bent down and put his hands beneath Billy's limp body then straightened up effortlessly to his full height.

"Give us a hand to get him settled and watch his head, I've got his weight."

Les held Billy's head and neck while John hoisted the lad over his shoulder in a fireman's lift and started to climb. Again the ladder sank until its top rung was only just level with the edge of the opening above, but there it stayed and John was able to ascend until willing hands lifted the boy clear and he himself was given a helping hand to climb out. By this time, a couple of jackets were already laid on the surface of the tip and Billy was receiving first aid from one of the miners. Les had cleared his nose and mouth so he was immediately placed face downwards on the coats with his arms extended and his face turned to one side. The miner attending to Billy knelt across the lad and placed his hands flat over his lowest ribs and threw the weight of his body slowly and gradually forward before raising himself to remove the pressure but without removing his hands.

—256—

This was repeated twelve times a minute without pause until Billy gave a little cough and started breathing more deeply and his eyes flickered open. John let out a deep breath of his own and placed a hand on the miner's shoulder.

"Thanks, Paul, that's a pint on me the next time I see thi in t' club – will he be alright, do yer think?"

Paul looked up; "It's them bloody fumes that's the worry; most of 'em would've escaped when the top caved in so I don't think he'll have come to much real harm. But Tommy Savage is the man to see – he's in t' pit rescue team and got more training than me, so have a word wi' him. He might advise a visit to doctor, and hey up – the lad's getting his breath back now and licking his lips, look, I bet the little bugger's thirsty."

Everybody gathered round as Billy raised his head, blinking in the light of the torches. He spat out black saliva then rubbed his lips with the back of an even blacker hand, which resulted in more spitting. "Where's our Les? He owes me a shilling," he protested and everybody burst out laughing.

Jimmy had also been brought up and was being attended to, while Walter had a protecting arm around the shoulder that hadn't been hurt in the fall. By the light of the torch beams, John looked down at Billy then to the men around him.

"Well, lads, what can I say?" His voice was humble.

"Nay, John, tha's no need to say owt." The men were

slapping each other on the back as tension gave way to elation. John shook each man warmly by the hand, thanking them as he did so. Billy made to rise to his feet but John indicated otherwise.

"I want thee to tek it easy till we've had a word wi' Tom and see what he has to say; I reckon I can manage to get a little 'un like thee back home."

Once again, Billy was lifted like a small child as John prepared to make his way down the tip.

"I can walk down, Dad, I'm alright," protested Billy.

"Aye, maybe so," John grunted, "but we're not taking any chances so shut up."

Billy knew it was useless to object any further and even though his head still hurt he would have preferred to walk, or at least be carried over his dad's shoulder, but not like a baby. The short distance from the end of the tip to the houses was soon covered and halfway down the avenue a group of housewives was gathered around Annie and Nora. As the flashlights approached, the women fell silent before uttering cries of consternation when John was seen striding forward carrying a boy in his arms. Annie surmised it must be Billy and her hand rose to her mouth before hurrying towards them. She reached out with outstretched arms as the figures drew near and she gave a little sob. John could envisage her anguish so he spoke up.

"Don't fret, lass, the lad's alreet apart from having a ton of muck on him."

There was a cry of relief from the group of women and Annie dropped her arms as she let out a huge sigh.

"Thank God, where's he been? What happened? Just look at him, are you alright, luv?"

The exclamations and the questions came in quick succession as Billy's face was pressed to Annie's bosom. When at last he could speak, the lad looked up with a woeful expression.

"Sorry, Mam, I've got mi clothes mucky."

Annie silenced the tale of woe. "A bit of muck's nowt our Billy, they'll wash."

She looked questioningly at John. "What's wrong with his legs? Not broken are they?"

John shook his head although he knew it was probably too dark for Annie to see this reaction, so he explained.

"Nay, he should be alreet, but Paul reckons it might be best to let Tommy Savage have a look at him, see if we need to tek him to doctor."

Annie looked relieved. "Right, come on then, let's hope there's enough hot water in t' boiler for a bath." But before leaving, she took a few hurried steps over toward Jimmy who was receiving the same attention from Nora.

"Your Jimmy alright, Nora? Apart from looking like a sweep, that is?" She bent down to cup Jimmy's black face in her hand.

"What are we going to do wi' you two? But then, it weren't your fault, that big soft son of mine should have known better so we can't blame you or our Billy. You sure you feel alright apart from that shoulder?"

"Yes thanks, Mrs Foster, your Billy came off worst when we fell in. Can we still go to Anston tomorrow?"

"See what your mam and dad say and let's see what Billy's like in the morning, or I should say later this morning; we can make our minds up then."

Annie gave Nora a hug and everybody said cheerio to everybody else before dispersing to their respective homes. Susan had been sent on ahead to prepare a big pot of tea for all the family and their next-door neighbours. About fifteen minutes later, an embarrassed Billy was sat in a bath, on the hearth, surrounded by onlookers all enjoying a well-earned drink. He couldn't make his mind up whether being in the bath in front of everybody wasn't worse than being down that hole. Well, maybe not.

CHAPTER THIRTEEN

The Village Fete

"How do you feel, Billy? Head still sore?"

Annie looked with some concern at her young son as he lay in bed, but he sat up fingering the lump on his head unconcernedly when he remembered it was Saturday.

"Still hurts a bit but not too bad."

He made no mention of his sore throat as that too could jeopardise his trip to Anston and the boxing contest.

"No, I'm alright, thanks, Mam," he affirmed.

"Well, we'll let Mr Savage have a look at you; you've nowhere else that hurts, have you?"

Billy shook his head as he licked dry lips. "Can I have some porridge for breakfast?" He reasoned porridge would be easier to swallow. Annie turned to leave the room, thankful that he had escaped with nothing more than a sore head but a bit puzzled regarding the porridge; he didn't usually ask for that.

"You can have a boiled egg and toast if you like; Jack is."

"Er, I think I fancy porridge, please."

"Fair enough, now I'm going to tek some hot water through to the kitchen so don't be long."

"Right, Mam, I'm coming."

Billy dressed himself, apart from pulling on his shirt, then he too went down and found Susan, Jack and Les all sat at the table. His father had already eaten and had gone to his pigeons.

"Hey up, Billy, Ma says you're feeling okay apart from that lump on yer bonce, is that right?" Jack had just taken the top off his boiled egg and was about to dip a 'soldier' into the yolk.

"Yeah, thanks Jack, I'm alright. Morning, Sue, morning, Les."

Susan muttered "Morning, Billy," but Les put his toast down to look earnestly at his little brother.

"Sure you feel alright, kiddo? Look … I'm sorry, I should've waited yesterday to mek sure you and Jimmy got down safe but I didn't want to get questioned by coppers; I should've hung on though, sorry, Billy." Jack nodded his head towards Les and gave Billy a wink. "Tell him not to forget he still owes you – you and Jimmy – and if I were you I should ask for a bit extra as danger money. Was it a bob you were promised? Well it must be worth a lot more than that for 'em not to get thrown in the clink, so charge 'em double, even half a crown! Go on, while he's still feeling sorry for yer."

Billy didn't answer but he did finger a lump on his head in a rather theatrical fashion that made Les grin.

"Alright, I'll have a word wi' lads, especially Arthur – he was on a winning streak before you whistled – so you'll get paid, and Jimmy."

Billy was pleased about that so he made his way to the kitchen where he found his mother and a pan of hot water.

"There's a new tablet of carbolic on the side there, though you shouldn't be mucky after the scrub you got last night; however that doesn't mean you can miss the back of your neck or behind your ears – you listening?"

"Yes, Mam."

"Now then, how about that boiled egg, don't you fancy one? I've managed to get some extra quite apart from the rations."

"Okay then, but I can go to Anston, can't I?"

Annie sighed; "When Mr Savage has had a look at you and if he thinks you're alright, then yes."

Billy dutifully washed and because his mother was still present, the lather went behind his ears and on the back of his neck.

On returning to the living room, he gave a little cough, fingering his throat as he sat to the table.

Jack gave him a quizzical look; "You sure you're alright?"

"I'm thirsty that's all; can I have a drink please, Sue?"

Susan filled his mug and Billy added sugar before taking a sip.

"Ah, that's better: best drink of the day, eh, Les?"

Les acknowledged with a wink before addressing Jack.

"Any idea who else is boxing this afternoon?"

Jack paused on a piece of toast. "I can take a good guess. There'll be them two Renshaw brothers, 'Basher' and the younger one, Pete. Then that farmer from Gildingwells who fancies himself – what's his name? Polkey. Too slow to catch a cold he is. Then me and maybe one or two more but I don't reckon there'll be any Bruce Woodcocks among 'em, at least I hope not."

Jack chuckled as he concluded his list of probable contestants and gave a nod towards Billy.

"But I shall be alright: I've got my two seconds to tek care of me."

Billy stuck his chest out. "Me and Jimmy will see you're alright, Jack."

By the time breakfast was over, John had returned and he indicated to Billy to get his jacket from the passage.

"Right, let's go and see what Tom has to say to thi, I dare say he'll have been told what's what so he'll be expecting us to call."

For Billy it was a case of trying to keep up with his father without actually running, as they made their way through a couple of alleys to Collier Avenue. The house they were visiting was exactly like their own so John's boots heralded their approach in the same fashion as they did on their own back yard. There was no need to knock and a voice hailed them from within as they neared the back door.

"Come on through, John, in t' middle room."

John removed his cap and stepped inside to be greeted by a stout lady with an ample pair of arms folded across an equally ample bosom. She met her visitors in the kitchen but turned to lead the way into the living room where she waved for them to move towards the fireplace.

"I've heard all about you, young Billy, you and your pal James. You'll not be doing it again I hope."

"No, Mrs Savage, once is enough." He looked towards the corner near the fireplace to where a rocking chair was being slowly canted back and forth by its occupant. He was a roly-poly of a man and his hairy arms rested on a bulge provided by a large abdomen that was spilling over his wide leather belt. A rotund face looked from John to Billy for a few seconds then the man spoke as he beckoned for Billy to step forward.

"Come here, lad, let's have a look at thi."

He waved to a chair in a rather regal manner with one hand while holding Billy's face with the other and addressed John.

"Sit yer down, John, could ye enjoy a spot of tea? Not tek but a minute."

John withdrew a wooden chair from underneath the table and sat down, but held up his hand with regards to the offer of tea.

"Thank ye, Tom, but I just want to know what you think we should do about lad here – you've heard what happened?"

"Aye, I have and it could have bin serious tha knows, but then, I've no need to tell thee that." He turned back to Billy.

"You and that mate of thine were lucky tha knows; do yer play on that owd tip? I bet you do. Let's have a dekko at thi."

Billy was standing between the man's chubby knees and Tom was still holding Billy's head.

"Fair owd bump on thi napper, in't it? Still hurt, do it?"

Billy nodded an affirmative so the man continued.

"Does yer head hurt if you don't touch that bump? Like a headache, or have a dizzy feeling?"

"No."

"I saw yer mate a while back, he said his shoulder was sore but it were nowt too drastic, I put it in a sling for him. He did complain of a burning in his throat though – what's thine like?"

Billy raised his fingers to point to his Adam's apple.

"It's a bit funny, but it's alright," he assured Tom and gave his father a quick glance but John's face was impassive.

"What's the cause of that then, Tom?" John asked.

"Well, it's all them fumes that'd be inside that hole; the lads were bound to have breathed some down 'em. That's why I said they were lucky." Tom rose from his rocking chair and took Billy to stand in front of the window.

"Open thi mouth wide."

Billy did as requested while Tom lowered his chubby face to peer within the confines of Billy's throat.

"Aye, just like Jimmy's." He pointed a finger at Billy's breastbone. "You sure you got no pain in yer chest?"

Billy shook his head so Tom returned to his chair and the rocking resumed.

"Well, I don't think there's bin much harm done, John,

but like I told Walter, keep an eye on him and straight to the doctor if he complains about his chest or starts coughing." He again pointed a finger at Billy. "And thee let yer mam and dad know if yer throat gets any worse or yer chest hurts, do you hear?"

"Right you are, Mr Savage, I will."

Tom looked up as the tall figure rose from his seat and approached the rocking chair, and John thrust his hand forward.

"I'm obliged to thi, Tom and thanks for yer time. Annie will feel easier now."

The rocking ceased for a few seconds as Tom shook the outstretched hand.

"I reckon he'll be alright, John. You still on days?"

John nodded.

"Right, well let me know on Monday how he is. I shall see thi in t' baths."

John turned to make his way through the passage with Billy following but paused and Billy received a dig in the ribs from his father. "Oh yeah, er thanks, Mr Savage, thanks a lot." He swung his gaze to Tom's wife who had sat patiently through the impromptu examination.

"You too, Mrs Savage, I'm sorry to have been a bother."

The pair of ample arms unfolded as the lady rose from her chair.

"Tha were no bother, Billy, but just be careful in future and remember me to thi mam." She nodded to John; "Cheerio, John, you did right in coming."

They made their way home where Annie was waiting in the kitchen for a report.

"His head is alreet but we've got to watch him for any trouble with his breathing. Apart from that he seems right enough."

Annie confronted Billy and put her hand under his chin.

"I thought you said nowhere else hurt; open yer mouth."

Billy tried to shake his head but wasn't allowed much movement, so with his mouth wide open he could only offer a faint gurgle until his mother released her hold.

"I'm alright, Mam ... I am," he eventually managed to say.

Annie stood scrutinising the freckled face.

"I bet it'd be a different story if it were school instead of that boxing palaver at Anston, so don't suddenly start looking for any sympathy on Monday morning, do you hear, my lad?"

"Yeah, okay, Mam; so can I go with our Jack then?"

Brown eyes twinkled among the freckles as he received a nod of consent. "Great, I'll go and tell Jimmy," and in a flash he was out of the door and on his way.

For a few hours, number sixteen buzzed with activity but it progressively grew quieter until it stood hushed and empty. Susan left to catch her bus to Worksop. Jimmy, with his arm in a sling, had accompanied Billy back to the house then he, Billy, Jack and Annie had all caught the same bus to Anston. Les saw them off, promising to get to the fete later after he had won his bus fare playing snooker. John too, remarked he would attend the festivities in the afternoon and he eventually departed, carrying a canvas bag. The house was hardly ever locked so the problem of who had a key or where to secrete one never arose.

At Anston, Annie bid cheerio to Jimmy and her two sons, adding, "Just be careful."

At the fete, Jack and his two seconds found things well under way, for as they entered the field they were just in time to hear a roar go up from the spectators who were giving encouragement to two teams, heaving and straining in a tug-o'-war. Heels were gouging great furrows in the turf as first one side, then the other, gained or yielded precious inches in an effort to pull the rope's knot over the winning marker.

Jack grinned at the toiling men. "Some of them poor buggers will have a job to lift a pint tonight; it's hard graft is that."

Any reply from Jimmy or Billy was drowned by another roar from the crowd as one of the teams made a supreme effort and hauled their opponents forward to be awarded a loud cheer in recognition of their victory, while their vanquished challengers collapsed dejectedly upon the grass.

Jack looked around as the clapping subsided. "There's supposed to be a team here from Bennington Working Man's Club; I wonder if Father's in it? You didn't hear him mention owt about it, did you Billy?"

Billy shook his head as two more teams lined up and dug their heels in, ready to take the strain.

"Nobody said owt to me, you know mi dad. By the way, what time do you think the boxing will be?"

Jack glanced around the site; "I'm not sure, but the ring is over there so I'll go and find out where the changing room is then I'll let you know. You two can have a look round and I'll see you in a bit." The boys decided they would watch the new tug-o'-war before having a wander round the numerous stalls and sideshows. Jack made his way towards the boxing ring near a large tent he surmised had to be for the contestants use, drew back the flap and stepped inside.

"Bugger me, watch yer pockets – the army's here!"

The greeting came from a young man wearing the uniform of a Naval Petty Officer and he shadow-boxed his way forward to shake Jack's hand. He was a wiry lad with a cheeky face, but much smaller than Jack which, in boxing parlance, placed him in the lightweight class. "I didn't think t' army could manage without thee, how's it going, Jack?" The young man's greeting was warm and sincere. Jack gave a hearty laugh as they stood pumping hands.

"Chippy, you sod you, don't tell me you've wangled a weekend pass just to win a bit of pork for yer mam? I wouldn't put it past yer." They stood facing each other, hands still clasped as Jack continued. "You're looking well, it must be a cushy number in that ruddy navy, – I think I'll ask for a transfer. By the way, me and our Les bumped into Tommy Riley last Saturday, in Worksop, so it's great to see thee too, Wilf."

"Same here, Jack, we'll have to meet up tonight for a few bevvies, providing we're in a fit state after this afternoon that is. By the way, what were you up to last week? A little bird tells me you had a bit of a set to in t' Red Lion, what happened? Somebody spill yer beer?"

Jack grimaced; "Oh that, you've heard have you? Well, there was this young squaddie really full of himself, shouting the odds and throwing his weight about and I lost mi rag and swung at the poor sod." Jack shook his head as he recalled the incident. "He was drunk and looking for trouble, but even so, I shouldn't have dropped him, I should've held back."

Wilf grinned and placed a hand on Jack's shoulder. "What if he's here today and brought half a dozen mates with him? Coldstream Guards, weren't it?"

Jack again pulled a face, "That's all I need, but my leave ends tomorrow, so I think I'll be guided by that owd saying 'He who fights and runs away, lives to fight another day'; there could be a bit of logic in that."

Wilf was about to comment but the tent flap was pulled aside and Vera's husband entered, and walked straight over to them.

"Hey up, Jack, I've just left yer Ma with our Vera, she said you'd all come on t' same bus; Billy not with you?"

Jack and Tim shook hands; they got on well together.

"How do Tim, our Billy? He's with a mate having a look round the stalls; they reckon they want to be my seconds – will that be alright?"

Tim smiled and nodded; "Aye, of course it is; we're not boxing for any Lonsdale belt are we?"

Jack gestured towards Wilf. "Did you know this reprobate was boxing?" Tim nodded but had to step back smartly to avoid a feigned left hook.

"Oh aye, he didn't get his name down until last night and he was pleased to hear you would be here. Mind you, I don't know if that would have been the case if you two were boxing against each other – which reminds me, Jack, I've got a bit of news for thi."

"Oh aye, good or bad?"

"Well you can decide on that, but I've found out that thi father's boxing."

"You're bloody joking, you must be."

"No ... straight up, Jack."

There was silence as the revelation sank in and it was a full half minute before Jack raised his hands as if in bewilderment.

"But why ask me to contest if you already knew Father was boxing?"

"I didn't, I didn't know," Tim protested. "I just saw three names on t' list from Bennington before I put thy name on it. There were them two brothers as usual, then Jos and another bloke, but only his initials which were J.A.F., but I didn't think owt about it at the time. Anyway, when I told the organiser you were boxing, then I found out that J.A.F. stood for John Arthur Foster. He hasn't said owt to thee then?" Jack's eyes were wide as he shook his head. "No!

How the hell can I box now? Can you imagine t' owd man and me in the ring together, fighting over a bit of pork?"

Tim smothered a grin, "Well I must admit it could be a crowd puller but you're in different groups. Your dad has had his name down a long time so he'll be in group A; the only way you can meet is if you both win your particular group and get into the final." Tim paused to let his summarisation sink in. "And if that happens then yes, it'll be thee against thi father."

Jack looked at Wilf who had a big smile on his face. "It's alright thee laughing but what am I going to do?"

Wilf chortled unashamedly and winked at Tim. "I know what I'd do if I were thee, I'd bugger back off to mi regiment pretty sharpish. Tell everybody the army has sent word it needs thi back because Hitler's about to invade." He gave Jack a slap on the back as he continued with his advice. "Let's put it this way, if I had to choose between taking on a German battleship at sea or facing thi father in that boxing ring, I'd put to sea every time; it'd be safer, don't you reckon so, Tim?"

Tim raised his hand as a sign of acquiescence but tried to act the diplomat. "Look, Jack, now that thi father knows tha's boxing, he might not even show up – let's wait and see, eh?"

"He'll turn up; if he's got his name down, he'll turn up." Jack gave a little nod, "I know my father." Tim looked at his watch. "Well anyway, the first bout will be in thirty minutes; you'll be one of the first, Wilf, against …" he perused his papers, "against Danny Weaver who, if I remember right, you beat last year?"

Wilf agreed so Tim addressed Jack after consulting his list once more. "You'll go on when their weight has finished but you'll be in the second group so your dad will box first, if he turns up."

"You wouldn't like to have a small bet, would you?" asked Jack.

Tim declined just as more contestants entered the tent carrying their bags, so Jack looked round for a place to store his, while he went to look for Billy.

Wilf pointed to a bench; "Put yer gear over there with mine, Jack; I shall be getting stripped shortly."

After placing his bag under the seat, Jack went to the tent entrance. He could see the two lads having a go at something on one of the stalls so he turned to give Wilf a wave and shouted, "Good luck." Wilf raised a fist and replied, "You too," but gave a wry smile as he continued under his breath, 'I think you might need it more than me, sunshine.'

Jack made his way towards the boys and reached them just as Jimmy was making a final throw with his last beanbag.

"Who's winning then?"

They both turned as Jack approached.

"Oh, it's not between us two, but there's a prize for who gets the most bags through that round hole on the board there. However, if any fall through the square ones then they get taken off your score, so me and Jimmy haven't done too good. I managed a total of four and Jimmy just two but the best score is eight so far, in't it Jimmy?"

"Yeah, but it's hard and this sling don't help," protested Jimmy.

"Gerra way, just because I got two more than you." Billy dismissed his mate's excuse then asked when the boxing was likely to start.

"Well the first bout will be in about twenty minutes or so, but you haven't seen Father, have you?" Both boys shook their heads.

"Is Dad in the tug-o'-war team then?"

Jack blew noisily in exasperation; "No, the sod isn't in the tug-o'-war, he's boxing. That means if we both get through our particular groups, it'll be him and me in the final bout."

Billy and Jimmy looked at each other wide-eyed and Billy had to adjust his jaw before he could speak.

"Oo-er Jack, what will Mam say? I bet Dad hasn't said owt to her, and hey up, speak of the devil: he's just come through the gate – look!"

The sentence ended in a whisper as Jack and Jimmy turned to witness the tall figure striding towards the boxing ring and its adjacent tent. John passed within twenty yards of the three motionless bystanders to give them a cursory nod before disappearing inside. As he vanished from sight, three pairs of eyes focussed on the soft earth near the entrance where deep imprints of size eleven boots bore witness.

Jack sighed; 'I knew the bugger would come … Well, I'm not standing down so it looks like me and thee, Father, if we both get through.' His private thoughts ceased and he addressed the lads instead.

"Right, now listen, the boxing is going to start in a bit so go and stand near the ring, before it gets crowded, then when it's my turn you can jump up into mi corner. Will you be alright with that gammy arm, Jimmy?"

"Yeah, I'll be alright, Jack."

"Okay then, I'm off; I suppose I'd better go and see what Father has to say for himself."

Jack made his way towards the tent just as the referee climbed into the ring to announce the start of the competition; there was a surge of people as the address was made.

Inside the tent, the heady smell of embrocation and sweat greeted Jack as he made his way through the milling contestants. Most of them were now in shorts and vests and either exercising or furiously boxing imaginary opponents. Jack weaved a careful path towards Wilf.

"They'll be knackered before they start; where's mi father?"

Wilf jerked a thumb to his right; "He's over there, still in his cap and muffler. Perhaps he'll keep 'em on to box in, boots as well."

Jack couldn't help but smile as he spiked his fingers through his hair.

"I'd better go and say 'How do', but I'm buggered if I'm going to wish him luck!"

John looked up from studying the ground as Jack approached.

"Why didn't yer say you'd already put yer name down? I wouldn't have entered if I'd've known."

"Don't mek any odds do it?" John replied. "Besides, I weren't to know tha would be home this weekend, so I put my name down. I fancy a decent joint of meat and I reckon I stand as good a chance as anybody."

John made a point of looking straight at Jack as he made the remark; he knew his son would take the bait and he did.

"Oh aye, well we'll have to see about that; I reckon that pork will taste just as good if I win it."

Jack spun on his heel and made for a seat on the bench beside Wilf who looked up enquiringly. "Well?" he asked.

Jack snorted; "Oh he's an annoying bugger. A proper jumped up twenty-two carat sod, he's ..." The words trailed off as Jack gritted his teeth and sat with his hands clasped behind his head. Wilf rose as the voice of the referee could be heard announcing the first contest, then he and his opponent were beckoned forward by a St John Ambulance member. There were cheers as they stepped from the tent, then more applause when they climbed into the ring. The crowd were under no illusions regarding the skills of the contenders and they knew they were going to witness more rough and tumble than actual boxing, but they were prepared to show their appreciation for the entertainment as the two men were introduced.

"Ladies! And gentlemen! The first bout of the afternoon

will be a lightweight contest of three two-minute rounds, fought according to Queensberry rules ... or as near as you're likely to get to them, between ... On my left in the blue corner ... Danny! Boy! Weaver! ... While on my right and last year's winner in this event ... The one and only Chippy! Marsden!"

Both boxers raised their gloved hands in the air as further cheers came from the crowd but spiced with juicy comments from some of the female spectators.

"If he hurts you, love, you come round to my house; I'll kiss it better, whatever it is."

"Ere, I'd go three rounds with any of them two; they both mek my owd man look like death warmed up."

It was all in good fun but the contenders were enthusiastic enough when the bell rang, and Wilf found he had to use plenty of manoeuvring to stay out of trouble. However, after three rounds of fast and furious activity there was no doubt as to who the winner was, so the referee raised Wilf's glove. This was to the approval of most of the crowd although a few catcalls were uttered, mainly by friends and relatives of the loser.

Wilf jumped down from the ring and made his way to the changing tent where John and his opponent were ready and waiting. He called "good luck" to them and had to smother a little smile when he noticed the contrast between the pair.

There was John, over six feet tall, thirteen stone and not an ounce of fat on him. His shorter contestant, at least two stone heavier was bulging in all the wrong places. He was the farmer that Jack had surmised would be participating.

After their introduction and formalities, John and Jos Pickering sat in their corners to await the bell. As soon as it rang, the farmer was out of his corner like a runaway tank, only not as smoothly. Neither he or John were boxers but at least John could execute a bit of footwork and he had no problem avoiding the flailing arms of farmer Jos, with the result that the first round ended without any real blows being landed.

Jos sat in his corner puffing and blowing but he was up and away again the moment the bell rang. John could see a repeat performance of the first round ensuing so he changed his tactics slightly. Instead of merely sidestepping to await the next charge, he spun on his left foot and as farmer Pickering lumbered past, he dealt him a savage blow behind his jaw. Such was its force that the man literally dived headlong into a corner post, all fifteen stone on a horizontal plane. The crowd oohed long and loud as Joss, with his arms each side of the post, flopped face down on the canvas like a defunct hippopotamus. The count to ten was a formality so two ambulance men were quickly in the ring to attend to the hapless man as John was declared the winner. When it came to Jack's turn to be in the ring, he had to be content with a point's win over one of the Renshaw brothers, but it was convincing enough to warrant high marks. Wilf congratulated Jack when he returned to the tent and handed him his jacket to put around his shoulders.

"Well, if nobody wins with a knockout in your group it looks very much like thee and thi father for the decider. Are you still going on with it?"

Jack glanced across at his father who was reading a newspaper.

"Look at him ... just look ... I wonder what he thinks I'm going to do if we do end up in the ring together, stand there like a bloody barm cake while he knocks ten bells out of mi?"

Wilf refrained from any comment and merely shrugged as Jack continued. "Well he's got another think coming, cos I'm going to win that leg of pork or whatever it is, and do you know, I can almost taste it now. Tender juicy meat along with a bit of stuffing and Ma saying, 'Thanks, Jack luv, I'm right proud of you, shame about yer Dad.' She would then look at Father; 'Would you care for another slice, John, or is your jaw still too sore? No perhaps not, but you'll have some more won't you, Jack?' Then I'll say, 'Don't mind if I do, Ma and don't forget a second helping for yourself, and of course Susan and our Billy and Les. Perhaps Father will be able to enjoy a bit of pork dripping in a day or two.' Oh I can just picture it, Wilf."

Jack sat there, rubbing his hands together and fantasizing, while Wilf buried his face in his hands to mumble through his fingers, "What kind of flowers do you like?"

"Well I am partial to cauliflowers," and both men burst out laughing.

As the afternoon wore on all the eliminating bouts were concluded, with Wilf going on to win in the lightweight class. It just remained for the winner of the heavier grouping to be decided and that was to be between the two boxers who had managed to accumulate the highest number of points. Billy and Jimmy waited expectantly as the referee studied his scorecards before stepping into the centre of the ring.

"Ladies! And gentlemen! We now come to the climax of this afternoon's boxing extravaganza: a final contest for the magnificent prize of a prime piece of pork." He had to pause to allow the whistles and cheers to die down before continuing. "The concluding contest of the afternoon between two worthy winners in the preliminary bouts and fully justifying their placement in the rankings: will you please welcome back, this year's contenders ... Jousting! Jack! Foster! And Jawbreaker! John! Thank you, ladies and gentlemen!"

Billy and Jimmy looked at each other as the crowd applauded, not knowing whether to join in or not.

"Cor, mi mam will have a fit when she hears," groaned Billy.

John and Jack were waiting at the entrance of the tent, now they both strode forward. John, impassive and a few inches taller than Jack, was in the lead. His son followed, beating his gloved hands together as they made their way through the crowd. Billy and Jimmy waited then all four climbed through the ropes, with three going to one corner,

John to the opposite. The crowd was now fairly quiet, apart from a buzz as they discussed the boxers' relationship to each other, but that too stilled as John and Jack were beckoned to the centre of the ring.

During the referee's obligatory instructions, John stared straight ahead, his hands by his side. Jack bobbed and weaved purely through habit, and when he and John had touched gloves, they retired to their corners.

The referee nodded to the timekeeper who checked his watch before ringing the bell, then father and son moved slowly across the canvas to face each other.

Their eyes locked in unblinking defiance as they circled in the centre of the ring with Jack in a classical boxing stance, while John still had his arms by his side. Suddenly he half turned, drew back a huge right hand and with a savage expression on his face he swung his arm to land the glove as light as a butterfly on the end of Jack's nose. Tension drained from the lad's face like water disappearing down a drain hole when he realized what the plan was and he quickly reciprocated by delivering a hugely exaggerated uppercut to land just as delicately on John's jaw. This had his father reeling back against the ropes in mock anguish but they came together again, placed their gloved hands on each other's shoulders and performed a little jig that rotated them through three hundred and sixty degrees. After an initial silence, the crowd, realising they were not going to witness any real conflict, roared with laughter and applauded the two men's antics until the bell signalled the end of the round. At this point they both turned to walk to their respective corners but before they could do so, a smiling referee grabbed an arm of each and raised them aloft, to signal not one winner, but two.

"Ladies and gentlemen ... I'm sure you will agree that in declaring this contest a draw, I have come to a fair and judicious decision. I therefore give you this year's winners of the 1940 Anston Fete heavyweight boxing competition and sadly, probably the last one until the end of hostilities with Hitler's Germany. Will you please give a big round of applause for Mr John Foster and his son, Mr Jack Foster. Thank you, ladies and gentlemen."

Billy dashed forward to unlace his Dad's gloves, then Jack's, hardly able to contain his delight at the outcome of the fight. "Awe, great eh, Jack? Nice one, Dad. That was better than knocking one another's blocks off. Can Jimmy come and have dinner wi' us tomorrow, if Mam cooks the pork?"

"Don't see why not, if it's alright with his mam and dad."

John allowed himself the vestige of a smile as he extended his hand to his son.

"Had thee going for a bit just then, eh? Come on, admit it."

Jack wiped the back of his hand across his lips.

"Well, I did think you were going to belt me one, but it would only have bin one, mind. What I can't understand is, why let me enter when you'd already got your name down?"

"Stands to reason that two bites at the cherry are better

than one, don't it? This way we had two chances of winning that pork, and I bet it's a fair piece of meat; tha can collect it and give it to thi ma then stand back and watch her face."

As he finished speaking they were joined by Les who had watched most of the boxing but had shied off when he realized that both his father and Jack were the finalists. He only returned after he had heard the result, so he now came forward with a happy smile on his face.

"Bugger me, Father, tha kept this little lot dark; why didn't tha let on?"

"Why? Does tha tell me everything tha's up to?"

As Les grinned and shook his head, John continued. "Right, well there you are then." He winked and tapped the side of his nose before glancing towards the tent. "Look, I'm going to get changed then I'm catching a bus back home; I'll see you all later." As he strode away, Billy spoke to Les.

"Hey, were you here when he clouted that farmer behind his ear hole? It were a real wallop, weren't it, Jimmy? The bloke did a flying header straight into a post – I bet he didn't half see stars." After receiving affirmation from Les, Billy switched his attention to Jack.

"Can we go and collect the prize? See how big it is."

"We'll go and get it just before we go home, I want to get changed then we can have a look round. I might have a go at them beanbags, see if I can beat you two."

After he had changed and dressed, Jack rejoined his brothers and Jimmy to spend the rest of the afternoon patronizing the different stalls. They collected the piece of pork just before leaving for home and when they arrived they could hear Annie talking to Susan in the living room. Billy was sent ahead bearing the parcel and there was a yell of excitement.

"Oh he won then bless him, is he alright? Not hurt is he, Billy?"

Billy laughed; "He's right as rain, Mam – he's here, look."

Jack followed Billy into the living room and his mother hurried forward to carefully inspect his face from every angle.

"You sure you're alright? They didn't hurt you? You've got some little cuts over your eyes and one on your cheek, look. I don't know, but well done, luv; shall we have a look at the joint? It feels a good size."

Jack smiled at his mother's obvious delight. "Aye, open it up but I have to tell you I didn't win it outright. I drew with this other chap but he said I could have it, so I reckon he knows you, perhaps he fancies you on the quiet."

"Don't be daft, but it was good of him; did you know him then?"

"Oh aye, I've seen him before," Jack winked at his brothers; "We've seen him before, haven't we lads?"

Les wasn't going to miss the opportunity to crack a joke and he replied in a flash. "Yes I recognized him because his face rang a bell when he was in the ring." This caused all three to collapse in fits of laughter.

Annie shook her head, "I'm glad you think it's funny but I reckon it was very good of him and tell him I said so." The boys were still laughing as Annie opened the parcel and its contents did indeed turn out to be a prime piece of pork, just as the referee had predicted.

"Oh just look at it – we'll have a real treat tomorrow. Sage and onion stuffing, apple sauce, crackling, the lot," enthused Annie.

"Can Jimmy come to dinner tomorrow, Mam? Dad said it's alright."

"You saw your Dad then? He wasn't here when I got back from our Vera's. Jimmy for dinner? Yes, of course he can come, now I'm going to put this away in the pantry then I'll get some tea ready. I bet your Dad is with his pigeons so you slip down there, Billy and tell him tea in about half an hour, there's a luv."

The rest of the evening traversed its intended course with Jack and Les, on this occasion, managing to get back home to their beds after a night out. The only detriment they sustained was to their depleted wallets and an ability to walk in a straight line, neither of which seemed to worry them unduly. In fact it provided Jack with an opportunity to philosophize during one of their many stops on an unsteady perambulation home. Slowly swaying, he scrutinized the few coins he had left in his possession and finally spoke as if endowed with the erudition of Solomon.

"Have yer noticed Leslie, money is made round? Perhaps that's so it'll go round. It goes from me to the pub, from pub to bank, from bank to t' army, then back to me again. Have yer noticed that Les?"

Les gave a hiccup and inspected a few coins from his own pocket.

"Yer right Jack, that's because if it were square it wouldn't go round, cos it would get stuck in the corner of yer pocket like. Tell you what, you have what I've got cos then, what I haven't got, I can't spend cos I haven't got it ... have I?" They were standing face to face and Jack blinked trying to fathom out the logic of what he had just heard, but after a while he gave up.

"No, sod it, I don't need money, what do I need money for? I've got my return ticket back to camp so why do I need money?"

He raised his face to the sky and swaying dangerously he lifted his palms to the stars. "The Lord will provide, that's what they say, Leslie, the Lord will provide."

Les joined him in looking at the night sky. "That's what they say, Jack, and perhaps right now, this very minute, he's shovelling money into a bucket to lower it down. No, no, no! I'm sorry, I mean two buckets, one for thee and one for me."

They rocked back and forth for a few minutes but after a while, Les shrugged his shoulders. "No, well perhaps not, he's probably busy, handing out wings or something important, so never mind, let's go home."

He placed an arm around his brother's shoulder but who was helping who to walk home was a debatable point, but eventually it was achieved.

CHAPTER FOURTEEN

It's Back To Camp

Sunday, one thirty in the afternoon and everyone at number 16 Jubilee Avenue had enjoyed their extra special dinner.

"Ma, that was first class. I don't care how many more meals I eat, I shall always remember that one, thanks."

Jack winked at his mother as he placed his knife and fork on his plate purposely smacking his lips. He was dressed in his uniform and Annie beamed across the table.

"I'm glad you enjoyed it, after all it was you who won that lovely bit of pork, or should I say you and this other chap?" The final part of the sentence was delivered with great emphasis and she looked round the circle of faces with exaggeratedly widened eyes as everyone laughed. John leaned back in his chair and scrutinized the ceiling for it was obvious someone had put Annie wise so he dealt with the matter in his own way.

"Would yer say that joint was a fine piece of pork, Annie?"

"Yes, John, very nice."

"And do yer reckon everyone enjoyed it?"

"All the plates are clean."

"Any chance of us having owt like it if we hadn't won it?"

"Shouldn't think so, John."

"Then, would tha say it were worth a few cuts and bruises?"

"Oh alright, but you and our Jack fighting each other for it, I ask you."

"But that's the point, Annie, we didn't fight, did we, son?"

Jack shook his head in confirmation. "No, Ma, in the end it turned into a bit of fun and the crowd enjoyed it, honest."

Annie looked from husband to son several times ... "Oh very well, in that case I suppose I'll have to let you both off and yes, it was a real treat."

Everyone round the table gave a cheer and Annie had to smile but her eyes saddened when she looked at the clock. "What time will you have to go, Jack?"

Jack looked down at his wrist. "Well the train isn't until four but I've got to get to Retford and it's a Sunday service for the bus, so it'll have to be half past two from the square."

"Right, mash a pot of tea, Susan, while I clear away and you can get your things ready, Jack."

"I'm all packed up, Ma. I'll just have a cup of tea with you, then I'm on my way and I don't want anybody to come to the bus with me."

Billy looked downcast. "Aw, can't me and Jimmy come, Jack? We can help carry yer stuff."

Jack looked at the freckled face and remembered the search on the tip. "Just you and Jimmy then."

Billy's face altered; "Thanks, Jack."

Jimmy however, butted in to say he had instructions to

return home straight after the meal because he had to go with his family to visit his gran.

Billy returned his gaze to Jack; "I can still come with you though, eh? Please."

Jack hesitated; "Go on then, but I don't like goodbyes so at the bus stop we shake hands then tha comes straight back home, okay?" His voice was gruff and Billy nodded in agreement.

When everyone had drunk their tea it was virtually a repeat scene of ten days ago, as handshakes, hugs and kisses were exchanged. This time however, the atmosphere was different, instead of 'Welcome home, Jack,' it was 'Cheerio'.

Jack gathered his kit and stood looking at the ring of faces. "Now then, no coming to bottom of the yard, do you hear?" And he looked especially at his mother and Susan. "I'm only going to catch a bus; you ready Billy?"

They made their way outside and Stan came to the door when he heard boots on the concrete.

"You off then Jack? Tek care mate, see you again soon, I hope."

They shook hands and Billy tried to shoulder the kit bag but it was nearly as big as him and he buckled under the weight. Stan laughed, which helped take the edge off the occasion. "Want me to get thee a barrow, young Billy?"

"No thanks, I can manage."

Jack however, took hold of the kitbag and held out his Lee-Enfield instead.

"Here, thee carry this, be careful mind."

Billy's eyes sparkled as he slung the rifle over his shoulder and they set off, Billy falling into step as they made their way along the avenue and he glanced back as they neared the top.

"They're all stood at gate, Jack."

"Aye and I told them not to; I can't turn and wave so just keep going."

They crossed over the main street and apart from one little incident their walk to the bus stop was completed with time to spare. The 'incident' in question was effectively dealt with by Jack in his own inimitable way.

"He shouldn't be carrying that tha knows." The comment came from a man walking his dog.

Jack slowed his pace, "Oh, does tha reckon he's likely to shoot some bugger then?"

"No, but he shouldn't be carrying it."

"Tell me why not." Jack's voice was like the thrust of a rapier.

"Well he …" The words trailed away as the man observed the look on Jack's face and he quickly hurried on his way with his dog.

"Some people just can't keep their noses out, can they Billy?"

"No, Jack."

When the bus pulled in, Jack stored his kit on a seat then returned to stand with Billy on the pavement. He knew it would be a few minutes before the bus resumed its journey.

"Now then, Billy, I want thee to shake hands then get off back home, will tha do that for me?"

Billy's eyes watered; "If that's what you want me to do, Jack."

He extended his arm and they shook hands, almost like two barely acquainted colleagues bidding each other farewell.

Billy stepped back as he saw Jack's jaw tighten, but he held his brother's gaze.

"Jack."

"What?"

Billy's eyes glistened as he looked forlornly at his brother.

"You won't go and get killed, will yer Jack? Please."

Jack gritted his teeth and swept the boy into his arms.

"I'll try not to, Billy lad, I promise."

He spun the young lad round and gave him a push. "Go on home," he said softly.

Billy took a small step backwards, so Jack boarded the bus to return to his seat where he sat staring straight ahead until the bus pulled away. Out of the corner of his eye he could see Billy, still there on the pavement, raise his hand in farewell and then run in pursuit as the bus rounded a corner. A few seconds later, he looked back to see the young lad still waving and swallowed hard as the figure faded from view.